MELANIE LEAVEY

Soul of The Sea

THREE RAVENS
PRESS

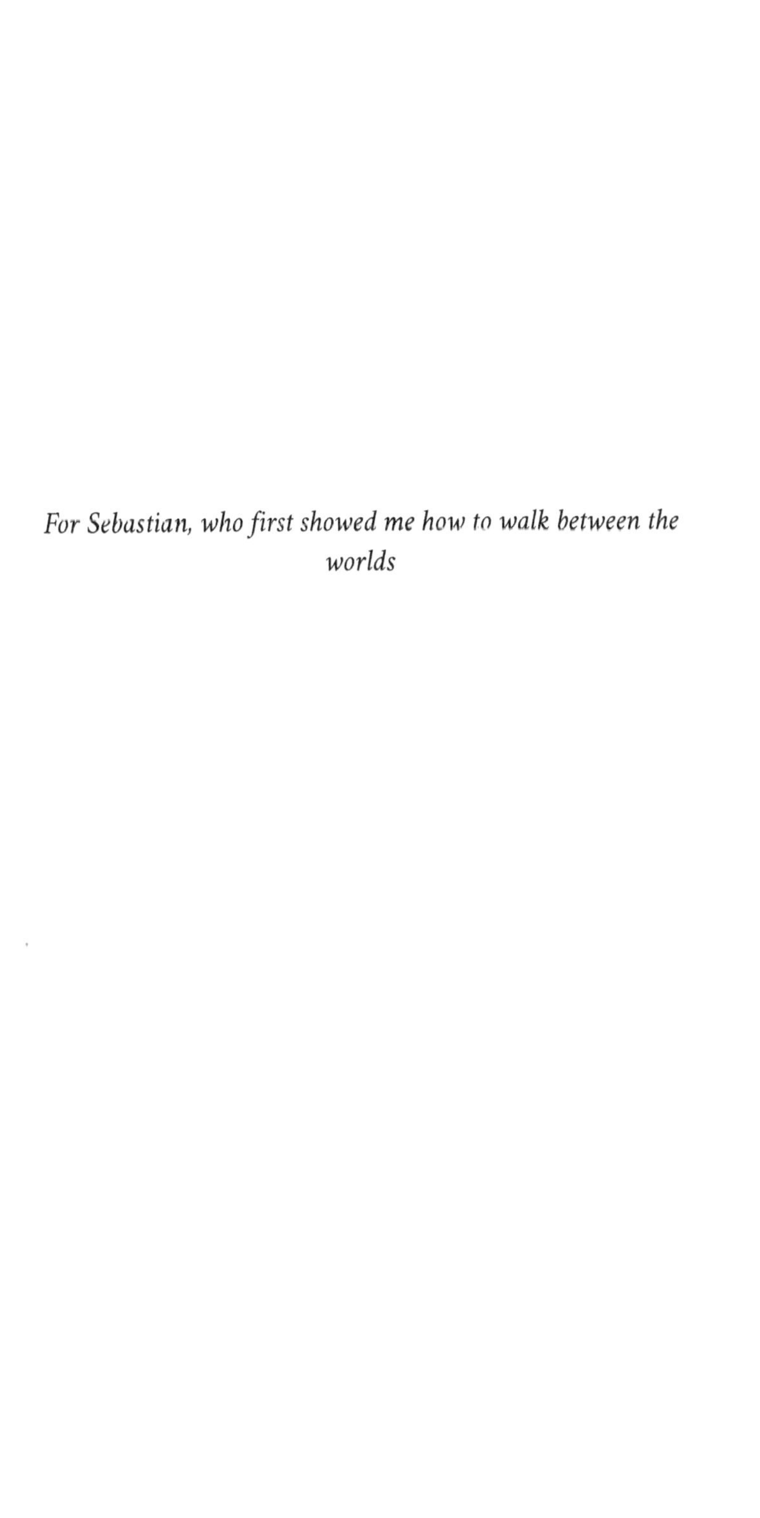

For Sebastian, who first showed me how to walk between the worlds

Remember your name.
Do not lose hope - what you seek will
be found.
Trust ghosts. Trust those you have
helped to help you in their turn.
Trust dreams.
Trust your heart and trust your story.

NEIL GAIMAN, INSTRUCTIONS

Contents

Acknowledgement

When *Skelly* was released in the spring of 2020, the world was only just beginning to know the scope and magnitude of the COVID-19 pandemic. Six months and three books later, things still aren't anywhere near what they used to be - in a lot of ways they are much worse.

Writing these books has been, in the words of Cliona, the wardrobe I've escaped through during some very difficult days. If you, Dear Reader, happen to find some small respite in these pages, then I have done all that I've set out to do.

* * *

Many thanks to Karin DiBiase of Lakeside Books & Art, for her support and encouragement and for being a champion of independent creators; to my husband, Brandt, for dreaming far bigger than I would ever dare and to my children for reminding me to come back through the wardrobe.

Special thanks to Lynna, for telling me to keep going, right when I didn't think I could and to everyone who has taken a chance on this humble writer's daydreams.

Chapter 1

" I wish it could be different, lass. I honestly do."

The head teacher's eyes bored into her and Trudy had to fight hard to maintain contact. After a brief, and what she hoped was sufficient, time, she looked away. It was going to take all of her will to not burst into humiliating tears.

"We've loved having you, and so have the children. Unfortunately, there's not enough of them. The MacGregors are leaving at the end of the Christmas term and that's five children. I've already had the superintendent after me for keeping you on after the Wainwrights and the Colsons left over the summer break."

Terrific, thought Trudy, *now I feel like I've been outstaying my welcome as well. As if I wasn't feeling horrible enough.*

"The young families just don't want to raise their children on Glencarragh these days," continued Mrs.Wright, with a heavy sigh, "They think there aren't enough opportunities for them here and for a lot of the parents, often with one of them having to work off-island, the ferries…well, it's just too much of a strain, having families always divided like that."

Trudy glanced quickly back at Mrs. Wright, who had paused in her justifications to look out of the window. The rain slanted down, obliterating the view across the school playground. The children had been allowed to leave early, knowing the trek home for some of them would be arduous. Even after being dropped by the school bus, some of them had a hard slog across the moor to reach their remote farms.

Thankfully, thought Mrs.Wright, shooting a guilty look back at Trudy, who had followed her gaze, *there aren't many of them left to have to make such a journey. Poor wee souls, it's no life for a young person here these days. The superintendent is doing the lass a favour, sending her back to the mainland, to civilization.* She suppressed a brief shiver and turned back to the matter at hand. It was never an enjoyable experience, having to let someone go, and the young woman standing before her had been a blessing when she'd arrived. The budget hadn't allowed for a fully qualified teacher and they'd been through a long string of unsuccessful assistants before young Miss Erskine had landed on their doorstep. A strange, anxious sort of person, she'd blossomed with the children. They were naturally drawn to her and she seemed to genuinely enjoy their company. There was something very child-like about her, Mrs. Wright had mused aloud in the tea shop, not long after Trudy had arrived, she seemed to understand their wild imaginations.

Trudy stood, staring out of the window, her brain only partially taking in what the older woman was saying. She stared past the streaked windows, over the playground and onto the moor that started on the other side of the hawthorn and bramble hedge that had been planted at the school boundary. Her hand made its way into her cardigan pocket, where her fingers closed around the smooth surface of the stone she carried there. She felt its familiar calming presence as her mind's eye saw past the veil of rain - because on

Glencarragh, the rain was a mercurial creature and it could be pouring in the village but clear up on the moors. There, on the other side, was an old, shepherd's croft, a curl of smoke spiraling out of the chimney. An old man shuffled around outside, accompanied by a smaller person - a child, probably - gathering lumps of peat into a basket. Sheep dotted the moor around the croft and it didn't occur to Trudy that it was either unusual or unlikely that any of it should be there. Her imagination was the place she went when she felt she couldn't cope, and this was definitely one of those times.

Mrs.Wright gave her a sideways glance. The young woman's usually pale skin was even more so, and the older woman worried if she might be going to faint. Trudy's face held a blank, calm expression but she noticed the way the young woman gripped the back of the chair with one hand, her knuckles white with strain. She saw the tears brimming in Trudy's eyes and looked quickly away. She busied herself tidying papers on her desk.

"Anyway, lass," she said, brightly, "it's not all bad news. The superintendent has arranged for you to start at a brand new comprehensive that they've built on the mainland. It's big and bright and modern and I imagine they don't depend on peat fires to heat the classrooms, eh?"

Trudy blinked, reluctantly bringing herself back to the room. She smiled a weak smile and nodded, just as she was expected to do. It was an automatic response, doing whatever would make others feel most comfortable.

"Yes, that's lovely," she replied, her voice wooden. "I appreciate that. You must thank her for me."

She stood, awkward and unsure, not certain what she should do next. What she really wanted was to bolt from the room and never return; waves of humiliation and embarrassment washed over her and she felt the heat rising in her face. How could this have happened?

Mrs.Wright fixed her with a pitying look. The poor girl was obviously in shock.

"Tell you what," she said, stacking up a pile of papers that would need unstacking and sorting again later. "I was just going to take myself down to the tea shop before I go home. Mr. Wright is on the mainland for his meal today so I've no cause to rush. It's a miserable old day for walking, shall I give you a lift into the village? You can come and sit with us old bats and have a cup of something lovely and hot to soothe the shock of this."

Trudy nodded, numb. She fought the overwhelming urge to return to the comforting scene in her mind.

Mrs. Wright bustled around her classroom, checking the windows, tucking in a towel that was soaking up the leaks, poking a finger into the soil of the classroom plant, tutting as she did so. She walked over to the blackboard and made a note for someone to water the fern.

Trudy watched her, barely taking it in. Instead her attention wandered around the room. She loved this little school, despite its peat fires and leaky windows. It was ancient and drafty, like most of the buildings on Glencarragh, made of the weathered grey stone that formed the craggy cliffs and littered the moors like a child's discarded building blocks. She'd spent every holiday on Glencarragh when she was a child, visiting a distant aunt of her adoptive family. They were the only memories of her childhood that were clear - full of joy and freedom; staying with her kindly, free-spirited aunt she had been free from the disapproving glances of grown-ups and the taunts of classmates. Glencarragh was a place where she'd felt, for the first time in her troubled young life, that she belonged and that she was safe. It had taken her years to find her way back to the island. All she had ever wanted was to live here. And now it was being snatched away.

"Ready?"

Mrs. Wright stood expectantly at the classroom door, one hand hovering over the light switch, the other clutching several bags and a set of keys.

Blushing, Trudy nodded and scurried to the door, slipping through and into the cold hallway. The central heating was coal-fired and not terribly efficient. At the behest of several parents and the Ladies Auxiliary, the old fireplaces that were in each classroom were refitted for peat stoves and they helped to keep the rooms warm during the worst of the wind and rain. The children quickly learned not to linger in the hallways.

The two women walked out of the large oak doors into the onslaught of wind and rain. Clouds scudded across the sullen grey sky and the trees were bent sideways against the buffeting force of the wind. It grabbed Mrs. Wright's headscarf immediately, pulling it upwards into a high peak as she struggled with her bags and the car keys. Trudy watched helplessly on, wanting to come to the older woman's assistance but feeling awkward at the idea of asserting herself into the situation. Her anxiety bubbled to a rolling boil as she reached out and withdrew her hands several times before Mrs. Wright simply thrust a bag of papers into her hands. The lashing rain disguised the tears that were welling from Trudy's eyes as she stood waiting for Mrs. Wright to unlock her car.

As the little car made its way through the puddles of the

parking area, windshield wipers waving madly, Trudy began to regret her decision to accept the offer of a lift into the village. Sitting in such close quarters with someone she knew as an authority figure felt strange and uncomfortable. To be in the head teacher's car felt like a familiarity that she didn't deserve. Then again, she reminded herself, Mrs. Wright was no longer her boss. She bit her lip and dug her fingernails into the palms of her hands, swallowing down the wail that threatened to erupt. She stared out of the car window instead, letting her gaze move through the streaking rain, back to the shepherd's croft where the old man and the small child were carrying peat indoors. *The child must be his grandson*, thought Trudy. *How lovely that they're spending some time together. The old fellow probably appreciates the help and it's good for the young ones to feel useful.*

"Trudy? Did you hear me?"

Trudy started and turned away from the window, blinking. Mrs.Wright was glancing at her, a small frown on her face. Seeing the look of confusion on Trudy's she smiled, indulgent now that she was no longer an employee.

"Away with the faeries again, were we?" she asked, her eyes twinkling. "The children are going to miss your stories, that's to be sure."

Trudy winced. She'd been teased her whole life for her absent-minded, daydreaming ways. It hadn't helped that she'd insisted her stories were real. At least until she'd had that beaten out of her by the bigger girls. Every school report and then, in adulthood, every workplace review she'd ever had, had made mention of her tendency to be distracted and to daydream which lead to more discipline and more teasing until eventually the people around her had given her up for a lost cause. Which, as far as Trudy was concerned, was perfectly fine. She hadn't seen any members of her adoptive family for almost seven years and it hadn't bothered her in the slightest. Cards and perfunctory telephone calls on the holidays and birthdays was the extent of their contact. She'd been content to live a solitary life and it wasn't until she'd moved to Glencarragh that she'd developed friendships with people her own age. She'd met the few young people through the various school and village fundraisers and while she felt that she still didn't exactly fit in with the vibrant, chatty group, she'd come to enjoy their company, especially Cliona and Frances. Folk on Glencarragh, she'd soon realized, especially those young ones, were more forgiving of strangeness and eccentricity. The painter, Frances, had once made a joke about entertaining angels which had made the others laugh, but even Trudy had noticed it wasn't an entirely joky laugh.

"I was just telling you about the new school," said Mrs.Wright, with mild frustration. Trudy may no longer be her employee, but her vague expression really was infuriating. She sometimes wondered if she was all there. If it hadn't been for her incredible work with the children, she might have suspected Trudy was a bit deficient in her mental faculties. She really was disappointed to be losing her. And so, she thought darkly, would be the remaining parents.

"Oh?" said Trudy, pasting an interested expression on her face. "I'm sorry, I was daydreaming. Tell me again, it sounds like a marvelous place."

Mrs. Wright beamed and launched into a lengthy description of the newly constructed school.

By the way she's going on, thought Trudy, making a concerted effort to pay attention, *you'd think she wanted to go there herself.*

She shot a sideways glance at Mrs.Wright and realized that she was correct in her assumption. The thought filled her with a crushing feeling of unfairness. Mrs. Wright would gladly leave Glencarragh - her children were grown and gone, and Mr. Wright worked off-island much of the time anyway. She felt a stirring of something like anger but quickly pushed it back down.

Thankfully, the trip into the village wasn't a long one and Trudy escaped from the confines of the car, almost before it had come to a complete stop. Even the coldness of the rain was a welcome relief from the stifling atmosphere of the vehicle. She closed her eyes and inhaled deep, recharging lung-fulls of the crisp air. They'd parked down close to the quayside, so the air was charged with salt and seaweed and a slight tang of fish. Trudy felt it seeping into her, settling the roiling emotions that were crashing around in her chest. The rain had eased and she would far prefer to take herself for a walk along the beach than sit in a crowded room listening to people say consoling things, but she was already committed. Changing her mind at this point simply wasn't an option.

"Come on, lass," said Mrs. Wright, clutching her handbag with one hand and her headscarf with the other. "Don't dawdle, you'll get soaked."

Without waiting for Trudy, she headed towards the tea shop, side-stepping puddles as she hurried up the small incline, away from the car park.

Sighing, Trudy gave the sea a wistful glance and turned to follow her.

* * *

It was exactly as she'd expected it would be.

The women who frequented the tea shop at that time of day were mostly the wives of fishermen and men who worked off-island. The few farms which were left on Glencarragh were too far flung to make it easy for those women to come into the village every day. They were a kindly sort; maternal and bossy, but in a generous-hearted, well-meaning way. They were exactly the kind of women Trudy had wished she'd had in her life when she was younger, but because the warm inclusiveness was such an alien concept to her, she found herself always off-balance around them. She couldn't always tell if they liked her or were exasperated by her. Which, to be fair, was generally most people's response to Trudy.

Immediately upon hearing Mrs. Wright's grave announcement, the women set about petting and consoling her. They bought her a whole pot of tea and a selection of scones, most of which sat untouched on the plate in front of her. There had been commiseration and righteous indignation and then they'd moved onto finding the bright side of the whole affair. Wasn't it just marvelous to have such an opportunity as a place in the new school? They'd listened with rapt attention to Mrs. Wright as she extolled the virtues of new construction and modern teaching practices. In the end, they'd decided it was For The Best and Things Would Be Grand before moving on to other topics, leaving Trudy, blessedly alone.

She glanced out of the steamed-up window of the tea shop. The weather had taken a turn for the worse again, the persistent drizzle shifting back into a lashing downpour.

Self-consciously, she pushed a strand of wet hair behind her ear then folded her thin, red, fingers around the hot teacup.

"...what do you think, Trudy?"

"Hm?" she started and blushed, instantly annoyed with herself for doing so.

"I was asking what you think of our newest tourist boat. Haven't those been just the answer to all of our troubles?"

Hilda Burns fancied herself the spokesperson of the village, the entire island, actually. It was she who'd invited the Eco-Tours scout to a town meeting in the first place and was, evidently, taking full credit for the success, past, present and future, of the island's tourist industry. The newest boat was set to take the first load of eager bird and seal-watchers out into the bay just as soon as the season turned. Donal Stewart had finally been convinced to sell his brand new trawler, a replacement for the one lost to the sea, in the last Great Storm. The same storm had claimed the life of his only son, Ewan, and he'd been understandably reluctant to part with the boat. Now, everyone was delighted to think there'd be more opportunity to separate the tourists from their money.

"Oh, I'm sure it'll be lovely," lied Trudy, softly. The boatloads of tourists with their bright, expensive, waterproofs and fancy, oversized, cameras disturbing the peace of the island's wildlife made Trudy wince, which she then attempted to disguise by reaching up to scratch her nose.

"Ah, Trudy! Would you ever have a bad word to say about anything?" exclaimed Hilda, clearly delighted.

The gathered women laughed kindly then turned their attention to discussing the strange artist-woman who made the odd paintings that all the tourists wanted to buy, although heaven knew why because they were the oddest-looking things.

Trudy retrieved her still-dripping mackintosh from a peg near the door. She hadn't bothered to say goodbye to the women, she doubted they would even notice she'd gone. Sliding gingerly into her wet coat, she slipped her hand into the pocket, as she always did, making sure her stone was still there, and stepped out into the driving rain.

Chapter 2

Cliona swore in frustration.

Climbing down off the large boulder, she tucked her long skirt up around her waist and stepped carefully into the bog, using hummocks of wet grass as stepping stones to reach the place where the page from her notebook had landed. Thankfully, it had caught around the skeletal remains of one of last summer's bog lilies. That had slowed the seeping brown water that was wicking up to claim it. Plucking it from the grasping tendrils of the dried flower, Cliona made her way gingerly back to the stone where her sketchbook and pens were waiting. She pressed the damp page between the folds of her handkerchief and clambered back up to her perch.

"I don't know why you bother coming out here when the wind is as wild. Wouldn't it be easier to go and sit in the nice warm tea shop or even the Oracle? Surely that mad old git would let you set up your bits on one of his tables."

"Surely, Iain MacGreive, wouldn't it be easier for us all if you just threw yourself into the bog and disappeared?" replied Cliona blithely, without looking around.

"Och, now. I'm sure you don't mean it," said the tall, black-haired, young man. "After all, aren't I the catch of the day?

What would all the lovely tourist ladies do without me to take photographs of?"

Iain sidled around the rock and leaned to look over Cliona's shoulder. She closed her notebook with a snap.

"What? Don't you want me to admire your drawings, then? New postcard pictures, is it?"

"Sod off, Iain," she replied, stuffing her notebook into the scuffed brown satchel that she'd tucked under her left leg. Despite having decided to return to her artistic efforts, she was still very uncomfortable with other people seeing them. Her friend, Frances, was an accomplished painter and produced gorgeous painting after gorgeous painting, seemingly effortlessly, while Cliona still struggled with producing what she thought of as useable sketches. As least, that was how she saw it. Feargus, who had first started buying her illustrated cards and postcards a couple of years ago, had insisted that her botanical drawings and watercolour landscapes were gorgeous. Not that she didn't doubt his sincerity, but she did wonder about his qualifications. Still, it was for Frances that she had returned to her little experiments and she was willing to persevere for the cause.

She fixed a mock scowl on her face and directed it towards her childhood friend, who was holding out his hand. "It'll be a sad day for Glencarragh when all we have to recommend us is your weasely face showing up in some rich old bat's holiday snaps."

"Shall I walk you back, then?"

"Aye, go on, you great pain in the arse!"

She took his outstretched hand and let him help her off the boulder and onto drier ground. He sketched a bow as she landed beside him.

Cliona laughed and gave Iain a shove

"Come on, let's go to Feargus, yeah? There's bound to be a cuppa going and you can tell the mad old git himself about how you're going to save the village with your smile and your clothes stinking of fish."

"As well I should, you know. Besides, it's not the weather that'll draw the punters so it might as well be the dashing young fishermen, aye?"

Cliona frowned.

"Is it…"

"Aye," said Iain, the laughter fading from his face. "It's bloody pissing down."

Cliona glanced up at the cloudless blue sky. They were only a half hour walk, at most, from the village. She felt her stomach clench and a brief stab of pain lanced behind her eyes. Rain concentrating itself over the village couldn't be a good thing.

"Any news from Frances?" asked Iain as they made their way down the steep hill towards the village. They'd walked in silence for most of the journey across the moor, the strange weather patterns setting each of them wandering through memories of the last Great Storm that had changed all of their lives. So much had happened then, and in the intervening months, that the memory of what life was like before it happened seemed lost to the mists of time. The people they'd been and the lives they were living belonged to someone else; they belonged to people who hadn't had their world torn apart and turned upside down.

Cliona shook her head.

"Nothing, yet. Well, not of the wee fellow, anyway. She's seeing plenty of the other lot about, but not Moss."

"That's a rotten shame," said Iain, his shoulders sagging. "I thought for sure she'd have seen him again by now. Getting the school children to do that show was genius. What faery could resist a bunch of kids singing and dancing and painting dragons?"

Cliona chuckled.

The First Annual Glencarragh Children's Art Exhibition had been a resounding success. She smiled at the memory of Frances trying to explain to the head teacher why she thought it would be an excellent idea. Mrs.Wright, a lovely but fairly unimaginative creature, had simply passed it over to the teacher's assistant, who, to everyone's astonishment, took the project on with great enthusiasm. Not only had she not questioned the difficult explanations of why they wanted to do it in the first place, but had embraced it with such seriousness that both Frances and Cliona had started wondering if perhaps the shy, slightly awkward young woman might become a true ally in their quest to bring Moss home. In the end, they'd decided it was worth a try and told her everything.

"A house brownie?" she'd repeated, when Frances had told her the tale of her lost friend. "You had a house brownie?"

Cliona and Frances exchanged worried glances. They'd invited Trudy to the tea shop under the guise of discussing the possibility of making the children's art festival an annual affair. Sitting across from her, seeing the sparkle of tears welling in her eyes and her pale, worried expression flickering and shifting rapidly, made each of them wonder if perhaps they'd made a grave error in judgement.

Trudy had seen them looking at one another and cursed

herself. She needed to calm down, her emotions were galloping around like crazed horses, colliding with one another in the tightly controlled, confined space of her heart. But she could barely believe her ears; it wasn't so much that the two women were talking about faeries as if they were simply a regular part of everyday life, but they genuinely seemed to believe, what Trudy herself had longed to, but never allowed herself to believe - that it was all true.

She'd taken a deep breath and tried to get her thoughts in order. This had happened before, she reminded herself; people liked to tease her. Maybe someone had told them about her daydreaming, and they were trying to have a bit of fun. Trudy swallowed down the knot of screams that threatened whenever the memories of her past trauma welled up in her mind. She dug her fingernails into her palms as the familiar swimming feeling drifted into her mind, the hazy, blurry invitation to let her thoughts take her to happier places. She fought the urge to look out of the window where she knew she'd see, not the cobbled streets of the village and the bobbing boats down at the quayside, but a green expanse of moor and an old, shepherd's croft. She thought, with fleeting panic, of her calming stone, which was in the pocket of her coat, all the way across the room.

"Are you alright?" Frances had asked, starting to become genuinely alarmed. Trudy's face had turned a frightening shade of grey and her eyes were staring wildly at the two women.

"Are you true?"

It came out in a croaking whisper, Trudy's lips barely moving. Frances frowned at the strange formality of the question. The structure of it was so familiar. A person didn't spend large amounts of time in conversation with faery folk without becoming accustomed to their way of speaking.

Cliona raised her eyebrows, opening her mouth as if to say something, but Frances silenced her with a slight shake of her head.

"I swear I am true," she said, her tone soft and mimicking the sing-song lilt of the fae, "I swear upon the first blossom of spring's return, I am true."

Trudy nodded, the unshed tears slipping free to stream down her face. Her thin, red fingers clenched and unclenched, her breath coming in short, rasping gasps.

"Here, love," said Cliona, leaning across the table to pass the shuddering woman her handkerchief. "Take a deep breath now, that's it. You're safe here with us. Everything's alright. You're alright now, that's it."

They'd waited for a few more minutes while Trudy's breathing steadied and she wiped her tears.

"I'm terribly sorry," she said, her voice trembling. "I don't mean to cause a fuss. It's just, well…people haven't always been kind to me, you see, and I suppose it's just a bit of a shock to know that it's all true."

She shot them a glance, the look of a frightened hare, caught in a trap.

"It really *is* true, isn't it? You're not just having me on?"

Frances felt something in her chest give way, tears pricking at the back of her own eyes. She heard Cliona take a sharp breath before she forced out a chuckle.

"Bloody right, it is," she said, reaching over to squeeze Trudy's hand. "And aren't we glad of it?"

It had all come out then. Frances told Trudy the story of Moss and how he'd come to live with her and then of how and why she'd lost him. Cliona told her about Skelly and the wind singing and what had really happened in the Great Storm that folk eluded to in hushed tones.

Trudy had sat, letting her tea get cold, a look of pure enchantment on her face.

"I can't believe there was a time when you weren't making those beautiful paintings," she breathed in absolute wonder. She'd seen Frances' work in Dorothy McShane's gift shop. In fact, she'd gone in so often, just to stare at them, that Dorothy had eventually harassed her into buying something. Her assistant's salary didn't lend itself to extravagant purchases, so she'd had to settle for a small postcard print of her favourite painting - the one depicting a young woman standing at the edge of a menacing sea while two strange-looking creatures appeared in the storm-leaden sky above her. She'd spent hours simply staring at it, memorizing the details - the foam-flecked shapes of sea-black horses in the surf, the ghost of antlers rising from the forehead of one of the sky creatures, and the faint, almost undetectable outline of a dark-haired woman in the leaden clouds.

Frances had grimaced, thinking back to the months in the damp outbuilding studio that she'd called home. After a crushing review at her first exhibition, she'd decided she was no longer going to paint and had returned to doing graphic design. She'd enjoyed the work well enough, but it wasn't what she was meant to be doing. It had taken the devious machinations of an old sheep farmer to show her the error of her ways. That, and losing her dear friend Moss.

"I know," she replied, her eyes downcast. She fiddled with a teaspoon. "Not the best time of my life. But here we all are, right?"

Trudy nodded, still sniffling.

"Yes," she'd said, her voice firm. "And you can count on me to help you in any way that I can."

"Penny for them," said Iain, jostling her with his shoulder. "You've got that look on your face that Trudy gets. Have you gone off with the faeries as well?"

Cliona stuck out her tongue.

"You leave our Trudy alone," she said, slapping him affectionately with her satchel. "She's alright. She's had a horrible go of things, poor sod. No wonder she's an anxious mess."

Iain's expression sobered, recalling the stories he'd been told of the terrible bullying Trudy had endured as a child.

"Aye, you're right. Poor wee thing. She's a grand one with those kids, though, isn't she? I can't believe she managed to pull off that concert, fairly much all on her own."

Cliona laughed, thinking of the rows of children, proudly bearing standards with haphazardly painted flags declaring them Citizens of the Imaginarium. It had been a marvelous performance and young and old folk alike had left the school gymnasium with stars in their eyes. Frances had been convinced that it would have brought Moss home. The magic was fairly thrumming that night. But it hadn't, and here they were, clearly on the brink of another storm.

The rain had started as they'd come down the hill into the village, or rather, they'd walked into the rain as they came down the hill. It had slowed to a misting drizzle but they both knew, from experience, that it was only a lull.

"Come on," said Cliona, elbowing Iain. "Let's pick up the pace a bit, or we're going to get soaked."

* * *

"So you're managing then?" asked the forest lord, nodding towards the stretch of moor, dotted with bursts of purpling heather and white splotches of sheep.

The old sheep farmer smiled grimly.

"Aye, you might say," he said, squinting against the sun. He took in the pressed wool trousers, tweed cap and waxed jacket of the man standing before him. "Bit of a dandy, aren't you?"

The forest lord laughed, a deep, earthy, chuckle and glanced down at his outfit. "I thought I was blending in with the local gentry," he said, wryly. "Have I overdone it?"

"Ah, I don't know," murmured Skelly. "'Tis very Country Gentleman's Quarterly, I suppose. Not my particular fancy, but then I've never been the one for following the latest fashions." He gestured at his patched corduroy trousers and worn overcoat with its giant pockets.

The two sworn enemies roared with laughter. The wind carried the sound high over the edge of the distant cliffs and out onto the foaming waves where it skipped across the surface like a hunting bird.

After the laughter died away, Skelly glanced warily at the old god.

"Cernach, you rotten old bastard. I've not seen you for more years than I've the inclination to count, and when last I did, I wanted to kill you."

The other man smiled at the old shepherd.

"Yes, I do recall the occasion," he tilted his head and regarded the other man thoughtfully. "However, I'm counting on the passage of time to have mellowed your vengeful nature."

Skelly grinned, a wicked glint in his green eyes.

"Bit of a risk, that, isn't it?"

The dark-skinned man shrugged and opened his hands in a gesture of surrender.

"I'm still standing here. You haven't blasted me off a cliff."

"Yet."

"Yet," he acquiesced, merriment creasing his angular features.

"And I believe I have shown you the goodness of my intentions of late, have I not? My delivery arrived safely, did it not?"

Skelly scowled.

"Safe, mebbe. But not exactly sound. What happened to the wee man, then?"

Cernach shook his head slowly, his eyes out over the horizon.

"It's best we not discuss the details of such matters. If it weren't for the rise in magic that day, well…let's just say it would not have ended well. As it is, I took a great risk in showing my hand, as it were, so the less you know, the better for all involved. Particularly your house guest."

Skelly sighed and spat into the heather.

"Will you come and sit by my fire, then?" asked Skelly, waving his hand toward a distant dwelling that hadn't been there moments before.

"Yes," said the lord of the forest, his face creasing into a sharp-toothed smile. "I believe I will."

"Why now, then?" asked Skelly as the two men walked across the moor towards his croft. The sun had begun to set, and the golden glow cast long shadows behind them. Anyone with an eye for such things would see the faint outline of antlers sprouting from the silhouette of his companion's head. Skelly himself cast only a shadow of his earthbound form. "This cursed island has been in need of your help for long before this, why turn up now?"

The forest lord, who called himself Cernach, walked in silence, the question hung in the air between them. There was no hurry to answer it. They were used to having plenty of time.

Eventually, he spoke, his voice a rumble of stones.

"There are forces gathering again," he said, choosing his words carefully. "Forces that neither of us have reason to favour."

Skelly snorted.

"If you mean Lira, she's been 'gathering her forces', as you put it, for centuries. There's nothing new in that. We just replay the same old battle over and over again and one day, one of us will win."

"True," said Cernach, "but this time she has reason to worry and when Lira gets worried, we all suffer."

"You're content then?" Cernach asked, shoving his hands deep into the pockets of his coat and rummaging until he produced a clay pipe. He proceeded to knock the old tobacco against the heel of his hand, glancing out from under his cap to look at Skelly. The two men were sat in tattered armchairs on either side of a peat fire, which blazed merrily in a scrubbed stone hearth. In the reflection of flames dancing over the Skelly's face, he saw a grimace - a twist of pain that settled into a soft frown of sorrow.

"Aye," said Skelly, leaning forward and clasping his hands

around a jar of honey-coloured liquid. "I am."

"Then why did you bind the painter? And why help the wind singer?"

"I've got no choice where the wind singer is concerned, as well you know it," retorted Skelly. "Those young lasses found my bit of glass all those years ago, I had no choice. Where were you then, I might ask," he added bitterly, "if I didn't already know the answer."

"And the painter, then?"

Skelly shrugged.

"Lira took the sea from me. She took my people and she took my home. But I've never forgotten, and I've never stopped wanting to find my way back. The song of the sea is as strong as ever it was, but my people - our people," he glared accusingly at the forest lord, "are fading from the mortal world. And with them go any chance at all of the rest of us surviving. 'Tis only right I do something if I'm able. Pan knows I've nowt else to do."

Shrugging, he added, "Besides, she keeps me near the sea."

Cernach nodded.

"So, by binding the painter you solved two problems?"

"Aye, I suppose I did."

"Good."

Skelly looked at the forest lord. He wore the face of a man whose features were muted and shadowed, the eye tending to involuntarily glance off and away from his direct gaze.

"What do you mean by that?"

"It means not only have you not lost hope; you're far from the contentment you claim."

Skelly scowled; his narrowed eyes full of suspicion.

"Supposing you're right, how's that a good thing?"

"Because I dare say, whether or not you think your erstwhile queen will emerge victorious, you'll go along with what I have in mind."

"Which is?"

"There's someone else in Glencarragh you might find to be of interest."

"Oh, aye?"

Skelly tilted his head like a curious bird, but he still regarded the old god with deep suspicion. Time may have passed but he knew that Cernach, by his very nature, wasn't one to be entirely trusted. If he was showing an interest in Glencarragh, after so many years, there was likely to be something in it to benefit himself.

"Yes," said Cernach, taking a deep draw on his pipe. The smoke wreathed around his head, winding between the tines of the antlers that ghosted in and out of view.

Melodramatic sod, thought Skelly, sourly. *He does that on purpose.*

"Consider this to be my contribution," continued Cernach.

"Contribution?"

"To the Three."

Skelly blanched.

Cernach chuckled, a deep rumbling sound, his dark eyes catching the firelight making them glow.

"You can't fool me, you old sea devil," said Cernach, wagging his pipe stem at the old farmer. "As if I'd believe you'd sit back and let that miserable harpy keep you here for a thousand years. And to use humans? Excellent. It gives it all a delightful sense of poetic justice, doesn't it?"

Skelly scowled.

"I never had a proper plan," he said, defensive. "You make it sound like I masterminded some plot. All I had was a notion and I took the opportunities when they arose. But it's not going to work. The wind singer is a fiery bit that won't do as she's told, she'll be years coming into herself, and the painter, apart from essentially being free of my binding by now, is still all broken-hearted over her lost house-brownie."

A shadow stirred in the corner. Cernach glanced over then back at Skelly. He raised a sculpted eyebrow but Skelly's face remained impassive.

"Neither one of them is strong enough," continued Skelly, his gaze fixed on the flames of the hearth fire, "or disciplined enough, for that matter."

"Perhaps," acknowledged Cernach, "but what would you say if I told you there was another way?"

Skelly glared at him.

"If you're meaning the exchange, then you're more out of touch than I thought. There's not a mortal about that would give themselves over. There might be believers, and those two are about as believing as they come, but that only goes so far. As far as the rest of their lot, most don't think much of the old stories, they've no' got any imagination at all."

Cernach chuckled at the bitterness in his old foe's voice.

"So, you've tried, then?"

Skelly grinned, showing a row of sharp white teeth.

"Aye, maybe I have." He glanced around the tiny cottage and his face clouded over. "Not to any success, obviously."

"You've lost your charm, old boy," said Cernach, teasing. "Who would have imagined? Maybe you should pick a different persona," he gestured towards the worn corduroys and shock of white hair. "The kindly old fellow obviously isn't doing the trick."

Skelly scowled.

"It works well enough," he retorted. "I bound the painter, didn't I?"

Cernach regarded him for a moment, then looked around the cottage. It was lit only by the fire and one single oil lamp. Small, but surprisingly clean, it had the air of temporariness that one might find in an inn or lodging house. It was somewhere to live, but it wasn't a home. The glass at his elbow had mysteriously been refilled. He glanced over to the shadowed corner from where a sense of something lingered, but he decided to ignore it. Whatever Skelly believed, that whole enterprise had likely been a wasted mission. There had been damage sorely done. Still, it had amused him to play the hero.

He turned his gaze back to Skelly who was staring, mutinously into the flames and he made a decision. He'd wanted to see how things really were with his old enemy before he played his hand.

"Have you time for a tale?" he asked, bowing his head to accompany the formal request.

Skelly looked up at him, surprise mixing with scorn on his face. He raised a shaggy eyebrow and gestured with a gnarled hand.

"Suit yourself," he grunted, then, at the look of disapproval that crossed Cernach's handsome features he sighed wearily and returned the bow. "A tale would be welcome," he replied, "The dark has risen and it's a long night we're in for."

Cernach smiled, satisfied, took a sip of the honeyed wine and settled into the telling.

"As well you know, my preference has been to keep moving," began Cernach.

Skelly grimaced, biting back the retort that rose to his lips. *Good for some*, he thought, sourly, taking a large mouthful of wine. The sweetness burned his throat and brought tears to his eyes.

"However, from time to time, it has served me to remain in certain places. You may be interested to know, that, for a time, one of those places was Glencarragh."

Skelly raised a questioning eyebrow but said nothing. He had only been able to return to the vicinity of Glencarragh because of his bond with the painter, Frances; he was still not able to move about in the rest of the mortal world with any ease. The curse that had resulted in his exile meant that any proximity to the sea caused him excruciating pain, which was why he preferred to spend most of his time in, what was known as, the In-Between. Also known as the Borderlands, it was a time and space that existed between the mortal world and the Otherworld and was a place to which many of his kind had retreated when humans began to lose touch with magic.

As it appeared that he was to get no response from Skelly, Cernach continued with his story.

"It may also interest you to know, not that you'd let on, I can see, that another of our kind frequented this place during those particular years." He didn't bother to wait this time but carried on. "The Old Mother set herself up in a little hovel, not unlike this one, on a coastal hill, not unlike this one, and it was to she that our significant personage came to visit."

Skelly felt a stab of reluctant interest. If the Old Mother had an interest in this person, then they must be of some power. She tended, even less than most, to get involved with the affairs of mortals.

Cernach caught the flicker of curiosity on Skelly's face and smiled inwardly, warming to the tale. He couldn't bear a disinterested audience; it was an affront to his pride.

"For a number of years, during the high season, a small girl came to visit the island with a family not of her blood. This particular girl, a mortal, I remind you, had, *has,* the gift of Traveling,"

Skelly perked up at that. Traveling, or the ability to move into the In-Between without faery assistance was a rare talent in mortals.

"Was she of faery blood, then, this one?" he asked, unable to maintain his air of indifference. "You said her family wasn't of her blood. Surely that's the only way she…"

Cernach smiled, his features slipping distressingly. The long snout of a fox shifted into the hooked beak of a raven then back to the handsome, dark-skinned man. A rack of antlers shimmered and solidified, reaching almost as high as the low cottage roof.

Skelly scowled.

"Never mind that bollocks," he said, "I'm not impressed with your amateur theatrics. Just answer the bloody question."

Impervious to his difficult audience, Cernach ignored him and continued with his tale. It did not serve his purpose to answer Skelly's question and so he would not.

"In the course of time, I made myself known to the young girl, seeing in her, a certain potential."

"You mean you wanted her in your pocket," said Skelly, leaning back in his chair. "So much for your not getting involved."

Cernach stifled his irritation. Skelly's commentary was disrupting the flow of his tale. He was used to a more rapt audience and found such critical assessment to be highly distasteful. He frowned at his old enemy who simply grinned and cocked his head, challenging him to retaliate.

"It would behoove you," he said, stiffly, "to keep your comments and remarks until the tale is told. I see you haven't lost your innate bloody-mindedness."

"Would I have survived this long if I had?"

Cernach bowed his head, antlers ghosting out of sight.

"The girl," he continued, "could not only pass into the In-Between, but did so almost effortlessly and would dwell there for substantial amounts of time, seemingly without ill-effect. And so, I, with the blessing of the Old Mother, sought to engage her in conversation."

"Did you not frighten the life out of the wee lass?" said Skelly, regarding the powerful, broad-shouldered frame and the uneasy features of the old forest god. He waved a hand down at himself. "Sure, you can see the wisdom of my old sheep farmer now?"

Cernach grinned his fox-faced grin.

"Ah, but what wee girl who walked freely in the In-Between would be afraid of a talking fox?"

"You never did?"

"Yes, indeed. And not only did she find me charming, she brought me tasty morsels from the mortal world. We dined on jam sandwiches and currant buns. Once, she even brought me a sliver of roast beef, wrapped in her own darling little handkerchief."

Skelly snorted.

"Leave it to you, you old dog, to charm the poor wee soul. What did you promise her then?"

Cernach drew himself up to his full height, which, even

seated in the armchair, was substantial.

"I made no promises," he said, his voice low and serious. "That is a lesson I have no wish to repeat."

Skelly frowned, his thoughts returning to long-ago promises of his own. He glanced at his fireside companion who was gazing into the flames, seeing far beyond the flickering stack of peat.

"So, you made friends with a wee girl," prompted Skelly. "Then what?"

Cernach shook himself free of his memories and shrugged. His interest in spinning the tale was waning, as it was wont to do. The unwelcome memories had taken the enjoyment from the moment.

"I gave her your daughter's sea glass," he said, fixing Skelly with his black-eyed stare.

Skelly blanched. His fingers gripped the arms of his chair. Something clattered in the shadowed corner but neither faery acknowledged it.

"Why?" croaked Skelly, his voice barely above a whisper. It had been hundreds of years since he'd allowed himself to think of the child he'd had, the child he'd lost, when he'd been cast from the sea. She'd been cast out along with him, although her fate wasn't quite that of the rest of the merrin who had angered Lira. In the end, it was her sacrifice which had allowed the rest of her kin to survive, albeit as selkies, neither of sea nor of land, but always trapped somewhere in between. It had been that or destruction for them all.

"Why?" he repeated, "there's no chance of finding her, you must know that."

He regarded Cernach with some pity. The forest god had fallen deeply in love with the beautiful merrin that had been

Fia, Skelly's beloved, only child. Their unwise marriage had been the beginning of everything that had gone wrong since. Skelly found it hard to believe that Cernach would be so foolish as to hold out hope and said as much.

Cernach winced as the words fell from Skelly's mouth. In his heart, of course, he knew it to be true and that was never his purpose in giving the girl Fia's glass. His purpose leaned far more towards revenge than reunion, but hearing Skelly say it out loud made him aware that perhaps he had held onto a small hope that he would see her again.

"Of course not," he said, summoning a light tone. "My intentions were far more calculated."

"Oh aye?"

"Aye, as you say," said Cernach, warming up to the big finish. "Because that wee girl is now a grown woman and has made her way, as I expected she would, to the shores of Glencarragh."

Skelly raised his eyebrows, leaning slightly forward in his chair.

"And, my old enemy, she has what we need to break Lira's curse, once and for all."

"And what makes you think she'll have any inclination to do that? I happen to have a bit of experience in these affairs and I can tell you, mortals aren't the most co-operative of creatures."

Cernach smiled, his teeth gleamed white in the flickering darkness.

"Because it was she, old man, who made *me* a promise."

Chapter 3

The rain had turned sideways.

The wind whipped the hood from Trudy's head and the water ran in icy rivulets down her neck.

Why, oh, why didn't I just go straight home? she thought to herself, tugging ineffectually at her mackintosh, trying to regain control of her wayward hood. *I could have been under a blanket with a cup of tea and my book by now.*

The harbour was deserted, the unsettled weather of the past week having forced most of the fishermen to remain at home. The markets were not so desperate for fresh fish that men were willing to risk life and limb. They had learned some difficult lessons over the years. Indeed, what few fishing families remained had secured alternate employment to fill the gaps. It wasn't possible to earn a living from the sea anymore, they said, the storms had made sure of that. And having to do odd jobs wasn't the end of the known world. It certainly was a blessing on weeks when the sea raged, encouraged by the gusting north wind that never seemed to relent of late.

The brightly painted boats bobbed up and down with the surging waves. *The Maid of Glencarragh, The Cormorant, The Sea Sprite*— the names were as familiar to her as the families who owned them. It was her habit to take the harbour route on her way home from school each afternoon and the sight of the boats, safely docked, filled her with a contentment she found hard to explain. She had been born and raised in a bustling city on the mainland, there wasn't a grain of salt in her — as the tea shop ladies were fond of reminding her. Yet she always found a strange peace in the nearness of the wild sea and it was to the shore that she invariably came when things became more than she could manage. Which, she would unhappily admit, was more often than not.

She fought the battering wind down to the edge of the quayside. She thought, briefly, of keeping going and picking up the cliff path that would eventually lead her down to the beach, but recognized it would be unwise. The sea was contained in the harbour by the clever construction of strategically placed seawalls but beyond those boundaries, Trudy knew it would be raging.

She glanced around, convinced that if she were to look back she'd see the faces of the sensible women with their sensible advice staring through the fogged windows, laughing at her foolishness. *Of course they wouldn't,* she reminded herself. Nobody would be watching. She had been marked as odd from the very first day she'd arrived in Glencarragh, all of those years ago, long before she'd come again to answer the post of teaching assistant at the primary school. Trudy gripped the smooth stone in her pocket and let her mind wander back through time.

At five years old, Trudy had finally been adopted. She'd been a foundling, a squalling infant wrapped in tea towels, tucked into a wicker trug and left at firehouse number seven. Her story had captivated the public for a week or so as her mother was searched for but never found, but then she was absorbed into the foster system and duly forgotten.

A strangely silent child, with large pale green eyes and mouse-brown hair she hadn't recommended herself to prospective adoptive couples. She'd been reluctant to meet people's eyes and had an unnerving habit of staring off into space in the middle of conversations, despite them being largely one-sided on the part of adults. There had, briefly, been talk of assessments and diagnoses but bureaucratic wisdom had decided it would simply add to her burdens. And so, she had been allowed to fade into the background and bumble along on her own. When, at age four, she suddenly began speaking in full, complex sentences and showed a remarkable talent for storytelling and other imaginative activities, the wise bureaucracy congratulated itself on letting her 'get there in her own time' and once again she was pushed to the front of the adoption line. After all, who wouldn't want a bright, talkative child to join their family?

The Erskine family already had two children but felt it their Christian duty to take in another, less fortunate creature. They were immediately taken by the small, chatterbox who told them tales of faery realms and talking crows and, after the paperwork was sorted, Trudy joined their family, moving from the only home she'd ever known to a tall, brick semi-detached house in a row of identical tall, brick semi-detached houses.

Her adoptive siblings were disinterested from the very beginning. They hadn't seen the necessity of adding to their perfectly comfortable arrangement and although they were never outwardly cruel, they weren't kind, either and Trudy learned very quickly that it was better to be as convenient and unassuming as possible. She also learned that stories of her adventures in the land of fauns and brownies and talking deer lost their charm after age nine or so. At that point, it was decided by her teachers and parents, that she needed to "get her head out of the clouds" and that imaginative activities ought to be limited to the completion of school assignments. All others were firmly discouraged.

No-one really noticed when she stopped talking unless asked a direct question, and her general nervous disposition was sighed over and discussed and then attributed to her 'difficult beginnings'.

School had been a nightmare. The children there *were* cruel, and she'd suffered horribly at their hands. There was no room in their world for a child like Trudy - silent, awkward and difficult to place in a convenient category. So it was easier for her to dwell in her imagination. She had friends there and adventures and it was a far more enjoyable place than the real world.

The only part of the real world where Trudy felt at home was in the three weeks every summer when the Erskines packed up their car and drove five hours north to the edge of the mainland, then onto a ferry and across a churning sea to the island of Glencarragh. Trudy was smitten from the very first glance at the craggy cliffs and stretches of moor. The rest of her family stayed with Aunt Iris down in the village but it had been decided that it might be better if Trudy stayed in a tiny cottage on the edge of the moor with Aunt Calla. Aunt Iris had even less patience with Trudy's oddities than the rest of her family, who were more or less used to her, having declared her 'a bit simple but harmless'.

Terrified, at first, of being shoved off, alone, into the care of an unknown aunt who, if the glances and whispers were to believed, was as much of a pariah as Trudy herself, she soon recognized a kindred soul and the time spent with Aunt Calla was the only bright point in her distressing and traumatic childhood. With Aunt Calla, she was allowed freedom to roam the shore. She was given flasks of tea and packets of sandwiches and squares of dark, rich chocolate to take on solitary rambles across the moor, with no further warnings given than not to make bargains with the faery folk and be sure to be home before the sun went down. Coming from a world where she'd been told what to do and what to think almost every moment of her life, the freedom that Aunt Calla gave her felt like the greatest gift she'd ever been given. For three weeks every summer, Trudy truly belonged somewhere.

A blast of needle-sharp rain jolted Trudy back from her memories. Sighing, she wiped the streaming rain from her face and pulled the smooth stone from her pocket. It gleamed dully in the grey light of the harbour - a mottled green-brown colour that sometimes glimmered with a strange iridescence. She'd found it one summer on Glencarragh and had carried it with her ever since. Her calming stone, she called it. With her child's imagination, she had imbued it with magical powers that helped her deal with taunts and bullying and making telephone calls. She stared at it for a moment longer, feeling it grow warm in her hand.

"I'm not leaving," she whispered to herself. "Whatever I have to do, I'm not going. No-one can make me. I won't."

She felt a sudden surge of confidence, then. It was as if

whispering the words aloud had affirmed what was truly in her heart. It wasn't going to be easy. Being convenient and accommodating were the habits of a lifetime and wouldn't go gently, but for the first time in recent memory she'd actually acknowledged the fact that she wanted something different from what others were telling her. In the wake of this revolutionary thought, she made another decision. She wasn't going to skulk off back to her flat, she was going to visit a friend.

Taking advantage of a lull in the wind, Trudy pulled the cold, dripping, hood up over her sodden, wind-ravaged hair, stuffed the stone and her hands into her pockets and set off back towards the direction of the town center. Feargus would be getting ready to open the bookshop for its afternoon hours and she fancied a friendly face to go along with a hot cup of tea. Thursdays usually guaranteed a fresh bun as well and she suddenly remembered that she hadn't eaten since breakfast.

So it was one of Feargus' famous cinnamon buns, oozing sweet, cream cheese frosting that was occupying her thoughts when she tripped over the small, green-skinned, boy who was huddled behind a pile of nets.

* * *

"Have you gone quite mad?" cried Feargus, his eyes wide as he stood with his back pressed against the pantry door. He pointed a shaking finger at the shivering bundle that sat dripping in the middle of his kitchen floor, "You can't bring that in here!" his voice rose to a quavering shriek and he passed a hand in front of his eyes in a theatrical gesture of disbelief. Feargus O'Rourke had been a figure in classical theatre before retiring to Glencarragh and was fond of reliving his thespian days whenever a crisis - real or imagined - arose.

"What was I to do, Feargus?" asked Trudy, her eyes as wide as his own. "I couldn't just leave him there, could I? The poor soul is clearly frozen. He would've caught his death sitting out there in that," she gestured toward the rain-smudged windows. The north wind whistled a high keen through invisible gaps in the masonry. "Yours was the closest place I could think of."

That wasn't entirely true. The tea shop would have been closer and the ladies there would have undoubtedly sprung into immediate action. Trudy would have been instantly absolved of responsibility for the small boy. She'd considered that option for only a second before bundling her little charge towards the Oracle.

"Well, first off, that's not a *him,* that's an It! Saints preserve us, Trudy, have you any idea what you've done?"

"What do you mean? Done? I've brought a small boy in from the cold, that's what I've done. And I would remind you of your own policy of hospitality, Feargus O'Rourke." Trudy folded her arms and tried to appear stern. Feargus was one of the few people with whom she felt completely at ease. For all of his bluster, he had a warmth and greatness of heart that was immediately obvious to those who chose to notice such things and Trudy, after a lifetime of feeling confused and lonely, was one of those people.

"That only applies to humans!" wailed Feargus. "Did the small detail of its green skin escape you?" He edged around the counter toward the telephone. "I'm going to have to call in the police, Trudy."

"Which branch of the police would that be then," asked

Trudy, with an air of innocent inquiry. "Would that be the Special Constabulary Regarding Small Shivering Children? Or perhaps the Inspectors Branch Pertaining to Waifs and Strays?"

"Oh, very clever, my dear," said Feargus. "But you're appealing to the wrong person here. I have it on good advice that the presence of such…. entities…in the harbour is a desperate omen and I'll wager that there's not a fisherman in the village that wouldn't rejoice at seeing this one packed off - and quickly."

Trudy glanced down at the shivering child. His strange, mottled green-brown skin had a luminescence to it - like sunlight rippling across still water. His hair was a deeper shade of green, a snarled collection of bits of seaweed and pieces of shell. He wore no clothing other than what looked like one of Eleanor Granger's best tea towels, tied around his waist. Trudy smothered a grin when she imagined Eleanor's discovery of a missing towel - although why she'd have her washing out on a day like today escaped Trudy's understanding.

The child hadn't responded when she gently asked him why he was there and where were his people. She was certain she knew all of the small children on the island, at least the ones from the village, so assumed that he had strayed from one of the tourist cottages or perhaps the Bed and Breakfast on the high street. It wasn't exactly peak tourist season but people visiting family often stayed in other accommodations as many of the village dwellings were painfully small. Standing over him in the lashing rain and wind, she hadn't really questioned the colour of his skin or his lack of appropriate clothing. It was as if she hadn't actually noticed. Which, if she was to be honest, she hadn't. Frowning, she tried to retrieve the memory but couldn't. Shaking her head, she brought her thoughts back to the kitchen and Feargus' hand poised over the telephone as he flipped through his address book.

"What are you doing?" she asked, striding across the room and snatching the book from his hand with uncharacteristic assertiveness. "You can't phone Roddie, he wouldn't believe you anyway."

Feargus stared at Trudy's pale, drawn face. Her green eyes were large and bright above dark smudges and tightly pressed lips. Tears began to well and she swallowed hard.

"Please, Feargus. Whatever you think he is, he's still just a child,"

"Trudy, pet," he said gently, placing a warm hand over her cold, trembling ones and giving them a squeeze. "It's not what I think it is, it's what I *know* it is."

"He," she muttered. "He's a little boy,"

"No, Trudy. He's not a little boy, far from it,"

"What then? What can you possibly be getting at? And what does it matter?" she cried.

"A selkie, love. You've brought a selkie into my home."

Chapter 4

Trudy stared at Feargus, disbelieving.

She glanced down at the green-skinned boy who sat huddled on the floor, his eyes cast down.

"A selkie? You can't be serious, Feargus. Aren't selkies supposed to take the shape of women…or something?"

Trudy frowned, searching her memory for stories about selkies. Since coming to Glencarragh she'd been inundated with them, seeing as how they were the main tourist attraction of the island. Or, at least that's what the brochures would have people believe. Seals had long made Glencarragh Bay their home and if mainlanders wanted to believe they were selkies then the islanders were only too happy to accept their money for the privilege.

Feargus chuckled, placing a long-fingered hand on Trudy's shoulder and squeezing it.

"Aye, lass. So the stories go. But the women are only half of the population, right?"

Trudy blushed.

"Now, now. Don't get yourself worked up. It's a common misconception. The selkie women get all the attention as they're the ones that make the best stories. And, to be fair, your one there probably isn't actually a wee boy, he's just appearing that way because it was the best way to get your attention."

"*My* attention?" said Trudy, still processing the idea of a diverse gendered selkie population. "Why me? I'm the least likely person to approach if you need help with anything."

"That's enough of that," admonished Feargus, gently. He regarded the young woman with an expression of imperceptible sadness. "You do yourself a great disservice, talking like that. What have I told you?"

Trudy swallowed.

"That I'm capable and resourceful and a credit to myself," she quoted, somewhat woodenly.

Feargus sighed.

"One day you might actually believe that," he muttered, turning his attention back to the trembling heap that was dripping all over his kitchen floor.

"Anyway, regardless of how or why, here it bloody well is," He spread his hands wide in a gesture of melodramatic despair. "And what, pray tell, do we do with it now?"

"Feargus!"

Cliona called out merrily as she pushed through the small blue door that led into the bookshop's back passage. Stacks of old tea crates and vintage tinware lined the narrow hallway. The worn wooden floorboards creaked as she and Iain squeezed through.

"Do you wonder if he'll ever do anything with this lot?" Iain gestured at the precarious piles. On top of a particularly high pile of dented treacle tins sat Feargus' runny-nosed cat, Malcolm. He regarded the pair with an air of indignation that only a cat could muster as the cold air from the street blew in and ruffled his patchy, beige fur.

"I expect he has…"

"A system?"

Cliona laughed, turning the doorknob that led to the upstairs flat. Feargus was constantly telling them of the importance of having organizational systems, despite seeming to lack all semblance of them himself.

Iain squeezed through, past the last heap of wooden crates, narrowly missing toppling them over. Malcolm hissed loudly at the disturbance and leapt down, snaking between Iain's legs and dashing up the stairs ahead of them.

"Oh! Hello, Trudy. Lovely to…what the…"

"Jesus-wept, Feargus! Have you lost your bloody mind?"

Feargus smiled weakly as Cliona and Iain looked between him and the huddled, dripping form on the floor.

"You might want to sit down. Trudy has a story to tell you.

Cliona sat across the table from Trudy. They both had their hands wrapped awkwardly around dainty china cups of tea, but neither one had yet taken a sip. Iain leaned against the counter, his arms folded, and his shoulders hunched. A faint scowl creased his features.

"You're telling me you found it down at the quayside?" he asked Trudy.

"Can we please stop calling him an 'it'?" said Trudy, avoiding Iain's glare. She knew he didn't mean to sound cross; Cliona had warned him to watch his tone, knowing how it affected Trudy, but she could hear the spikiness behind his words. Still, she felt very strongly about the way the selkie child was being spoken about as if he didn't matter. "And yes, for the hundredth time, that's where he was. Behind the stack of torn fishing nets, across from Ned Finlay's toolshed."

"Did he have anything with him? Any sort of...bits of anything?" Iain leaned in towards Trudy, searching her face for untruths. "Think carefully, lass. It's truly important,"

"Why, Iain?" asked Cliona, tucking a wayward strand of red hair back into her ponytail. "He's obviously not got any clothes, why on earth would he have any 'bits of anything'?"

"Iain wants to know if the creature has taken anything from any of the boats," said Feargus. "There's a story told among the old folk, that the selkies in the bay know the will of the sea and that if a boat is ill-fated, they'll lay claim to it. Well, not so much the boat as the souls of the drowned..."

Feargus stopped abruptly, a flush of colour rising from his collar. Trudy's eyes widened in alarm and she shot a furtive glance across the table. Iain simply sighed.

"Oh, don't be ridiculous!" said Cliona, ignoring Feargus' blunder. "Half of those selkie stories are just foolish old fish-wives' tales, embellished for the sodding tourist brochures."

"Really?" said Iain, raising an eyebrow. "Are you quite one to be questioning the existence of selkies, then?"

"Iain!"

"No, Feargus," persisted Iain, waving an accusing finger at Cliona and Trudy, "These two are just being a pair of soft-hearted women. And at this moment, they're also half-wits."

Iain turned his attention to Cliona who had drawn herself up into a quivering stance of righteous indignation. Trudy shrank down in her chair, avoiding both of them as they glared at each other. In response to the rising tension, she felt her focus slipping so she gripped her teacup tightly, letting the heat of it ground her.

"Of all people, Cliona, you should understand the seriousness of this," continued Iain, seemingly oblivious to the sparks of fire crackling around his friend. "The rain, woman! You know it's not natural. And," he gestured toward the boy. "the last time one of his lot were spotted, Ewan…"

Cliona pushed away from the table and slammed her cup down, sloshing tea all over the scrubbed pine. Trudy hummed softly to herself, a ballad that her Aunt Calla had sung to her when she was a girl. The words had something to do with May queens and summer wine.

"Iain MacGrieve, you're still as much of a numpty as you were at five years old! Don't you ever, EVER, talk about what happened to Ewan in the same breath as some ridiculous after-the-fact rumours. I can't believe you! Giving any credence to Hilda Burns' hateful gossip. There weren't any seals in the bay that night and you know it. You know as well as I do, it was the storm that wrecked our Ewan's boat, not a bloody selkie!"

Trudy closed her eyes, willing the headache that she felt creeping up to go away. She felt hot and fuzzy-headed and wished she could turn back the clock and start the day all over again. The first thing she'd change, she thought to herself, was agreeing to go to the tea shop with Mrs Wright. It was so tempting to let her mind wander off for a moment. But she had to think of the little selkie boy. She needed to focus.

Opening her eyes again, she saw Iain and Cliona locked in a crackling glare at each other over the table. The air still sparkled with Cliona's anger. *I wonder if she knows how pretty it is,* mused Trudy. *And how it shoots right through the swirling haze of blue and grey of Iain. He'll never best her,* she thought, smiling inwardly. *I don't know why he bothers to try.* She blinked and looked away. She had to be mindful not to stare. Looking around the kitchen, she saw Feargus dry-washing his hands over by the sink. He had his eyes on the green-skinned boy who, in turn, was watching the exchange between Cliona and Iain. Quiet and still, his strange, liquid, eyes darted between the two as they remained locked in each other's furious gaze.

Nobody even acknowledged him, she thought. *They just set about arguing over him. I know how he must be feeling.*

She placed her cup gently on the table and rose from her chair. Moving carefully, she stepped over to where the boy sat huddled near Malcolm's water dish. Surprisingly, the curmudgeonly old cat seemed unperturbed by the visitor. In fact, he had placed himself between the boy and the kitchen table and sat with his tail wrapped around his front paws, staring unblinkingly at Trudy.

"You know he's harmless, don't you?" murmured Trudy, soothingly. She inched closer to the two of them, acknowledging and returning Malcolm's slow blink. The boy's gaze shifted from the other three, who were now arguing in barely restrained whispers amongst themselves. His black eyes glittered with an odd light, but he remained still.

"It's alright," said Trudy softly. "I won't hurt you. And neither will they. They just have a passion for disagreeing with one another; it's what cements their friendship."

"Does it even understand English?" demanded a voice over her shoulder. She flinched, feeling the sharpness of the words like prickles over her skin. Without looking around, she replied,

"Iain, if you insist on calling him 'it', I'm going to have to ask you to…."

"Yes, Iain. Show a little respect for the fearsome evil that sits huddled before you."

Cliona moved to stand beside Trudy, putting herself between Trudy and Iain, giving her a small smile. Trudy smiled back, grateful, as Iain stepped back, contrite.

"Sorry, lass," he said, realizing his mistake. He rubbed a hand over his face. Trudy saw his fingers trembling slightly and the frowning glance he kept directing at Cliona. She understood now; he was just worried for his friend.

Hunkering down, Cliona held out her hand, palm facing up.

The boy regarded her for a moment then reached out his own. His mottled green skin glimmered oddly in her ink-smudged hand.

Trudy smiled as he stood up, and reached out for his other hand, which he took without hesitation.

The three turned to face the two men, differing expressions on their faces; one of triumph, one of quiet determination and one quite unreadable.

"Right then," said Cliona brightly. "Why don't you get lost and go have your photo taken," she said to Iain. Then, nodding towards Feargus, "You can open up your shop and *we* shall go upstairs and find our friend some warmer clothing and get him something to eat."

Marching past the two staring men, she pushed open the kitchen door, to the stairs that led up to Feargus' bedroom. "I trust you have some bits and pieces we can use for clothes, Feargus?" she called back, without waiting for a reply.

Iain and Feargus stood in the empty kitchen, looks of stunned amazement on their faces.

"Well," sighed Feargus, "they've got us beaten."

"Again," grumbled Iain as he ran a rough-knuckled hand through his tangle of black hair. "What're we going to do,

Feargus? What can it mean?"

"It means, my friend, that you guessed right. We must be in for one of those terrible storms."

He sighed and started collecting the teacups.

"I find it highly unlikely that the wee creature just turned up for tea and biscuits. Skelly very likely has a hand in this. And as well you know, no interference by our esteemed friend goes without some meteorological catastrophe of a supernatural persuasion. We need to find out why he sent the bloody thing before anyone else sees it. There'll be pandemonium if anyone finds out. That old gossip Hilda Burns really started something with that nonsense about the selkies appearing right before poor Ewan's boat went down."

"Do you really think it was Skelly that sent the wee beast? It isn't actually some awful omen or the like?"

"Good heavens, Iain! Don't tell me you fancy those old gossipy tales? No, the selkies are in Glencarragh for one reason only and it's got nothing to do with wrecking fishing boats. Well, not as the first order of business, anyhow. And as I said, they don't make themselves known without good reason."

"And by 'good reason' you mean?"

Feargus nodded.

"Aye, I do."

"Disaster."

Chapter 5

" I 'm sorry that Iain comes off as such a horse's backside sometimes," said Cliona, rifling through Feargus' wardrobe. She withdrew a pair of knee-length, tartan golf-shorts and held them up against herself. "He's mostly a lot of hot air, there's no real harm in him. What do you think, my little sea-skinned cherub? Do you fancy looking like an old-man-o'-the-greens?"

The boy sat on the floor by the door where they'd left him, his eyes closed and his head bowed, as if in some form of silent prayer.

"I'm not sure he understands what we're saying," said Trudy, with a furrowed brow. Suddenly, she slumped into a heap on the floor, leaning against Feargus' narrow wooden bed, her pounding head cradled in her hands. "Oh, Cliona, what've I done? What if Feargus and Iain are right? What if I've unleashed some terrible fate on the village?"

Cliona threw her head back and laughed. She tossed the golf-shorts onto the floor with a pile of other discarded items and lay across the bed so that she could wrap her arms around her friend's neck. She planted a kiss on Trudy's hot cheek and gave her shoulder a squeeze.

"Don't you be taking any of that ridiculous bluster to heart,

Trudy. You know how the menfolk like to be all trial-and-peril and go on about the savage sea. It's all a load of superstitious nonsense that ignorant people made up to explain things they'd rather not acknowledge. Everyone knows there've been selkies in Glencarragh since time immemorial. Why do you think the tourists want to be here? Surely not for the great climate and the culture?"

Trudy managed a weak smile.

"But has anyone ever actually seen one, you know, that's not a seal?" asked Trudy, massaging her temples, the force of her thumping head making her eyes ache. Fighting to stay present was taking its toll. Every cell in her body was screaming for the drifting escape of a daydream. "Have you? You know, because of what you are and that fellow Skelly…."

She faltered and looked at Cliona from under a damp curtain of hair.

Cliona smiled and then rolled onto her back and stared at the ceiling, frowning. The first and only time she'd had to sing the wind she'd seen a selkie on her way up to the cliff edge. She'd given him a piece of sea glass so that he could get safely back to the sea before the storm came to full force. Everything that happened after that was a nightmare she had no desire to relive.

"Nope, I haven't seen one," she lied, squashing down the memory of that terrible night. "Not in seal form, nor in green-skinned boy form. And Skelly? Well, now that he's finished raking me over the coals and back again with his wretched training sessions, he's only likely to be in my head these days, rather than roaming about the place. And even then, only if there's a need for the wind song, which, please-Mary, there won't be. As for anyone else - not that I know of - although there've been plenty of stories. You know, the punters love to have Actual Testimonials and any of those silly old bats down at the teashop are more than happy to see their names in a brochure. I mean, why let the truth get in the way of a good story? The way they tell it, we employ the selkies like tugboats and they've saved at least twelve children from drowning in the last five years alone. Not to mention the bountiful cod harvests and the practically pain-free childbirths the women of the island enjoy." She laughed, bitterly. "If only the stupid old cows knew the half of it, it'd be enough to curdle their custards."

Trudy rested her head against the embroidered bedspread; Cliona's voice was muffled and far-away.

Maybe if I just doze for a minute, my head will clear, she thought, sleepily. *Maybe the headache is because I'm getting ill. I must've caught a chill standing out in the rain for so long.*

"Yoohoo, earth to Trudy. Don't drift on me now!"

Cliona's teasing voice penetrated the fog and Trudy reluctantly pulled herself back to see her friend attempting to entice the selkie boy into a tartan jumper; he seemed reluctant.

"I don't think he likes the way it rubs," said Trudy, feeling her attention wavering again. She looked at the selkie boy and he gave a slight nod. His black eyes drew her into their depths and she saw a flicker of silvery fish reflected in them. She smelled a familiar tang of salt and ozone and heard a deep rumbling of waves against rock. A sudden gust of wind rattled the windowpane and Trudy started, tearing her gaze away from the selkie. "He's probably not used to something so scratchy against his skin," she added, confused. A wave of nausea rolled over her and she closed her eyes.

Cliona sighed and threw the jumper onto the bed, flopping

back down beside it.

"I give up," she said. "He'll have to settle for the tea towel. Although I can't say as I blame him, Feargus has a very, how shall we put it? Eclectic fashion sense? A veritable symphony of tweed and tartan."

Trudy forced a smile. For the thousandth time, she wished she'd gone straight back to her flat. From some place far away, she thought she could hear the sound of people singing.

"Tell me about your stone," said Cliona's voice, sounding loud and oddly out of place.

Trudy blinked, confused.

"You told me I'm supposed to ask you a question if I think you're drifting off," said Cliona, her voice soft and soothing. "You said it would ground you."

Cliona placed a hand against Trudy's flushed cheek.

"It's alright, pet," she said, soothing. "It's going to be alright. You needn't work yourself into a state. We'll take care of our wee friend, you'll see."

Trudy managed a quick nod. Tears rose in a burning lump at the back of her throat.

She doesn't know the half of it, she thought. If only it was just the selkie boy she had to worry about. Trudy hadn't had a chance to tell them she'd been sacked and that she was being told she had to take the job on the mainland by everyone that knew what was best for her. Because that was it, wasn't it? No-one had ever believed she could know what was best for herself. Her anxious disposition and strange, socially awkward ways had defined her as being slightly less than competent, someone who needed looking after. And, to be fair, she was just as much to blame because it had simply been easier to go along with things. She found it hard to understand when people were upset so she'd learned it was better to just do what people wanted. That way she could be sure she'd done the right thing and no-one would be cross with her.

"Your stone," prompted Cliona, gently but firmly. "Tell me how you found it."

"But you already know the story," said Trudy, confused. "I've told you before, the first time we ever met. I found it here, on Glencarragh, when I was little."

Cliona nodded, encouraging. It was true, the stone was the second thing she'd noticed about the pale, slightly trembly young woman with the startling green eyes. The first was how she had suddenly lit up, seemingly from the inside, when Frances had explained what they wanted for the children's art and music festival.

"I know, but surely there must be more to it than just picking it up on the beach. You tell a great story; you could recite your shopping list and make it interesting. And who knows, maybe our little green-skinned guest would like to hear it too."

Trudy smiled a weak smile and tried to collect her thoughts. Telling a story, after all, was just like losing herself to a daydream.

It was the summer before secondary school when she'd visited Glencarragh. Packed off to stay with Aunt Calla while the rest of the family stayed with prickly Aunt Iris, she, as always, could barely believe her good fortune.

Aunt Iris lived right in the village, just off the high street, in a tall, terraced house that was as pinchy and narrow as she was. The first time she'd accompanied the Erskines to Glencarragh, Trudy had felt instantly uneasy in the winding, close passageways and steep staircases, and it had prompted all of her anxious mannerisms which, in turn, had instantly annoyed Aunt Iris.

"The child isn't normal," she'd announced on that first evening, as they sat at the tea table. Trudy had been sitting to her immediate right, but Aunt Iris spoke as if she weren't even there. That had been the habit of most people in her life. She had reasoned that people must have assumed that, because she didn't speak very much, that she also couldn't hear what they were saying, because surely they wouldn't say such things if they knew she could understand. Regardless, she was used to being dismissed as invisible.

Her mother and father had exchanged uneasy looks at this declaration. It wasn't the first time someone had said such a thing but as they'd generally adapted to her oddities, they didn't usually give them much thought. Having her strangeness pointed out upset their strategy of willful ignorance. Trudy did well with her studies and never got into trouble and because she didn't disrupt their way of life, they'd simply let her be. It had worked for years and allowed everyone to get on with their lives. This, however, seemed like it could be a disruption.

"I'm sorry, Aunt Iris," her mother had said, shooting Trudy a stern glare. Trudy flushed and dug her fingers into her palms. Had she been staring? "As you know, Trudy came from difficult beginnings and sometimes has trouble adapting to changes in her regular day-to-day life. I assure you, she's quite harmless. You won't find a more quiet, hard-working and respectful child."

Aunt Iris had snorted, in a very unladylike fashion that struck Trudy's siblings as riotously funny. The pair of them sniggered behind their hands, earning them a glare from their father.

"That may be so, Maureen, but I can't have that sort of behaviour in my house. All that humming and pacing about. She's like a caged animal. And the way she stares is very alarming. You know, I tried speaking with her earlier and she just stared right past me, completely ignoring me. Quite rude."

Trudy flushed a brighter shade of red, keeping her eyes averted. She could feel her mother's glare, rippling waves of irritation the colour of oil-slicked water.

"She can go and stay with Calla," continued Aunt Iris. "I've arranged for her to go first thing tomorrow morning."

Trudy felt her stomach drop. Aunt Calla was rarely spoken of and when she was, it was in hushed and furtive tones. Words like 'witch' and 'cunning-woman' were said with sideways, knowing glances which sent deliciously terrifying thrills through children and adults alike. To think she was being sent to stay with such a creature was enough to strike absolute panic in Trudy's heart. She gave her mother a pleading look but when Maureen averted her eyes, Trudy knew her fate was sealed. Aunt Iris brooked no argument and if it meant no further disruptions then her mother wasn't going to protest.

Trudy spent her first and only night in Aunt Iris' house in floods of quiet tears, sobbing into the musty feather pillow in her room at the very top of the claustrophobic staircase. She muttered fervent prayers that her family would come to her defense and stop her Aunt Iris from sending her away. As hateful as the narrow house was, and as indifferent as her family generally behaved towards her, at least there was familiarity in them. But her red-eyed, blotchy face had no effect on anyone at breakfast the next morning and so after picking at a bowl of uninspired porridge, she was deposited at the home of the mysterious and alarming Aunt Calla.

Aunt Calla's cottage by the sea was as round and welcoming as Aunt Iris' house was sharp and hostile. It was nestled in the lee of an outcropping of stones that Trudy imagined were the tumbled, forgotten dice of long-ago giants, its crooked stone chimney poking up above the boulders like a waving hand. Despite the salt air and punishing winds, roses climbed in wild abundance over the white-washed walls and the kitchen garden was a tangled riot of honeysuckle and cabbage, foxglove and tomatoes. Everything grew together in joyful chaos, with utter disregard to climate and soil. A small flock of striped hens pecked about the garden and a dark-eyed Jersey cow named Verbena grazed on the stretch of moor that met the edge of the sea cliff. Trudy felt the knot of writhing snakes that lived just below her ribs instantly relax.

There were no rules in Aunt Calla's cottage, only, as she called them, Guidelines for a Harmonious Existence. These included things like tidying up after yourself and asking the trees before picking a piece of fruit. Meals were simple and delicious, everything gathered from the garden or chicken coop and were often taken out of doors, perched on a handy rock or up-turned flower pot. Every morning, after she'd made her bed and helped Aunt Calla with the dishes, Trudy would be sent off to play, a large, flowery handkerchief wrapping a doorstep of freshly-baked bread and lump of Verbena's cheese. She would politely request an apple from the tree by the back gate then, having been granted permission, would gently take the shiniest one.

"Be home before the dark rises, darling pet," Aunt Calla would call from where she was working in the garden. "And what else do you need to remember?"

"Don't make bargains with the faeries!" Trudy would call back, delighted, and off she would skip, to spend the day exploring the moors and woods and tide pools.

It was when she was playing in the tide pools, one gloriously sunny afternoon, a few summers later, that she met the talking fox.

Chapter 6

"A talking fox?" said Cliona, her eyes wide. Trudy had said it so matter-of-factly,Cliona wasn't entirely sure whether she was serious or not. But, by the way Trudy shifted her eyes away from Cliona's surprise, she had a nagging suspicion that she *was* serious and that, in Trudy's mind, there really had been a talking fox.

A movement out of the corner of her eye drew her attention momentarily away from Trudy. The selkie-boy sat in the same position as the last time she'd looked but there was something that seemed different about him. Frowning, she turned back to Trudy, who was leaning her head back against the edge of the bed, her eyes closed. Her usually pale cheeks were bright with colour and the dark smudges under her eyes looked to have been made with charcoal.

"Yes," murmured Trudy, "a talking fox."

It wasn't the first time she'd seen the fox; she'd glimpsed him several times before, but it was the first time he'd spoken to her.

"Well met, Bright One," he said, bowing his head and bending one foreleg. "I see you've been a-gathering on the shore."

Trudy paused, her hand suspended in the action of placing a piece of sea-polished glass into the little rush basket that Aunt Calla had given her for just such collections. She looked at the glass in her hand and then back at the fox, her brain slow to acknowledge that the russet-coated creature, standing on the boulder just above her had actually spoken. Or had he?

"Indeed," said the fox, jumping nimbly down from the stone, his magnificent brush waving aloft. "I do, on occasion, like to exchange pleasantries with those who would listen."

Trudy felt a surge of excitement, followed quickly by doubt and confusion. Was this real, or was it one of her daydreams? She hadn't had one in ages; there was nothing to escape from when she was here with Aunt Calla. She regarded the fox, feeling the familiar unease of not being sure she was getting something right. It was all so muddling. Aunt Calla had said it didn't matter what anyone else believed, it only mattered what Trudy believed. And right then, Trudy very much wanted to believe that the beautiful beast, regarding her with mischief sparkling in his strangely human eyes, was talking to her.

"And would you, Bright One, be inclined to listen?"

Trudy nodded, still unable to speak. She was thoroughly charmed by the idea that such a thing could happen to her. She set down her basket and rummaged in the satchel she kept slung across herself, pulling out the handkerchief-wrapped bread and cheese and a bottle of blackberry cordial.

"Ah," said the fox, grinning toothily. "I see you brought provisions. Clever girl. Shall we, then?"

"So, lunch with a talking fox?" said Cliona, her eyes sparkling.

"And you were collecting sea glass? How amazing!"

She looked at the stone which Trudy turned over and over in her hand, her thin, red fingers delicately rolling it back and forth over her knuckles and then into the palm of her hand and back again.

"But that's not sea glass you have there," she pointed out. "I mean, it's very pretty but it's a regular stone, isn't it?"

Cliona frowned. Trudy spun the stone more quickly, her gaze fixed just below the window of Feargus' bedroom. The mottled green and brown stone flickered in the light of the lamp, the colours reflecting iridescence like the scales of a fish.

A crash from somewhere below them startled both girls. Trudy dropped the stone into her lap, her eyes wide and staring before she grappled with retrieving it and slipping it back into her pocket.

"Bloody Malcolm, no doubt," said Cliona, attempting to soothe the fright on her friend's face. "Probably knocked over one of Feargus' towers of tea tins. Never mind that, get back to the story. What did little Trudy and the fox chat about?"

Trudy felt a wave of red heat rise up from her collar and her scalp prickled. Cliona didn't believe it was true. She berated herself harshly. *Stupid girl,* she thought. *I've gone and done it again. It's no wonder people think I'm off my head.* But it had been so lovely to talk about it again, to go back in time and feel like she felt when she was Trudy-who-lived-by-the-sea. Coming back to Glencarragh had been her life's ambition, to recapture how it felt to be understood and accepted and safe. It had been the only contrary thing she'd ever done and now it looked like it was all going pear-shaped. Trying to relive the past wasn't the answer, especially as the end to that particular story didn't paint Trudy in the best of lights.

With a great effort of will, Trudy pulled herself back to the present. She smiled at Cliona, matching her twinkle, and shrugged.

"Oh, you know," she said, waving hand, airily. "This and that. He was very charming, as foxes usually are."

Cliona giggled and squeezed Trudy's shoulder.

"That's grand, Trudy. You know, you really ought to be writing these stories down. They'd make a great children's book. Those are the kind I loved when I was little. You know, the one where the child goes off and has all sorts of adventures in a magical land."

"Hmmm," said Trudy, nodding absently. The pain in her head was intensifying and her flushed feeling now seemed more fever than humiliation.

I really must have caught a chill, she thought, placing a cool hand against her forehead. The familiar swimming sensation was coming over her again, and she was too tired now to fight it. Serial catastrophe was exhausting. Her mind started to wander.

"But the trouble with those stories," she heard herself saying, "is that eventually the child has to go home."

She was vaguely aware of Feargus coming into the room and an alarmed look on Cliona's face.

The last thing she remembered was seeing a large deer walking past the window.

* * *

"Trudy! Trudy! Can you hear me?"

Feargus' voice barely penetrated the fog.

"Feargus?" she called back. "Feargus! I'm over here! Feargus, I can't see you…"

She had no idea where she was. This wasn't the way it usually went.

The last place she remembered being was Feargus' bedroom, although why on earth she would be there, she couldn't recall.

The faint traces of a headache floated behind her eyes and she felt achy all over.

I really ought not to have stayed out in the rain, she thought. *I'm sure I'm going to end up with a terrible cold. That's what this is, it's a fever dream.*

Strangely, though, the fog that swirled around her didn't feel cold, or even damp. It smelled faintly of earth and old, rotten leaves with an undertone of sweetness - like wind-fallen apples, she decided.

"Cliona always warned me not to go out walking in the rain," she muttered, nonsensically to herself. "She said the fog always rolls in after a heavy rain and that if I get caught out on the moors, I'll be wandering around for days."

Was it Cliona who said that? Trudy thought, idly moving her hand through the air, trying to get a feel for the strange mist. *Maybe it was Aunt Calla. No, she always said don't bargain with faeries. She didn't say anything about foxes, though. She should've mentioned that. She didn't mention the moors much.*

But I didn't go out on the moors, she argued with herself. *I'm sure I was on my way to the bookshop. Oh dear, I'm in a terrible muddle.*

"Feargus!" she called again, but there was no answering shout.

She swallowed back the tears that were gathering in her

throat and started walking towards the place where the fog seemed most thin. Surely then, she'd find a familiar landmark and she could make her way back.

But back from where?

I'm not lost, she told herself. *I just got a bit turned around in the rain and because I'm not feeling well, I wasn't paying close attention. I must be nearby; how else would I be able to hear Feargus?*

In truth, though, no matter how brave she told herself she was being, she was terrified. Nothing made any sense and she only scared herself more when she tried to sort it out. This couldn't be one of her daydreams. Her daydreams weren't frightening. They were where she went to get *away* from the things that frightened her. Like arguments and stern looks and difficult parents.

She felt as if she'd walked for days when finally, the mist started to thin, and she could begin to decipher shapes and outlines up ahead. She was just imagining what they might be - could that be the post-office? - when a small figure stepped out in front of her. She yelped in surprise and stepped backwards, almost tripping over her own feet.

"Sorry, miss." said a voice.

"Who? Wait a minute…"

Trudy reached into her befuddled brain for a memory.

"Yes, miss. It's me."

The figure stepped closer, the mist clearing around him.

It all came back to her then - being given her notice, going to the tea shop, the small boy and the argument in Feargus' kitchen.

"You!' she squeaked. "You're talking. Do you understand me?"

"Yes, miss. Only here, though. Only here in the In-Between. It's forbidden for me to speak in the mortal world."

"The what?"

The traces of headache seemed to magnify. Sharp, piercing shafts of light appeared behind her eyes and she felt suddenly nauseous.

The selkie boy reached out a green-skinned hand and steadied her.

"It's alright, miss. The feeling will pass. I'm sorry to have to bring you here like this, but you saw me, so you must be the one."

"The one what?" asked Trudy, almost dreading the answer.

"The one who's going to save us."

At that, Trudy collapsed in a faint.

*   *   *

She was having the most marvelous dream.

In it, she had found a faery creature down by the quayside - a small selkie-boy - and brought him back to the bookshop so that Feargus could help her sort out what to do with him. The dream got a bit fuzzy after that - scenes seemed to fade in and out, wavering like the air over the pavement when it's very hot - but she thought there might have been an argument and then she didn't feel well so went to lie down for a bit of a rest.

She was just marveling at the great comfort of her dream-bed - it was so very soft and enveloping, like the old feather mattress that Aunt Calla had on the bed in the front room - when the sound of voices began to drift into her consciousness. That annoyed her, because she was quite content to stay where she was. Her head didn't hurt so long as she stayed asleep.

"What'll we do, Iain? There's something gone terribly wrong here - I can just feel it. Oh, where on earth is Feargus? Not that he'd be any help, the pair of you numpties going on about the selkie child like it was some harbinger of doom, upsetting poor Trudy when she was only trying to help."

"Would you ever stop the theatrics, Cliona? You're not helping, besides it's not like you to be prone to the hysteria. Settle yourself. Shall I phone Frances?"

The voices wavered and muffled before fading again; which was just fine with Trudy, having suddenly got the notion she'd quite like to stay asleep forever.

"Come b'ye, lass," said a voice, lilting with a sound like the burbling foam of the tide across the sand.

"No thank you," said dream-Trudy, as politely as she could.

"It's time you were up and about, pet. You'll be no use to any of us if you let the dreaming take you."

Trudy sighed and opened her eyes. Stretching her aching limbs, she got up from where she'd been sitting, propped up against the trunk of a gnarled ash tree.

That's odd, she thought. *I could've sworn I was in a bed. A lovely soft bed...*

She remembered again; the blinding headache - which was now gone - the selkie-boy and the strange way Feargus and Iain had reacted to him.

She shook her head, clearing away the last of her befuddlement.

Well, she thought, *it doesn't much matter where I am or how I got here. The most important thing is getting back to where I ought to be.*

Trudy found it helpful to talk to herself in a no-nonsense

voice when feelings of panic started to rise. It was the same voice that Aunt Calla would use with Verbena when the cow had decided she was frightened of the milking stool. She found that if she was firm with herself, she could talk herself into behaving sensibly and calmly, without being swept away by large, inconvenient emotions.

Taking a deep breath, she surveyed her surroundings.

By all accounts, she was at the edge of the moor. She couldn't see the ocean but could smell the taint of salt in the air. The various buildings of the village and the quayside couldn't be seen either, but she was quite sure they were there, just over the rise of the undulating grass.

If I just follow the smell of the ocean, she told herself in a firm voice, *I'll be back in the village in no time. At least the rain has stopped. And my headache is gone.*

Feeling decidedly better for having convinced herself so, Trudy set off across the moor.

She'd walked for about ten minutes when she began to get the distinct feeling she'd made the wrong choice of direction. What had seemed like a rise in the near distance, seemed to be further away than she'd anticipated. The oasis-like quality was amplified by the fact that the scenery looked more or less the same no matter how far she'd walked. It was so odd. The places in her daydreams had never behaved that way before and she was sure this was a result of her having let her thoughts slip after all. It was the fuss with the selkie-boy and then the arguing, all of that combined with what she was sure was a burgeoning cold and she obviously wasn't able to hold on any longer.

It was to be expected, given the circumstances, I'm not to be cross with myself. Nevertheless, this wasn't like her usual experiences when she let herself drift away from the real world. As a general rule, she didn't actually *go* anywhere else. It was a matter of more interesting elements adding themselves to the scenery to make it easier for her to cope with difficult situations. There had been plenty of occasions, for instance, where a mischievous sprite would helpfully hold her attention while some person of authority explained to her why she wasn't behaving appropriately. If that also included the sprite tying the offending persons shoelaces together, then that was an added bonus. This, though, this was very different. She wondered briefly if she had actually lost her mind altogether. Her mother had warned her that would happen.

Quelling the first tremors of panic, she decided to veer off to the right - convinced that she would no longer be walking in circles if she changed direction.

Sure enough, after a few minutes, the landscape began to change. It still didn't have any recognizable Glencarragh features, but at least, she assured herself, she could be sure she wasn't wandering around the same patch over and over again if the sudden appearance of a hedge of scrubby hawthorn trees were any indication.

"Got yourself a bit turned around, have you?" said a vaguely familiar voice from behind a twisty-trunked tree.

Clutching her mouth to stifle a scream, Trudy whirled away from the sound.

"Bit flighty, aren't you lass?" said the weathered old man, his emerald eyes twinkling merrily.

"Sorry, yes." stammered Trudy, smoothing down her hair, wondering if she looked as ragged as she felt. "It's just I've been walking for ages and didn't think I was going to find another living soul. Gosh. I'm so glad to have run into you actually. I'm sorry I don't know your name. Would you happen to know the way back into the village? It's all a bit muddled but I think I've managed to get myself lost."

Trudy took a deep, shaking, breath and burst into tears.

"There, there, now. Don't get yourself in a state," the old man reached out a crooked fingered hand and led her to a large boulder, conveniently placed beside the hedge. He patted the stone and Trudy sat down, sniffing loudly.

"Have you a hanky, then, lass?" he asked, patting her arm awkwardly while she sobbed.

"Yes, of course. Sorry. I don't mean to be blubbering all over the place; I've just had the most awful day so far." Trudy reached into her cardigan pocket and pulled out a wrinkled handkerchief.

"You've naught to be sorry for. 'Tis many a brave soul comes to bits when they've got themselves wandering in a strange place, aye? 'Tis only natural to feel a bit out of sorts."

Trudy nodded and dabbed at her eyes. She really wanted to blow her nose but thought it the last intrusion on this lovely old man's kindness to be doing something so personal in his presence.

"Right, then. I was just about to have my elevenses. Would you fancy a cup of tea?"

He rummaged in the pockets of his overcoat and produced a flask and two large mugs.

Without waiting for an answer, he handed Trudy a steaming mug, smiling warmly. "Now, then lass. Why don't you tell me how you ended up to be here? 'Tisn't every day I have the pleasure of such a lovely lass in my own patch."

Chapter 7

"So you see," said Trudy. "It was all a bit of madness. I suppose it was the shock over the awful news that I'd been sacked. I ought never have gone to the tea shop with Mrs. Wright in the first place. And if I hadn't done that, then I never would have found the little boy and then I wouldn't have taken him to the Oracle and no-one would be upset with me."

She frowned down at her hands. She'd been folding the handkerchief into squares, over and over until it was a tightly-wound bunch. She sighed and set it down beside her on the stone.

"You must think me quite ridiculous."

She kept her eyes low. She couldn't imagine what had come over her. She *never* chatted with strange people so freely. The last time she'd done that it was when she'd first met Frances and Cliona, but they'd asked her about things she loved and so it was easy. There was something about this old fellow, though. He reminds me a bit of Aunt Calla, she decided, letting herself have an inward smile.

The old man laughed softly.

"Not at all, lass. You had an awful shock. You can't expect a body to act sensibly when they're in a state of upset. And as it happens, it were just one of those things where I needed the right sort of someone to find the wee lad and I had it on excellent authority that mebbe you were that right someone," he reached over and patted her knee before taking the wadded hanky from where it lay. "Because these days, 't'isn't just anyone as listens to the voice of the far-away places."

"Hmmm?" said Trudy, frowning slightly. "I'm sorry, did you say something?"

The old man smiled kindly and shrugged, glancing out across the vista of the moor.

They sat quietly for a while, sipping their tea. The mist had long since lifted and the sun shone golden in a cloud-studded sky. Curlews called from somewhere off in the distance and the heather rippled with the gentle breeze.

That feels much better, Trudy said to herself, feeling calm washing over her. *There isn't much that can't be managed after a cup of tea, and this lovely man makes a fine cuppa indeed. I don't quite remember ever seeing him around Glencarragh before. Perhaps,* she reasoned, *he's one of those hermity old sheep farmers that prefer the moors and sheep to village life.*

"Are you alright then?" the old man asked, breaking the silence and startling Trudy from her inner dialogue

"What? Oh goodness!" exclaimed Trudy, sitting up and pushing her hair back from her face. "Sorry, I was just turning things over in my head," she said, looking up to smile at him. A small "oh" of surprise formed on her lips when she saw the air shimmer around him and the fleeting image of a tall, blue-skinned creature sitting in his place. She squeezed her eyes shut and willed herself not to start panicking. She was mostly familiar with small faeries, having not encountered any of the larger ones in her various imaginal wanderings.

She was generally more comfortable with small things.

The old sheep farmer grinned and stood up, leaning on a gnarled wooden stick.

"Now then, lass, will you come sit by my fire?"

Trudy stared. Perhaps she'd imagined the blue-skinned faery. She looked where he had gestured with a wave of his arm. A small cottage sat some distance away, a curl of smoke spiraling out from its chimney.

"That can't be," she whispered, tears prickling the back of her eyes. "How can it be?"

From where they sat, it looked exactly like her Aunt Calla's cottage. Only Aunt Calla's cottage had been down by the edge of the sea and Trudy had only ever seen this one from a distance. She'd been watching it just that morning when Mrs.Wright broke the unhappy news.

Trudy looked back at the old man, who simply smiled, his teeth a startling white in his weather-beaten face.

"Surely you know the way of things here," he said, after a few more minutes of her open-mouthed silence.

"Here?" croaked Trudy, her eyes darting from the cottage to her companion. "What do you mean *here*? What is *here*?"

She felt her heart hammering like a trapped bird in her chest. She forced herself to close her eyes and breathe the way she'd been taught. *A square*, she said to herself. *I can breathe in a square.*

"Why, 'tis the In-Between. Or at least, that's one of its names. But surely you know that, lass. You've been coming here since you were just a wee bairn."

Trudy felt a stir of recognition. She'd heard someone say that recently, hadn't she? Then she remembered, the selkie boy. He'd called it that. Speaking of which, where was he? She put a hand to her head, the coolness of her palm felt pleasant against the hot skin of her forehead.

"I don't know what you mean," she whimpered. "I haven't been here before. I don't…"

She felt his hand at her elbow. A shock of tingling warmth shot up her arm, making her flinch. He gripped it tighter and she felt the tingling spread over her whole body in a sort of warm, comforting glow. She felt her muscles relax and her breathing steady.

"Come on, lass," he said, his voice lilted into a pleasant sing-song. He took the mug that had been dangling in her hand and tucked it into the capacious pocket of his overcoat. "Come sit by me and let's have a wee chat, shall we?"

* * *

Trudy felt a thousand thoughts colliding in her mind as she allowed the sheep farmer to guide her over the hummocks of heather towards the little cottage. As they got closer, she could see that it wasn't exactly the same as Aunt Calla's, after all. It wasn't covered in roses, nor was it surrounded by Aunt Calla's garden. There was no apple tree by the gate and no chocolate-coloured cow grazing on the moor. She wasn't sure if that made her feel better or worse.

"Who are you?" she said, finally finding her voice. The question blurted from her mouth before she could run it through the series of checks and filters she'd developed to avoid saying the wrong thing. She bit her lip and held her breath.

A low chuckle rumbled from beside her. She had her hand in

the crook of his elbow and his own gnarled one rested lightly on hers. The old-fashionedness of it was oddly comforting and she felt steady and confident, which was not something she experienced often.

"Surely you've guessed by now," he said, glancing at her sideways. His emerald eyes twinkled with a mischievous glint and he cocked his head like a curious bird. "Or do I need to dazzle you with another vision of my true form?"

Trudy blushed, without knowing why. It was true, she'd had her suspicions from the very beginning. She'd heard enough stories about him from her friends. She frowned as she remembered some of what she'd been told.

"Aye, 'tis me, lass. And I can see you've had some foreknowledge of my wickedness," he said, wryly.

"But how am I *seeing* you?" she asked, involuntarily looking down at his hand where it rested on hers. "I mean, I can touch you. Aren't you supposed to be in exile or something? Not allowed on Glencarragh, or by the sea?"

Skelly waved a hand dismissively.

"The wee lad brought *you* to *me*. Right after I sent him to find you."

Trudy pondered that for a moment. Her thoughts raced and a hundred questions tumbled over one another. Where exactly was she? How could Skelly be here, on Glencarragh?

"Why would you want me, though? Haven't you already got a, well, you know, a connection with Frances and Cliona. Surely they..."

"Canny lasses, both of them, aye," said Skelly, interrupting her train of questions. "And I'm very grateful for them. As, I'm sure, they are for me." he grinned wickedly.

Trudy smiled weakly, thinking of the stories her two friends had told her of the faery creature who, at once aided and exploited the two of them. It was a complicated relationship.

"Still, though. Me? I've got nothing at all to recommend me."

"Now, then," he said, patting her hand. "We'll have none of that nonsense. Like I said, I have it on great authority that you're a grand lass altogether."

"What on earth does that mean? Who would say such a thing? And to you, of all…people."

Skelly chuckled again. They were approaching the door to the cottage and he slid her hand from the crook of his elbow, giving it a squeeze as he did so.

"You underestimate yourself, lass," he said, lifting the latch on the weathered wooden door. "You do yourself a great disservice talking like that."

Trudy scowled. Platitudes, in her experience, were simply veils to cover up the fact people didn't really have anything helpful to say.

"Perhaps," she said, folding her arms, mutinously. "But you've left an awful lot of my questions unanswered and *I* have it, also on great authority, that you're not to be trusted."

Skelly sighed.

"By Pan's hoary beard," he swore softly. "Why is it that I'm forever remembered by my misdeeds?"

He rubbed a hand over his whiskered face.

"All I'm asking of you is that you listen to the tale I have to tell, and to learn the part in it that belongs to you. Now, will you come sit by my fire?"

The door was open, and Trudy could see inside to a sparsely furnished room. A fire crackled in the grate and an oil lamp cast a yellow glow.

Trudy shook her head, as if trying to dislodge something. *If I don't believe it, then it isn't real,* she told herself calmly. That was the advice she'd been given by various people over the years. Usually counselors and therapists who'd intervened when her behaviour had inconveniently interfered with other people's lives. *Simply act like you hadn't noticed any of it. Just like you were instructed. Remember what they told you: 'There are no such things as faeries and certainly no talking foxes. You need to ground yourself in the real world and cope with your problems like everyone else.'*

"I'm sorry, but I really ought to get back. Thank you for the tea, it was quite lovely. If you could just point me in the direction of the village?"

A look of something like anger flashed across the old man's features, then the air around him began to shimmer.

The old man was gone and, in his place, stood a tall, powerfully built faery with blue-green hair. His handsome, angular features were expressionless but for a flicker of a smile.

"The tears of a believer," he said softly, holding the rumpled handkerchief he'd taken from her. "Not quite the way I'd hoped this would go. I had a hope that perhaps you, of all of them, would…."

He stopped then, shaking his head.

"Never mind. I've no time to argue my methods with yet another one of you tiresome creatures."

He moved his hand gently in a sweeping gesture. The look of unease and confusion on Trudy's face was replaced with one of benign calm and understanding.

"Will you come sit by my fire?" he repeated, for the third time. He gestured towards the open door with one hand and held out the other. "I've a tale to tell and you'd be the one who needs to hear it."

What a lovely person, thought Trudy. *And how kind of him to invite me into his home.*

Smiling, she reached out and took his hand in hers and allowed him to lead her across the threshold.

* * *

"You feel a bond with this land," he said, a statement more than a question.

Trudy stared into the flames of the crackling peat fire. The small cottage, although sparsely furnished was clean and surprisingly cozy. There were unexpected homey touches - a vase of wildflowers, a crisp checked cloth on the scrubbed pine table, plump cushions on the slightly tattered, wing-backed chairs that sat at either side of the hearth. After her initial alarm had worn off, at suddenly finding herself sitting by the fire with a steaming mug of tea and a plate of sultana rock buns, she felt strangely at ease. The idea that Skelly had somehow tricked her into coming into his home was fading against the background of not now wanting to leave.

"I suppose I do," she replied eventually. "Although I hadn't thought of it that way. I just knew that it was somewhere I wanted to live."

She reluctantly remembered the events of earlier in the day and the sage wisdom of the tea shop ladies, and added,"Even though everyone seems to be of the opinion that I'd be better off elsewhere."

Skelly smiled a twisted, wry smile.

"Aye, well. There's always going to be someone who thinks they know better than you know your own self."

"That's not hard with someone like me," said Trudy, with her own crooked smile. "I seem to inspire people to take control. They think I'm dithering when really it just takes me a bit longer to sort some things out, mostly to do with how I need to say or do something so as not to offend. It makes me look a bit half-witted, I'm sure, so I imagine people feel they have to help."

She shrugged.

"Most of the time I don't mind. It's easier, sometimes, to have someone else do the heavy lifting."

"But not this time, aye?"

Trudy frowned.

"No, not this time."

They sat in silence for a few minutes before the sound of the door opening caught Trudy's attention. Skelly shot a quick glance at the door, then at Trudy.

She stared at the creature who was struggling in through the open door with a basket of cut peat. He was small, about two feet in height, and wiry in stature, with a tangled shock of nut-brown hair. He wore a rumpled linen tunic and trousers of a soft material, in hues of brown and lichen-green. His large brown eyes lifted to hers then quickly slid away, a look of fear and confusion crossed his face. The basket of peat landed with a thud as he hunched his shoulders and pressed himself against the door.

"'Tis alright, *bodach*," murmured Skelly softly. "She's a friend."

Trudy turned to Skelly, her eyes wide. Could it be?

She saw that he was smiling, a small contented smile, his

head tilted sideways in question.

"Is that Moss?"she asked, breathless with delight. "Surely it can't be?" she said, looking back at the little brownie who had retrieved the basket of peat and was moving about the cottage with quick, furtive movements. He kept his eyes averted and tended to melt into the shadowed corners. "I mean, he sort of looks like how I imagined him but Frances always goes on about how proper and fussy he is. That poor wee thing looks like he just crawled out from under a hedge."

Skelly nodded.

"Aye, well. He's had a bit of a time of it," he said, looking at Moss. "He was in a bad way when he came to me. A, uh, a friend found him wandering out by the edge of the moor. He's been here a wee while, but he's not much better."

A thought occurred to Trudy.

"When was that?" she asked, eagerly. "When was it that you found him?"

Skelly shrugged, avoiding her gaze.

"I don't rightly know," he said, frowning. "Time is different here, as you may know. So mebbe a few months?"

Trudy felt a surge of warmth. The children's concert! Surely that was what had brought him back. She couldn't wait to tell Frances. A clatter from somewhere in the cottage, followed by a shriek of rage and a stream of unintelligible chatter jolted her from her excitement. That didn't sound like the cultured, snobby Moss that Frances had described to them. That, along with his tattered and unkempt appearance tempered the joy of knowing he was safe.

"What happened to him?" she asked, not able to imagine what could have produced such a stark transformation.

Frowning, Skelly leaned forward to poke at the fire.

"'Tis better we don't talk about it," he said. "Suffice it to say, he fell into the wrong hands and he paid a steep price for his choices."

"Choices? You mean, choosing to live among humans?"

Skelly nodded, stiffly.

"But Frances said that he would often go and mingle with other faery folk. That he would go to the markets to get the things he liked. He never came to harm then."

"That were here, though," said Skelly, gesturing vaguely around the cottage. "Where he ended up wasn't anything like what's here. Deep Faery isn't a place many would go voluntarily."

Trudy frowned, struggling to understand.

"What do you mean by *here*, though?" she asked, looking around the room. "I don't understand. This cottage is obviously nowhere near Thistlecrag, where Frances lived. You know, where you met her. And speaking of that, how is it that you're here on Glencarragh? You never answered. I thought you weren't able to come by the sea."

Skelly's eyes widened.

"But we're not on Glencarragh, lass," he said, "I thought you knew that. At least not in the usual way."

Trudy's stomach gave an unpleasant lurch.

"What do you mean?" she whispered. "Of course we are. I'm in Feargus…I *was* in Feargus' bedroom…"

Skelly sighed.

"Where is it that you are when you're not in the world, lass? When you let your thoughts slip sideways and you leave go of things?"

Trudy felt her head spinning. She let her mug slip through her fingers where it clattered onto the stone floor.

"Now then, don't take on so. It's a simple enough question."

"But I'm nowhere," she stammered, thoughts whirring erratically. "I'm wherever I am. I'm a daydreamer. I just daydream. It's just my imagination. It's not real, not an actual place."

"And who are you trying to convince of that, *mo chroí?*"

Trudy hunched over, face in her hands, willing herself to sit still. It was all too much. She heard herself humming softly.

"And where did you learn that tune?" asked Skelly, his voice gentle. "Because if it's just your imagination then I wouldn't recognize it, would I?"

His voice joined hers, softly singing the words of the lullaby she'd learned from a dryad who lived in her favourite oak tree. The tree that grew in front of the library in the city where she was raised.

Tears rolled down Trudy's cheeks as it all started to fall into place.

Chapter 8

"What's the matter with her?' asked Cliona, frantic. "She just sort of keeled over. Has she fainted?"

Feargus leaned over and placed a hand on Trudy's forehead. At the sound of Cliona's shout, he and Iain had come running up the narrow stairs and burst into the bedroom expecting some sort of treacherous behavior on the part of the selkie-boy. Instead they found Cliona struggling to lift Trudy onto Feargus' bed. The selkie-boy sat motionless on the floor, apparently oblivious to the commotion.

"It's that bloody thing doing this," Iain insisted. "It's put some sort of spell on poor Trudy."

Cliona snorted.

"Don't be so ridiculous, you daft git," said Feargus, helping Cliona get Trudy's limp form into the bed. "Earlier, she said she'd a headache and her skin *is* awfully hot. She's probably got a fever. Maybe caught a 'flu or something from being out in the rain."

He tucked the bedspread more firmly around her and stood up, shifting quickly from hysterical mode to organizational mode.

"Cliona, can you stay with her? I'll pop 'round to the chemist and get some powders and a bottle of aspirin. I haven't got a thing in the house. Iain, you go and put the kettle on and fill up a hot water bottle. While you're at it, make a lemon-tonic for when she wakes up. She's going to have to stay here, at least for tonight. It's no fit weather to be out wandering about,"

Feargus was right. The rain had picked up into a steady downpour and the wind lashed at the windows. Without waiting for the young people's reply, he gave the selkie-boy one last, frowning look and left the room.

He descended the staircase and ducked through the small door that separated the bookshop from the rest of the building. Rummaging in the drawers of the huge and ornate table that doubled as his check-out counter, he pulled out a sheet of paper and scrawled a notice with a black, felt-tip pen.

Closed due to staff illness. Sorry for any inconvenience. Thank you. The management.

He smiled to himself. There weren't likely to be any tourists about in this foul weather and anyone local would just come around the back to the door of the flat if they had a desperate need of anything. Even that seemed unlikely, but even in a crisis, he felt it necessary to observe the proper social protocols.

Locking up the front door, he went into the back passage and pulled his rain gear out of the cupboard, put it on and let himself out into the foul weather. He paused for a moment, squinting up at the sky, then set off in the direction of the chemist. *First, though,* he thought to himself, *I'll stop in and see Mrs. Glenbogie. It's time we knew where things stood.*

* * *

Eileen Glenbogie despised under-done toast.

She had bought and given away no less than six toasters before she settled on the one into which she had just placed two slices of wholemeal bread. Still, even with the dial set all of the way to the maximum setting, she often would pop the toast back in for a "finishing off". Some things, she would say, could not be compromised.

Humming a Highland reel to herself, she opened two tins of cat food and divided them between three willow-pattern saucers. Shuffling to the back door in her tartan slippers, she paused to wrap her cardigan more tightly around herself before jiggling the latch in the particular way it required before it would open. Then, shuffling back to the bench, she retrieved the saucers, still humming as she balanced one on her wrist.

"Table for four today, is it?" she asked, wincing slightly as the wind sent a particularly sharp, rain-laden gust in her direction.

Four pairs of eyes regarded her unblinkingly from atop the dustbins. She'd had Iain put a little roof over the area where she kept the dustbins, her reason to him being it was nicer not to have to get wet every time the rubbish needed to go out, but no-one was fooled. She had been caring for the waifs and strays of Glencarragh for as long as anyone could remember - the two- and four-legged. No creature - be they human or animal - in honest need, was ever turned from Mrs.Glenbogie's door. Such a policy had seen a vast array of colourful characters wandering through over the years - some of whom had raised questioning eyebrows and some of whom were only spoken of in hushed whispers, if ever at all.

"She's a witch, true as true," Mona Gordon was fond of

saying. "Not that I've anything against that sort of thing, mind you. When you keep the company that she keeps, you would be wise to have a bit of supernatural assistance at times."

"Go on, then. I won't watch you," she said in a soft voice as she placed the plates on the ground."'tis not fit weather to be standing around anyway and I've a kettle to boil. Company's coming."

Smiling to herself, she closed the little door behind her. Turning back to peep through the cobbled glass, she could see the fun-house outlines of one black, one brown tabby and two gingers tucking into the saucers of food.

The toast had popped up from its first round of toasting and after close examination, she pushed the lever down again. Her movements were slow and deliberate as she moved around the tiny kitchen - filling the kettle and putting it on the hob. She pulled two mugs down from the cupboard and rummaged in the bread-bin for the bit of fruitcake she kept there for when she had visitors. Nobody ever ate any - it was at least six years old, by her estimation, but she always offered a slice to go with the tea. She was just spreading the butter on her perfectly toasted bread when Feargus rapped at the back door.

"Come in, Feargus," she called, her voice clear and strong. "You're just in time to spoon the tea into the pot. "Fancy a bit of fruitcake to go with it?"

"No thank you, Mrs. Glenbogie, but it's lovely of you to offer. Just the tea will be marvelous. It's wicked out there."

Feargus shrugged off his sodden raincoat and hung it around a conveniently placed chair by the fireplace. Mrs.Glenbogie's tiny cottage had somehow managed to miss the refurbishing project that the village council had implemented for the old folk living in the ancient dwellings. She'd been adamant that she didn't want any newfangled appliances and that she'd been cooking and baking with an old Aga her whole life and didn't need any fancy ovens or microwaves. She'd resisted the toaster for years before she finally admitted that she was wasting far too much bread for her eyes not being as young as they used to be and not being able to see the degree of toasting when she had it in the kitchen fireplace. It was Feargus who had patiently hunted down each model and design of toaster until she found one that did almost a good enough job of it.

Donning an oven mitt, Feargus pulled the whistling kettle from the top of the stove, and placed it on the trivet in the middle of the worn wooden table. He spooned three heaping spoons of tea from the canister into the teapot, added the steaming water then settled himself into a chair with a heavy sigh.

"So then, Feargus," said Mrs. Glenbogie, sitting herself opposite him with her plate of toast. The jar of perpetual jam, as Cliona was fond of calling it, appeared to be full of strawberry preserves. She placed a generous dollop on each slice and started to spread.

"You've got yourself an unwelcome visitor, is it?"

Feargus smiled. He was used to Mrs. Glenbogie's uncanny knowing of things and was not the least surprised that she knew there was some sort of disturbance.

"Yes, I'm afraid to say," he replied.

Mrs. Glenbogie slid the sugar bowl toward him and produced a spoon from her cardigan pocket.

"Nothing to be afraid to admit," she said, pulling a small, glass bottle of milk from the other pocket.

Feargus raised an eyebrow at that but said nothing.

Smiling still to herself, she tucked into her toast while Feargus poured them two mugs of tea.

When she was finished, she pushed the plate away and took her tea mug in both hands.

Feargus sat gazing at the flames in the kitchen grate, lost in thought while he sipped absently at his tea.

"Right then," she said, emitting a tiny belch. "Why don't you tell me about your selkie-boy?"

"Well, then," said Mrs. Glenbogie, once Feargus had filled her in. "Our wee lass from the school, is it? I can't say I'm surprised."

Feargus raised a questioning eyebrow.

Eileen shook her head then wagged a finger in Feargus' direction.

"You yourself should know, my boy, that you can't be taken in by a first impression. Young Trudy has a way about her. I've always wondered how she ended up here, you know. All that talk about visiting an aunt in the school holidays. I never let on, mind. Folk have their reasons. But when she got those children organized in that concert, well, that's when I knew I was right. They raised some grand magic that night."

Feargus let out a small chuckle.

"What on earth do you mean?" he said. "Surely you can't be telling me you thought all along that our little trembling Trudy was some force of supernatural power."

Mrs. Glenbogie scowled, leaning across the table to rap Feargus' knuckles with the back of her spoon.

"Watch your cheek, laddie," she said. "You'll be of a mind not to jest."

She sent a meaningful glance towards the kitchen window which was streaming with rain.

Feargus lowered his eyes, still suppressing a smile. She was a tiny wisp of a woman but had the power to suppress the biggest of bullies with a single glance.

"My apologies," he said, nodding his head in a gesture of a bow. "I simply don't see Trudy as a force of any kind, to be honest. She's a lovely lass, she has a heart of gold, but she's so painfully shy and skittish. I don't know that she'd hold up to the likes of Skelly and all that business. She scurries about in the wake of that fearsome Mrs. Wright and the tea shop harpies will have brainwashed her with the stories, no doubt. No, I don't see how this could be a good thing at all. You'll have to rally your two and knock Himself back into place. He's obviously stirring. To what end, who can imagine? You'll have to have the girls give him a talking-to. We can't have him upsetting Trudy with all of this. We just don't need any excitement of that sort."

He took a satisfied slurp of his tea, having decided that the matter was best left in the hands of people more suited to cope with it. He felt immensely relieved.

Eileen gave him a calculating look. Feargus had arrived on the scene in a flurry of excitement. His modest fame in theatre had made him something of a celebrity. No-one had ever ascertained why such a cultured personage would want to settle on Glencarragh, never mind open a bookshop full of antiquated books, but not for lack of trying. He'd been courted by every busy-body on the island, plied with plates of scones and cheese pies and hand-knit jumpers but no-one had come away any the wiser. In the end, it was enough that he was jolly and generous and a bit of a draw for the tourists.

Eileen had never been entirely satisfied, however, though not for any reason she'd ever been able to put her finger on and he'd become a dear friend over the years.

Sighing, she pushed the thoughts to the back of her mind, admonishing herself for her suspicious nature. There were more pressing issues at hand and Feargus had always been the soul of kindness. And who could blame a body for wanting an easy life?

"So you think it's Skelly then, as has a hand in the matter?" she asked, knowing full well the answer to the question but wanting a moment to marshal her thoughts.

Feargus placed his empty mug down on the table. He leaned back in the chair and spread his fingers over his ample middle. He pursed his lips and frowned.

Eileen suppressed a smile. The man loved a bit of intrigue.

"I can't see how it could be otherwise, Mrs.G. I mean, who else could have either the means or the inclination to have a selkie creature do his bidding? And there's obviously some weather brewing. It's stranger than ever. Our Cliona was just up the moor and she said it was as bright as a summer's day. The real question is, though, why would he bother sending a messenger? Doesn't he just have a direct line to Frances? And Cliona, too, if he was feeling particularly brave. Why send a wee beast when he could just have a chat with either of the girls?"

"Exactly," said Eileen, feeling a niggle of worry tapping at the back of her mind. "It's something to do with Trudy, that's for certain."

"But what?" said Feargus, his voice rising in indignation. "What in the world could he want with her? Poor thing would collapse in an apoplexy if he showed himself to her."

Mrs. Glenbogie frowned down into her tea.

"I've no notion at all, dear boy, but you can be sure I intend to find out."

Chapter 9

Trudy stared at the blue-skinned faery. He was everything his glamour wasn't; tall, broad-shouldered and powerfully built. His forearms snaked with a winding tattoo that shifted and writhed; a rippling pattern of leaves and curving shapes that looked like waving fronds of kelp, intertwined with an unreadable language. His hair was a shade of midnight blue, hanging in thick, dreadlocked ropes. Small shells, knotted into the strands, clicked and clacked together like bones as he turned his head. He wore a simple tunic of earth-brown and green, over matching leggings. His feet were bare.

He's beautiful, she thought, unexpectedly. *Why would he hide himself?*

Then she remembered.

Her mouth went dry and her chest constricted. She gripped the arms of the chair tightly, willing herself to breathe slowly. *What's happening to me?* she thought. She took a deep, shaking breath.

"Please, Skelly," she said, pressing her hand against her eyes. "I don't understand."

"Well, I suppose we *are* in Glencarragh, after a fashion," conceded Skelly, leaning back into his chair. He folded his hands across his stomach. He was the sheep farmer again. Without the voluminous overcoat, he looked even smaller. He wore a grey woolen vest over a collarless flannel shirt tucked into brown corduroy trousers. His clothes were as weathered as his face, but they were spotlessly clean and neatly mended. *Moss,* thought Trudy, oddly comforted by the idea. That would make Frances happy.

"That's not helping," she said, keeping her eyes closed. She envisioned a square and started to guide her breathing. Focusing in, she could feel herself get steadier with each inhale and exhale.

"It's quite simple, really," he said, holding up his hands to explain. "There's the mortal world and there's the world of faeries. They exist together, side by side. Once upon a time, they were the same thing but then things got complicated and now they're separate. But they're also not. Where we are now, is the In-Between. Sort of a borderland between the mortal world and Faery. Every once in a while, although not for a very long time, a mortal has the ability to walk freely between the two places - their world and the In-Between. For that person, the worlds become the same again. You happen to be that person."

"Simple, you say?" said Trudy, with uncharacteristic sarcasm. Her thoughts careened wildly but somewhere, deep in her heart, she knew that it was all true.

"Do you remember a talking fox?" he said, changing the subject abruptly. "From when you were just a wee thing?"

Trudy's eyes flew open.

She hadn't told anyone about the fox, at least, not until she'd told Cliona. Even Aunt Calla. *Especially, Aunt Calla,* she thought, shrinking at the memory. There was no way Cliona would have told Skelly. That conversation had just happened. Or had it?

"How do you know about the fox?"

Skelly shrugged.

"So you remember then?" he said, avoiding the question.

Trudy nodded, lowering her eyes. Skelly watched as her hand slid into her pocket. A small smile played across his lips.

"Will you tell me the story?" he asked, his voice soft and lilting.

She nodded again.

"I suppose there's no harm in it," she said, resigned. "Everything is a giant muddle anyway."

"I think you'll find that it gets clearer once you let yourself believe it's true," said Skelly. "It'll be far easier."

"Really? Do you think so? Because from where I'm sitting, believing that everything I thought was in my imagination is actually *real*, only makes my life more difficult. In case you hadn't noticed, I've already got more than a few social handicaps. The fact that I'm apparently able to drift about in two worlds at the same time, one of which apparently only I can access, does not help with my pre-existing difficulties."

Skelly chuckled.

"It's not funny."

"The fox?"

Trudy sighed.

"Fine, the fox. It was when I was visiting my Aunt Calla, maybe the third summer? I'm not exactly sure."

She *was* sure, though, because it was the summer holiday before she was to start secondary school and she was terrified.

Things had only become more difficult as she'd got older. People confused her more and more, especially the children her own age. The few friends she'd had had drifted away when they realized she didn't share their interests any longer. She found it easier and easier to let her thoughts drift away and take solace in her imagination. She understood the things in her imaginary world. There was comfort there, and a feeling of safety. Unfortunately, it also made her stand out as not only awkward and shy, but also strange and possibly a bit simple. It was a fatal combination in the world of pre-teens.

So it was with incredible relief that she heard the news that the family would be returning for their summer holiday on Glencarragh. As she walked into Aunt Calla's cottage that day, her worries and fears melted instantly away, and she could forget everything that loomed threateningly on the horizon.

"Had you seen the fox before?" asked Skelly, settling into the story. *The lass has a way for the telling, he thought,* quietly pleased. It had been a long while since he'd had the pleasure of a tale well-told.

Trudy shrugged.

"Sure, I had. Don't I have the gift of wandering about in fairyland?" she said, wryly.

Skelly laughed out loud, his head thrown back in genuine delight.

"That's the way, *mo chara,*" he said. "I knew there was a spark in you. Did he always stop for a chat?'

Trudy shook her head.

"No, I'd only ever seen him from a distance. I didn't think anything of it, really. I would often see wild things up close when I was out on the moor. Aunt Calla said that the creatures were less afraid because no-one bothered them all the way out there."

"Aye, she would say that," murmured Skelly.

Trudy opened her mouth to question that but decided against it. She was tired and headachy and really would rather just lie down and go to sleep until the nightmare was over.

Instead she shrugged and carried on with the story.

She'd been down at the tide pools looking for sea glass and shells and whatever else caught her eye. She had her basket and a picnic and instructions to be back at the cottage before the sun slid down over the horizon; the entire day stretched out before her, one of freedom and possibility and, more importantly of all, peace. She felt the expansiveness that only came with the utter contentment of one's lot, so she was only slightly bothered when the fox came and asked her what she was doing.

Of course, she would have rather spent the day in happy solitude, but as he was a fox and had impeccable manners, she forgave him the intrusion on her solitary world.

"I'm collecting treasure," she said, primly as she placed a piece of weathered driftwood into her basket.

"I see that," replied the fox, nodding his head in acquiescence. "And you have a fine eye for the most precious of items."

Trudy smiled, her hand pausing in the basket, as she smoothed her hand over the bits and pieces there. She was particularly taken with the rounded piece of glass. She picked it up. It fit perfectly into the palm of her hand, its curious mottled combination of colours - blue, green and grey -

set it apart from the other, less colourful pieces and it had immediately caught her eye from where it lay, glittering in a tide pool. It felt warm and cool at the same time and having it nestled in her palm filled her with a soothing sort of quietness. She exhaled happily, raising it up for him to see.

"This one's my favourite," she said, smiling down at it.

The fox eyed the glass appraisingly. He got up from where he was sitting and ambled closer to the basket with an air of casual indifference as he peered at the offered treasure.

"Indeed," he said, grinning. He cocked his head to the side, settling himself into a crouch beside her. "And will you be holding onto that one, do you suppose?"

Trudy nodded.

"Oh yes," she said, having just made the decision. "I usually only keep my treasures while I'm here visiting Aunt Calla. Then, before I have to go back to the mainland, I bring them down to the beach and give them back to the sea. Aunt Calla says we mustn't take things that belong to the sea,"

The fox shifted uncomfortably at that, darting a quick look in the direction of the old woman's cottage.

"She says we can have things for a short while, to enjoy them, but then they must go back."

Trudy frowned down at the glass, then looked back up at the fox who was regarding her with his glittering black eyes.

"Do you think it would be alright if I kept just this one?" she asked, her mind beginning to worry over the idea of breaking a rule. "It's just I rather like it and I think that having it will help me feel brave."

"Do you often find yourself in need of bravery?"

Trudy nodded, her eyes still on the stone. She blinked. Surely it had been sea glass a moment ago. She turned it over with her finger, frowning. No, it was a stone, but a lovely one, nonetheless.

"I'm starting secondary school in September," she whispered. She closed her eyes tight and willed the worrying thoughts away. She wanted to forget all of that. This wasn't the time for it.

"Ah," said the fox, rising to his feet. "Well, we can't have you facing such a frightening ordeal without a talisman, can we? All adventurers, even the bravest and most fearless, don't embark upon such a quest without a talisman."

Trudy felt her face stretch into a wide smile. That was exactly how being at school felt sometimes. Like she was a character from her favourite stories, being forced upon a harrowing quest into dangerous, unfamiliar lands. The idea of a talisman cemented her decision to keep the stone. She closed her hand over it and the fox smiled.

"Walk with me?" he said, leaping back onto the boulder from which he'd first appeared. "You can tell me of the perils you face in this 'secondary school' and then perhaps I can tell you how I may be of help."

Skelly regarded her face. She'd told the tale with her eyes on the fire, her gaze seeing not the flames, but the Glencarragh shore and the burnished red of the fox's coat.

"So he talked you into it, did he?"

Trudy pulled her eyes away from the fire and gave a small smile.

"I suppose," she said, "although, to be fair, I was ninety-nine percent of the way to having already decided. There was something about that particular piece, you see."

Skelly nodded, a wry smile on his face.

"And how were things for you, then, in the 'secondary school'? Did the stone ease all of your troubles?"

Trudy snorted.

"Not likely," she said. She slid her hand into her pocket and pulled out the stone, which was actually sea glass. The glamour that the fox had laid on it had held. To everyone's eye, including Trudy's, it looked like a smooth, polished mottled green-brown stone, unremarkable but for the vein of blue-green colouring that ran down the middle of it. "Although, I suppose I believed it did. At least for a while. It mostly helped me to stay calm when things got particularly upsetting. I used it to help ground myself, so in a way it did ease things a bit."

She pursed her lips, knowing she needed to ask but wishing she didn't.

"So, the fox is a friend of yours, then?"

It was Skelly's turn to snort.

"Aye, you could say we're acquainted," he said. "Although, we use the term 'friend' a bit loosely like."

Trudy nodded.

"And my stone? It's got something to do with why I'm sitting here with you and not still with my friends in Feargus house?"

"Aye, lass. It does indeed."

And so he told her what she'd done.

* * *

"I think it would behoove the solemnity of the situation if we were to conjure up an oath, don't you?"

The fox's eyes sparkled.

He's so full of fun, thought Trudy happily. She lay on the heather, the sun warming her face. She'd shared her lunch with the fox after they'd spent a delightful hour exploring a stand of hawthorns near the cliff edge. He'd told her there was a particular group of them, somewhere on Glencarragh, if one had the knowing of it, that could transport a person into Faery itself. Trudy had decided then and there to explore every last stand of the thorny trees until she found the portal to Faery. He had the most wonderful stories. He'd given her so many ideas of places she wanted to go to in her mind. He'd said she could visit there any time. All she would have to do was remember Glencarragh and she'd be whisked away from whatever was upsetting her.

"That sounds like a wonderful idea," she murmured, feeling more like she'd like to close her eyes and have a short snooze. The salt wind of the shore had made her deliciously sleepy. The mad scrambling over the moor, with its rocks that needed clambering and trees that needed climbing had only contributed to her blissful fatigue. And the fox had such a smooth, soothing voice."What sort of oath?"

"Well, since you've decided to keep the stone, the talisman, it means you're taking it from the sea, correct? And so I think it would even things up, and perhaps make you easier in your mind, if you made a promise to the sea in return. You know, just to inform the sea of your good intentions, in case it was upset that you're taking the stone. What do you think about that?"

Trudy thought that made the most marvelous sense. It was the perfect solution. As much as she wanted to keep the beautiful stone, her Aunt Calla's words of warning were niggling at her conscience.

She regarded the fox through half-closed eyes. He was

pacing around her as he spoke, his brush held aloft. *Such a handsome creature,* she mused. *I wish I could draw; I'd paint a picture of him just as he looks right now.*

"I think that's a wonderful idea," she said. "I wouldn't want the sea to think badly of me."

"Indeed," said the fox. "That would be an unfortunate thing."

"What do I have to do?" she asked, hoping it didn't involve getting up from where she was lying. She was so very sleepy.

"Not a thing," said the fox. "Simply repeat the words I shall whisper in your ear."

"Oh," she murmured, feeling a soothing warmth creeping over her. "That sounds easy."

"As easy as can be," said the silky voice in her ear.

Right before her eyes closed, Trudy thought she saw a shadow of antlers on the fox's brow.

So silly, she thought, as her mouth formed the words of a promise.

Chapter 10

"Have you heard from Himself, lass?" whispered Mrs. Glenbogie, as she pulled off her mackintosh.

Cliona suppressed a snort, turning into a muffled sneeze.

"Bless you!" chorused Iain and Feargus.

Mrs.Glenbogie raised a questioning eyebrow at her evasion of the question but Cliona refused to make eye contact. If Feargus had gone to fetch Mrs.Glenbogie and if Mrs.G had saw fit to come, it could only mean they were in serious trouble. And Cliona didn't want to think about the last time they'd had similar trouble.

Rattling the kettle against the stone sink, she made a noisy show of pouring out the spent water and refilling it. She clattered it across the counter toward the top of the stove where she lit the gas after several failed attempts to strike a match. The gathered friends simply waited.

"Why," she said finally, "do you insist on believing that I've got a direct line to Skelly? I only ever hear from him if he wants something. It's Frances you need to talk to, she's the one who shackled herself more or less permanently to the rotten bastard."

"Cliona! Now mind your tongue, lass. Your gran'd never

forgive me if she thought I'd let you take so familiar with our esteemed friend."

Cliona laughed, appreciating the relief of tension. She playfully swatted the elderly woman on the arm. "Right! And you and Gran never had a few choice words to say about him in your day?"

Mrs. Glenbogie grinned, showing a row of brilliant, white and perfectly sculpted teeth, a sharp contrast to her lined face and wispy grey hair. "Aye, go on then. I'll give you that one! Still…"

"It behooves us to observe a modicum of respect for the ancient and otherworldly."

"Oh, Iain, lad!" Mrs. Glenbogie cackled loudly at the very accurate imitation of Feargus at his most pedantic and condescending.

"Are you lot taking the piss again?" asked Feargus, good-naturedly as he emerged from the back passage. The sound of their laughter did him good. Things were getting far too serious for his liking. "Eileen, pet, have you seen what I did with the packet of chocolate biscuits? I could've sworn I left them in my shopping bag with the bottle of aspirin."

"Um, sorry," said a voice from the kitchen doorway. "Would these be them?"

A slim, blonde woman held up the slightly battered packet, a rueful smile on her face. "Really, Feargus. You ought not to leave your bag on the floor. You know their Angus' favourite."

"Frances! We were just talking about you!"

Cliona paused in her delight at seeing her friend, her face creasing into a frown.

Feargus and Mrs. Glenbogie exchanged worried looks and Iain busied himself tousling the ears of the excitable terrier who was dashing from person to person, much to the dismay of Malcolm.

Frances shrugged, an unspoken apology hanging in the air.

"Yes, I'm afraid so. He's wondering about one of his brethren you're apparently holding hostage?"

* * *

"What do you mean, Trudy is *with* Skelly?" asked Iain, after Frances had filled them in. "How is that even possible? I just looked in on her myself, she's fast asleep on Feargus' bed."

Frances wrapped her hands around her cup of tea. Her fingernails were embedded with paint and she had a smudge of something purple across her left cheekbone. She sighed heavily, shifting her position to accommodate Angus, who, having made the rounds and sniffed over every inch of Feargus' house, had joined in the conference around the table. "I don't understand really. I've given up trying to make sense of any of it, to be honest. It's obviously something very different to what he and I do. He just wanted us to know that she's alright but not to disturb her from where she is."

Cliona reached across the table and patted Frances' wrist. She knew well, the strangeness of having an ancient sea faery inhabiting her head - but at least, despite the unpleasant necessity of their relationship, she didn't have him echoing around in her thoughts all of the time.

Frances smiled weakly and pushed a hand through her hair.

"All I can tell you is that your selkie-boy up there has done something to send Trudy into a place that Skelly called the In-Between. It's where he is when he's not…. here." She waved a hand around her in a vague way.

"Aye, I've heard tell of it," said Mrs. Glenbogie. "It's somewhere between this world and Faery proper. You'll be familiar with the old stories of folk getting lost and wandering then turning up days or even years later? The In-Between would likely be where they went. As for Skelly's lot, 'tis easier on them to stay in the borderlands than try and always be in this world."

"Yes, that's it, Mrs.Glenbogie," said Frances, nodding. "He once told me that it takes a lot of energy to be in our world, especially for a faery his size and to hold a glamour. It's easier for the wee folk, as they can hide just about anywhere. I actually used to think that Skelly lived, you know, somewhere around Thistlecrag. I don't know how many hours Angus and I spent wandering around looking for his farm," she shook her head, chuckling at the memory. "I had no idea he just popped up there whenever the mood suited."

"You mean whenever he thought there was a likely chance to bend you to his will?" said Iain wryly.

Feargus kicked him under the table. "Give over, Iain. Anyone would think you didn't like the poor wee exile. Tortured soul that he is...."

"That's enough from both of you," snapped Cliona. "In case you've forgotten, we've got a couple of problems."

"Aye," said Mrs. Glenbogie, leaning back in her chair, reaching towards the counter. "Not the least of which is this soggy packet of biscuits."

* * *

Frances and Cliona left the men and Mrs. Glenbogie talking over tea and the salvaged chocolate biscuits. Angus clattered up the narrow stairs ahead of them and pushed into Feargus' room. The dim glow of the lamp illuminated the still form of Trudy where she lay, tucked tightly under the covers. Angus gave the sitting form of the selkie-boy a quick sniff, a friendly wag of his stumpy tail, then jumped up onto the bed and burrowed in tightly next to Trudy, his head resting on her stomach.

"Well, that's Angus' take on the situation, then," said Frances, offering Cliona a strained smile. "I suppose that means our little green-skinned friend isn't a threat."

Cliona grunted.

"It's not him I'm worried about," she said, walking around the bed. She pulled up the wooden chair that sat in the corner of the room, tipping off the pile of clothes that were draped there before doing so.

Frances put her hand to her mouth in mock horror.

"Cliona! You've upset Feargus' chair-drobe. You'll wrinkle his tweeds."

Cliona suppressed a giggle.

"Shhh!" she said, "You'll disturb the patient."

Frances grinned and came to perch on the edge of the bed, opposite from Cliona. The two of them gazed at the face of their friend. To the casual observer, Trudy was simply asleep. Her features were smooth and relaxed and her breathing steady. The dark smudges that shadowed her eyes and the paleness of her skin were the only clues that perhaps all was not well. Her hands were clasped across her stomach, thin fingers wrapped around the stone she always carried in her pocket.

Cliona stared intently at the stone, as if willing it to provide some sort of clue.

"It's something to do with that stone," she said, finally.

Frances raised an eyebrow.

"I knew as soon as ever I saw it that it wasn't just an innocent beach pebble. I don't even think it's a stone, to be honest." She frowned. "It's just, something Trudy said earlier when she was telling me about how where she found it and she said she was collecting sea glass, but she was talking about the stone, I'm sure of it. Can a stone have a glamour, do you suppose?"

"I don't know," mused Frances, pursing her lips. "I daresay it could. You hear tell of entire buildings being obscured by glamours. You know, the beautiful rose-covered cottage that's actually a damp ruin. I imagine it wouldn't take much to glamour a stone. But why and who's holding the glamour?"

"What do you mean, holding it?"

"Well it can't put a glamour on itself, can it? Someone, some*thing*, has to be holding it."

"Skelly?"

Frances shrugged.

"I doubt it," she said. "I had no idea he'd any dealings with Trudy until today. I'm sure he would've mentioned it."

"Are you?" said Cliona, folding her arms. "I mean, would it serve his purpose to tell you that he had some a connection to Trudy?"

France sighed.

"Oh, Cliona. You're too suspicious by far. Even if Skelly hadn't told me, surely Trudy would have? I mean, she's heard us talk about him all this time and never once has she said she had dealings with him. If anything, she found the whole thing fascinating and slightly beyond belief."

Cliona's eyes narrowed. She didn't want to believe it, but it must be true.

"Aye, you're probably right. Our Trudy wouldn't be the sort for pretending she didn't know something when she did. But who then? And how did she come to have the stone in the first place?" She broke off, waving a hand in a dismissive gesture. "I know where she got it, she told me the story, though I got a slightly more embellished version earlier."

Frances grinned.

"She does have some good ones, doesn't she? It must be a grand thing to be a child in her classroom. No wonder they did so well for her during the concert."

"Sure," said Cliona, moving on. "A grand story it may be, but it doesn't really give us the facts, does it? I mean, foxes aren't in the habit of actually talking, are they?"

Frances looked at Cliona, waiting. Her friend's face twisted into a frown then she puffed her cheeks and blew out a long, slow breath.

"Oh for heaven's sake," said Cliona, slumping back into her chair. "You don't really believe she really *was* chatting with a fox, do you?"

"Why would she say so if she didn't?"

"Because it's Trudy and she's odd and awkward and lovely," said Cliona, a hint of exasperation in her voice. "It's just what she does when she doesn't want to actually deal with things, isn't it? She just wanders off into a story. You know she had the most wretched of childhoods, poor soul. Can you blame her for wanting to make it something better, even if only in her own head?"

Frances reached out to smooth a strand of hair from Trudy's forehead.

"I think, Cliona," she said, carefully, "that you and I both know that things, and people, aren't always what they seem. Not only that, there's more to be gained from having an open mind. Especially on Glencarragh."

Cliona groaned and scrubbed a hand over her eyes.

"Bollocks," she said, throwing her head back and staring at the ceiling. "I hate it when you're right."

* * *

"You're not wrong, Mrs.G," said Feargus, twirling a butter knife on the table. "There's definitely something more to our Trudy than I think any of us had imagined. There has to be. Let's face it, Skelly has practically *summoned* her. Not only that, she's actually managed to go to him in this In-Between place. Surely that's not a common occurrence."

Eileen Glenbogie shook her head.

"No, it's not. Especially as she's gone to him and left her physical self behind. That says a powerful lot about how strong she is.'

"How strong she is?" repeated Iain, his eyes wide. "What, is she some sort of sorcerer or something? A witch?"

Feargus chuckled.

"Settle yourself, laddie. No, she's neither of those things. She's an ordinary lass, just like any other."

"Well then why is she able to do what she's doing?"

"It must be partly Skelly's influence," explained Mrs.Glenbogie. "He drew her to himself using the selkie-boy. Like a sort of bridge, aye? As long as our wee friend is upstairs, he's acting like a sort of…well, yes, bridge."

"A conduit?" offered Feargus.

Eileen smiled.

"Aye, go on then, that."

She leaned over and poured herself another cup of tea, stirring in a spoonful of sugar.

"But she'd still need to have some sort of knack for seeing the faery folk in order for Skelly to bring her along."

"So, like Frances, then?" said Iain, struggling to understand. He'd come a long way since Cliona had discovered her ability to harness the wind, but his pragmatic self still wrestled with the more esoteric points.

"Yes and no," said Mrs. Glenbogie, taking a sip of her tea. A gust of wind sent a clatter of rain against the windows, making them all jump. "Our Frances sees the wee folk because they make themselves known to her in the real world. Those faery creatures are here, in our place. What I think maybe our Trudy can do is go *there,* to where they are. To the In-Between."

Iain groaned, dramatically clutching fistfuls of his unruly hair.

"But why then did Skelly have to use the selkie-boy to make her go there if she can do it on her own?"

"Perhaps," said Feargus, piping up. "It's a matter of will. Perhaps Trudy can't control how she travels between the worlds. Maybe she can't do it on purpose."

"Then so he used the selkie-boy to force her there against her will?" Iain's face flushed and his eyes glittered. "That's it, isn't it? He's doing the same thing as he did to Frances. He's going to hijack her somehow, isn't he?"

Mrs. Glenbogie reached over to pat his arm in a soothing gesture.

"No, pet. I don't think he bears any ill intent,"

"This time," agreed Feargus.

Eileen nodded. "Aye, this time. Besides, as I figure it, I think our Trudy would have the ability to resist his summons."

"So she *is* there by choice?"

"And choice is everything," muttered Feargus, passing a weary hand over his eyes.

Chapter 11

"I have a choice then?" asked Trudy, when she learned what she'd done and what it all meant.

"Aye, lass. Of course you do."

During the telling, Skelly had got up from his chair by the fire and gone to stand with his back to the window. He needed to move away from her, to sort out the strange conflict of emotions that churned in him. They were unfamiliar and unwelcome. *Too much time away*, he thought. *Too much time interfering in the business of mortals.*

He turned away from her, towards the window, speaking softly so that she couldn't hear.

"In this, it truly has to be your choice."

Trudy stared at his back, a million questions flitting through her mind. It was awful, she ought to be devastated. Just the idea of it should have been enough to send her into a panic. *But,* she reasoned, *that would only be the expected reaction if I believed I'm even remotely capable of doing what was being asked of me.*

"I think you've both made a terrible mistake," she said, finally. "You've picked the wrong person entirely."

Skelly spun around.

"There's no 'both' in this at all. Cer…the fox worked on his own. I had no knowledge of it until just recently. I'm only trying to minimize the damage."

Trudy shrugged.

"I don't know why it matters to you, but it still doesn't make the slightest difference. The point is, I'm the wrong person to be doing this. You'd best find someone else."

"It has to be you," said Skelly, his jaw set in a stubborn line. "You made the oath, so it's you. The crafty bastard knew what he was doing. You're the one that took the glass."

"And what's so special about my stone, for heaven's sake? And for the hundredth time it's not sea glass, it's a stone. And even if it was sea glass, people collect it all the time."

"It *is* sea glass," said Skelly, mutinously. "Playing with perception is just one of the…fox's tricks. One minute you see it, the next minute you forget it ever was."

She pulled the stone from her pocket, held it out on a flat palm. He glanced at it then looked away quickly.

"Look, see here?" she demanded, losing patience. "It's really just a stone." The subtleties and nuances of unsaid things hanging in the air were draining her. "And even if I go along with your version of the story, then it's still just a piece of sea glass. And like I said, people collect it all of the time."

"It's not the glass," he said, "it's who it belongs to."

"Do the others know about this? Do they know what we, *I*, have to do?" Trudy asked, folding thin, red, fingers around the enamel mug. It had been quietly refilled while she was arguing with Skelly. She sat huddled close to the peat fire, suddenly finding it difficult to get warm despite its comforting glow.

Skelly sighed heavily and leaned back in his chair. The wood creaked in protest.

"No, lass. Not as such."

Trudy frowned.

"Is that another one of your evasive faery answers?" she asked. "Because I have to tell you, I've got no energy left for that."

Skelly scowled.

"Well?"

He snorted.

"No, 'tis the truth! They have no knowledge of it. I told you, even I didn't know about it until just now. Before."

He waved a hand dismissively, muttering something about time.

Trudy thought for a moment.

"What about Mrs. Glenbogie? Does *she* know?"

The old farmer chuckled.

"Not that I've told her, but I learned long ago to never underestimate that one. I warrant she knows a lot more than she lets on, even to you three lasses."

He studied her closely, seeing the questions in anxious eyes that seemed huge in the pinched, white, face. The air shimmered and the glamour fell away.

"What does it matter *mo chara?*"

Trudy flinched at the sudden change. "Stop calling me that," she said, shifting in her chair. "It's not even slightly endearing."

Skelly smiled, sharp white teeth gleaming in the firelight.

"Despite what the lasses have likely told you, I don't bite. I'm the same, no matter what you see standing in front of you."

"Perhaps," she said, setting down her mug. "But I've a lot to take in, you must see that."

She looked at him, narrowing her eyes. She found that she was sorry she wouldn't be able to do what was asked. She was sorry because there was nothing she wanted more than to be able to immerse herself in his world.

Reaching out a tentative hand, she let her fingers touch the tracing of the tattoo on his forearm. "I need you to know…" she faltered then cleared her throat. "I need you to know that I'm sorry it can't be me. I'll take whatever consequences there are but I've no illusions about myself, you see. I know I'm not world-saving, curse-breaking material. Besides, there's a good chance there's more like me out there."

"Do you truly imagine yourself not able to the task, pet?" he said, softly.

Trudy blushed her eyes filling. Gentleness wasn't what she'd expected of him and she didn't deserve it. Not after she'd broken the only rule her Aunt Calla had ever set for her.

"Don't make fun," she whispered. "I really mean it."

Skelly stood up and walked back to the window. Outside, the weather had changed; clouds scudded across a moody, storm-heavy sky.

Without turning, he said, "I've walked the earth now, nigh on nine hundred of your years. I've been bound to tread the soil and feel the burning touch of sun and wind on my face. I'm forbidden the presence of my people and my home."

When he turned to face her, it was as the weather-worn farmer, his lined face hard and his eyes cold.

"Do you not see, lass? Do you not see the horror of *that*? Do you not see that you're the first glimmer of hope I've truly had in centuries? Don't think I've come to any of this lightly. I've as little choice and even less inclination to do what's expected of me as any of you do. Not to mention the company I'm required to keep to do what's needed."

"Then why *are* you doing it?" asked Trudy, stiffly. She felt as if she couldn't find her footing with him - he was unpredictably kind and cruel. And now he was getting angry with her. "Why don't you just finish out your thousand years, or whatever it is, and leave us to cope with our own part in it?"

He laughed at that, a deep, throaty chuckle that seemed to shift his mood.

"Do you really think that Lira will leave it at that? Besides, yon red-headed piece would be away and wild with the wind without my help and as for that faithless painter and her constant fretting…"

"You are quite possibly the most arrogant beast I've ever had the misfortune of meeting!" snapped Trudy, suddenly at the end of her tolerance. "Here I am, being told that a silly, childhood bargain I made with a talking fox to take a piece of stone from a beach that would help me feel safe from bullies now means I have the obligation to hand myself over to this nasty sea-faery woman-person in exchange for the end of some stupid curse caused by some stupid squabble between you and her, all of which constitutes a major life-altering decision - benefiting everyone *but* me, I might add - and you're acting as if you're the one great gift to us all, like we couldn't manage without you!"

Slamming her hands down on the arms of the chair, she stood, breathless and red-faced from her outburst. She pulled her coat from the peg where Skelly had draped it to warm.

"Where might you be going, lass?" he asked, his voice soft and full of quiet menace. He moved to stand between her and the door of the cottage.

"Home," she replied, more firmly than she felt. "I've made my decision and I'm sorry, but I just don't trust you, Skelly. No matter what my..." she paused, struggling for the right words. "...*talents* may allegedly be. All I have are silly childhood daydreams and your word that any of it is real. All I really know for certain is that I'm chronically feeble and incapable of making decisions without someone telling me what to do. But not this time. I've no idea from one minute to the next whether you're on our side or just using us to serve your own purpose. How can I even know this isn't just some part of another, more intricate plan? Picking on the weakling, turning her head around, telling her some fanciful tale to make her believe she's important...."

She broke off and stared at him, unflinching but tearful in the power of his green gaze.

"Aren't you forgetting something, lass?" he asked, holding up her handkerchief, still damp with her tears.

She blinked and swallowed hard.

Tears of a believer. Aunt Calla had said that tears held immense power.

"But you said..."

"I know what I said, lassie," he smiled, impossibly white teeth in the creased, brown face. "And you know I need to make this right, one way or t'other."

"How is that any kind of choice?" she said, shoulders slumping as she leaned against the wall. Her face felt flushed and the uneven plaster felt cool against her hot skin. "How can you even *call* it a choice if you're just going to use my tears against me?"

"Och, lass, and there you are calling *me* arrogant!" He reached over and tucked the damp handkerchief into her clenched fingers. "I never said it was all *your* choice, did I?" He paused, letting his statement sink in. "Now, will you sit down and listen to what else I have to say?

***

"Are you able to visit your Aunt often? Now that you're living on Glencarragh? That must be nice for the two of you."

Skelly had made the remark, very casually, as he'd guided Trudy back to a chair by the fire.

"What?" she stammered, bewildered by the sudden change of conversational direction.

"Your Aunt," repeated Skelly, leaning back in his chair, fingers laced across his stomach. "the one you stayed with in the summertime when you were a wee girl. Calla, I think you said she called herself."

Trudy blinked rapidly.

"Yes, my Aunt Calla. She…" Her voice trailed off as she grappled with her scurrying thoughts.

"Only I thought mebbe you might have a word with her about all this."

Skelly cast a sly, sideways glance at Trudy. Her colour was high and she knotted her fingers in her lap. He felt a momentary pang of unease before pressing on.

"It seems she might have some advice for you, that's all. Help you get things sorted in your mind, like."

"I don't know…" she faltered, eyes wide and brimming with tears as a strange awareness descended upon her. She unknotted her fingers and wrapped her arms tightly around herself. "She, my mum told me…"

Trudy's mind raced. Why *didn't* she visit her Aunt Calla? Moreover, why wouldn't she be staying with her instead of living in the little flat over the fish and chip shop? Surely her cottage would have been a better option. The memories of her summer visits flashed through her thoughts as she searched them for answers, the sun-drenched hours of delight and safety, of feeling finally welcome and accepted. A cold, dull ache began to spread upwards from her belly as, time and again, she lost the fragments of memory that surrounded each departure. It was as if she were there, with Aunt Calla and then, in an instant, she was in the back of the car, sandwiched between her brother and sister as they drove down the ramp of the ferry that had brought them back to the mainland.

She raised tearful eyes to Skelly's face. He stiffened slightly at what he saw there, his fingers gripped the arms of his chair as he nodded.

"Aye, lass," he said, softly. "You got there in the end."

Trudy shook her head as the tears spilled silently from her eyes.

"No, I won't believe it. I know what I did and what I saw. I was *there*," she said, choking.

"Did anyone else from your family ever mention her then? Do any of them visit with the old girl?"

"They were never close to her like I was," said Trudy, grasping firmly to a logical thread."They all thought she was strange and even a bit mad," her voice faltered again. "A bit like me," she added with a whisper.

"And you never told me why you don't go and visit with her now," prodded Skelly. The slamming of the cottage door startled them both. "*Bodach*," he growled, glaring at the closed door. There was an answering crash of a metal pail before silence fell again.

"I think…. I was told…. she moved to the mainland, to look after Aunt Iris when she fell ill. Yes, I seem to remember my mum telling me that at some point. Anyway, what does my Aunt Calla have to do with any of this?"

Skelly sighed, tilting his head back and looking at the ceiling.

"First off, I think mebbe you might want to have a word with that woman who calls herself your mother. And secondly, your Aunt Calla has everything to do with this. And thirdly, it's time you stopped dithering and applied that clever brain of yours to what you've been told. There's no passing this off to someone else to sort out for you, not this time."

Trudy flushed and opened her mouth to respond before pressing her lips together in a firm line. She took a steadying breath and stood up, chin high and shoulders back. Skelly remained seated, his head tilted, an unreadable expression on his face.

"Aye, go on," he said, waving a hand towards the door. "You're no prisoner here. I think I made that clear."

She gave him a curt nod.

"Yes, you did. Thank you, also, for making me aware of my situation. I shall take everything you've said under careful advisement."

Skelly's mouth quirked into a smile that didn't reach his eyes.

"Aye, do that, lass," he said, his voice barely more than a whisper.

Trudy moved towards the door, fighting the urge to look back at him.

"Oh, and you don't have to march out in a strop," he called to her, as a shimmer of movement in the corner caught her eye. The selkie boy bowed his head in acknowledgement as the cottage vanished.

* * *

"She's stirring," said Iain, moving to the side of the bed where Trudy lay. "Trudy? Are you awake?"

"What a numptyish question! Do you suppose she'll answer if she isn't?" snorted Cliona, elbowing him out of the way. "She's ever so cold. Have you another quilt, Feargus?"

"Yes, yes," he replied, rummaging in a chest at the end of the bed. "What about an electric blanket? Will that be better do you think?"

"Oh, for heaven's sake. Men are absolutely no use at all in times of crisis," muttered Mrs. Glenbogie, pushing past with a hot water bottle in her hands. She tucked it under the covers at Trudy's feet. "Warm the feet and you've warmed the soul," she said firmly.

"Cliona?" whispered Trudy. "Is that you?"

"Now who's asking numptyish questions?" muttered Iain under his breath, avoiding the glare he knew would be coming his way.

"Yes, lovey. It's me. Frances is here, and so's Mrs. Glenbogie."

"Aye, and so's the cat's dinner," remarked Feargus, huffily. "Come on lad, let's go back downstairs. Clearly we're surplus to requirements."

The circle of women ignored the two men as they banged noisily out of the bedroom and clattered down the stairs.

"I saw Skelly," said Trudy, pushing herself into sitting

position as Cliona lay the electric blanket across her knees.

"Oh?" said Cliona, faintly, the plug dangling from her hand. "And how was that, then?"

Frances sat down beside Trudy and took her cold hand in hers.

"He didn't harm you, did he?"

"Blessed Mary, Star of the Sea...." murmured Mrs. Glenbogie.

"How did you know?" asked Trudy, her eyes filling with tears, realizing that Frances had spoken it as a statement, rather than a question. The enormity of what had just happened crashed over her in a suffocating wave.

"Because I can feel it," replied Frances. "You're like an echo - not as obvious as him, but I can feel a sense of you here," she tapped a finger to her temple then paused, tilting her head as if trying to catch a sound "It's different though, not like when Cliona is there...." she frowned at Trudy who looked down and began smoothing her fingers over the blanket. "Anyway, it seems he left his mark on you, but not in any permanent way."

"I'm sorry," said Trudy, wild-eyed with fresh tears trickling down her cheeks. "I knew better - I remembered what she'd told me, but he was so kind, and I wanted the stone. I thought it would help me. I didn't mean..."

Her voice trailed away, and she fixed her far-seeing gaze towards the rain-fogged window, silent, wracking sobs heaving from her chest.

The three women exchanged worried glances. Cliona opened her mouth to say something but Mrs.Glenbogie laid a warning hand on her arm.

Leaning over, she cupped Trudy's cheek gently, turning her

face and forcing her to look into her kind blue eyes. Trudy took a deep, shuddering breath and her shoulders sagged as her own eyes came back into focus.

"Rest now, lass," continued Eileen, her sing-song voice lulling Trudy into soft sniffles. "There's plenty of time for the telling. You've had a grand adventure, aye? You stay tucked in tight. Everything else can wait."

Chapter 12

"Well we can't just sit here doing nothing," said Feargus, getting up to pace back and forth in front of the stove.

Angus whined in agreement, toenails clicking on the flagstone floor as he paced back and forth in front of the door leading to the stairs. He'd left the bedroom with the two men, thinking there might have been snacks to be had in the kitchen. Not only was he disappointed on that score, he was now stuck downstairs, which was not where he felt he was needed.

"What do you propose we do, then?" asked Iain, folding his arms. "You know as well as I do, there's not much reasoning with that lot when they've got themselves all up in a state over that bloody faery."

"That's the problem though, isn't it?" said Feargus, his voice rising and his hands punctuating his indignation. "Bloody Skelly and all his bloody nonsense!"

"Steady on, old bean," said Iain, mimicking Feargus' dramatic gesture. "You'll give yourself an apoplexy if you don't settle down. You don't have to convince *me* he's the problem. I've often wondered exactly how much he enjoys the havoc that follows him wherever he goes."

"Of course he bloody enjoys it! Isn't he just made for this

sort of thing? Scheming swine! You can't tell me that selkie-boy just happened to be lounging around the quay in the teeming rain and that no bugger else happened to catch sight of it until poor Trudy tripped over it."

"Despite the fact it was in a direct, harridan's-eye view of the tea shop? Aye," nodded Iain, thoughtfully. "I had thought of that. That clutch of harpies doesn't miss anything. So, you really do think Mrs.G has the gist of it, that Skelly was after Trudy all along?"

Feargus sighed heavily.

"I wouldn't put it past him."

"What do you suppose he wants with her, then? I mean, no offense to her, she's a grand lass, but she's not like our Cliona with the wind singing, or even Frances with her paintings."

"He wants her because she's a believer," said Mrs. Glenbogie, coming into the kitchen and sitting wearily down. "That's all I can say for certain. The lass has a heart the size of this island and she believes with all her soul in the magic of the place."

"There's lots of folk who believe in magic, Eileen," said Feargus. "Surely aren't they coming in droves now with the tourist boats, hoping for a glimpse of a selkie?"

"Aye, Feargus, that may be so. But for yon lass, the magic isn't something separate, something that comes and goes. It's a part of who she is. For all of her nerves and dithering, she has a feel of power in her. You see it when she's telling those lovely stories or the way she drifts off in her mind when you're trying to have a serious word. And you know as well as I do that there's something in the land here. It's claimed her, the way it claims all of us who're meant for it. I hadn't thought it common with an off-islander, though, 'til our Frances came along. Still, I'm mystified as to why and how it could be so strong in Trudy. She's a right puzzle, that lass."

She rubbed hands together, massaging her arthritic fingers. The rain and damp seeped into her bones.

"And now Skelly's claimed her as well. For all intents and purposes anyway."

The three sat in silence, pondering. Angus paused in his pacing to sniff at a crack between the floor and the wall. Sighing, he conceded to lie down on the clippy mat by the door and await his mistress.

"I'll tell you this, lads," said Mrs. Glenbogie, breaking their reverie. "She must be more of a power to Skelly than Frances and our Cliona put together. Somehow, he's got wind of that. He wouldn't've gone to the bother of sending the selkie-boy otherwise. 'Twas a dangerous thing for him to do and for the wee laddie himself, for that matter. I can't imagine Lira missing the surge of magic that must have produced."

Feargus frowned.

"What do you mean, Eileen? What could he possibly be after?"

"I've no notion just yet," replied the old woman grimly. "But you can be sure I'm going to find out before he gets it."

* * *

The blue-skinned faery and the horned god stood on the edge of the cliff, overlooking the sea.

"This is the easiest I've felt at the edge of it since those lasses found my bit of glass and summoned me," said Skelly, breathing deeply of the salty air. "And even then, it only lasted a moment. How is it, d'you suppose, that I'm not doubled over in agony?"

He glanced at Cernach whose gaze was far out over the horizon.

"Not that I'm of a mind to complain, you understand," he added.

Cernach smiled but didn't turn to look at him.

"It's because of the girl," he said. "The one who can travel between the worlds. She's bound to the land here, the Old Mother saw to that, and so she's connecting us all. Even Lira can't dictate that. It belongs to something more powerful than any of us which is why it's to that we must tether our hopes."

"But she was tricked into it," said Skelly, musing on the truth of it. "She was just a wee bit of a thing. Still is. Does that not taint it?"

Cernach shrugged, turning to look at his once-sworn enemy.

"There was a time when you wouldn't have asked such a thing, *mo chara.*"

There was no answer for that. For either of those things.

Skelly spread out his arms, tilting back his head until the long, ropy, strands of his hair caught the wind and lifted around him.

"Will it always be?" he asked, quietly, afraid of the answer. "Will I be able to stay this time?"

Cernach bowed his antlered head.

Without a word, he was gone.

Skelly turned to see the bushy tail of a red fox disappearing behind the scrubby, stunted rowans that clung to the cliff's edge.

* * *

"How is she?" asked Iain as Cliona and Frances clattered into the kitchen.

"She's properly asleep now," said Frances, fending off Angus' mad excitement. "Silly boy, I've not been gone that long. It'll do her the world of good. She's had a terrible upset, poor thing."

"Cup of tea, pet?" asked Feargus, going to fill the kettle.

"Please," said Cliona throwing herself into the chair beside Iain. He put a hand on her forearm and gave it a squeeze. She responded with a quick smile and a brief rest of her head on his shoulder.

Good, thought Frances. *At least those two won't be bickering anymore.*

"Well," said Feargus, once the large teapot and tray of cups were on the kitchen table. "What do we think of all this, then?"

Cliona groaned, her hands grasping handfuls of hair, elbows on the table, propping up her head.

"Where do we even start?" she asked. "This whole thing is far too strange. And poor Trudy is up there babbling about her stone and what someone had told her."

She broke off and waved a hand.

"I don't know what to think."

"What is it about the stone, then?" said Iain. "She's never without it, that's for sure. I thought it was just one of those worry stone things."

Frances shrugged, gratefully accepting the cup of tea he handed to her.

"That's what I thought too. It's something she picked up off the beach when she came to Glencarragh as a child. I had always assumed it was just a souvenir from a day at the beach."

"You'll have to ask her to tell the whole story about it,"

interrupted Cliona. "It's fantastical. She'd told Fran and I the basic gist a while ago but she gave me a more detailed version earlier."

Frances took a sip of her tea, nodding.

"Yes, it's a good one, especially the bit about the talking fox."

"A talking fox?" said Iain, incredulous.

Cliona nodded. She turned to the puzzled faces around the table. "It's a brilliant story. She ought to make it into a children's book or something."

Iain frowned.

"Well is it a story or is it real?" he asked.

Frances and Cliona exchanged a look.

"If you'd asked me that this morning, I would've told you it was a made-up story," said Frances, reaching down to tousle Angus' ears. "Based on fact, sure, only embellished to make it more interesting. But after today, I really don't know what to think."

Mrs. Glenbogie pushed away from the table.

"Never mind that for now," she said, brusquely. "If we're to sit vigil for the poor lass, we'll need some food in our bellies. Feargus, have you a large pot? I fancy we can conjure up a soup of some kind with the scraps of what you've got lying around. Come on, it'll give us something to keep our hands busy."

And so began an assembly line of soup-making. Feargus peeled and chopped potatoes and Iain tended to carrots and onions. A rummage in the deep freeze produced a jar of vegetable stock and it was thawed in a saucepan and added to the large pot. A slightly wilted bunch of leeks were chopped and tossed in, along with a cup of dried lentils and for a while, the worrying events of the day were forgotten in a haze of steam and garlic, herbs and laughter.

"This'll be perfect for Trudy when she wakes up," said Frances, peeling a clove of garlic and passing it to Cliona for crushing. "Whatever else has happened, she will have caught a chill standing out in the rain like that. This'll warm her through."

"What on earth could have possessed her to do that anyway?" said Cliona wiping down the cutting board. "Seems like a silly day to take yourself off for a walk along the quayside, what with the wind blowing a hoolie and the rain coming down in sheets."

"I imagine she wanted to get away from the harpies at the tea shop," said Feargus brandishing a wooden spoon. "And can you blame her?"

"Well that makes you wonder why she was in the tea shop in the first place, doesn't it? She's hardly one for the after-work gossip group, now is she?"

"Mebbe you lot should concentrate on getting that soup put together instead of speculating on the goings-on of our wee lass," scolded Mrs. Glenbogie. "You're no better than those kind souls you're calling harpies with your gossiping and nattering. Like a bunch of magpies you are, chattering away. Now Feargus, have you a lump of that bread dough I gave you in the fridge? I feel like a fresh loaf would be just the thing with this soup."

Iain glanced over at the two girls, his eyebrows raised in silent question. It wasn't like Mrs.G to be so short with them. Frances frowned. If Eileen Glenbogie was worried, then things were far worse than she imagined. Squashing down that thought, she concentrated on filling the sink with hot soapy water. Washing dishes reminded her of Moss and how he always complained about her excess of suds. And at that particular moment, a pleasant memory was welcome.

So it was a scene of domestic camaraderie that Trudy came upon as she stood in the doorway, Feargus' quilt wrapped around her.

She'd woken up from a strange dream that she couldn't remember and was momentarily disoriented, not knowing where she was or why. Then it all came flooding back to her and her first instinct was to bolt away from what was troubling her. She would pack her things and leave Glencarragh as she'd been told to do by the ladies at the tea shop. She would take the teaching job on the mainland that had been offered and be happy for it. The strange story that Skelly had told her could be easily pushed into a corner of her brain that she didn't acknowledge. After all, he'd said it had to be her choice and for once, she was doing what she wanted. Or at least what was the most sensible option. As she'd told him, she was hardly world-saving material. She'd be doing them all a favour if she just slipped quietly away and let them find someone else.

She had it all planned out in her head when the faint aroma of something delicious cooking drifted up the stairs and into the room. More memories came flooding back to her, this time of sitting in Aunt Calla's kitchen, tying bundles of herbs for drying. It had been a week after her conversation with the fox and two days before she had to leave to go home and back to school.

"You'll be alright, lass," Aunt Calla had told her. "It won't be easy, mind. It never is for the likes of us. But you've got a power of good on your side that'll watch over the worst of it."

She'd fixed Trudy with a meaningful gaze, which, at the time, Trudy thought was intended to make sure she brooked no argument with the well-meant words of a grown-up who really didn't know how awful it could be.

Looking back on it now, Trudy began to wonder. She sat up in the bed, pulling the quilt tightly around her. The wind was a wolfish howl through the old windows and the rain drummed steadily.

She glanced around the room, lit as it was by the yellow glow of the oil lamp. She smiled at Feargus' old-fashioned choices in furniture and clothing that clashed with his image of cosmopolitan grandeur, his inherent sophistication at having come from London and the theatre. His arrival had, by all accounts, truly bewildered the people of Glencarragh but in the wake of his generosity and kind spirit, his oddities and flamboyance were looked upon with indulgent affection. He had them enthralled. Now there was a person who didn't seem as if he ought to belong in a place like Glencarragh, thought Trudy, fiddling with a stray thread on the quilt. He just came as he was and let his good nature speak for him. That, it seemed, had been enough to guarantee him a place. For a brief, glorious moment she imagined how it would be to let herself do the same. To feel as if she truly belonged to Glencarragh, and it to her. The promise she'd made to the fox that long-ago day on a windswept beach had meant she'd had the benefit of the sheltering magic of the island, but did that constitute belonging? She wasn't sure. It felt more like an exchange of service. And now, according to Skelly, it was time for her to do her part. Shuddering, she felt an unusually pressing need to be around other people. No, she corrected herself as she crept down the kitchen stairs, to be around her friends.

At the sight of them, bustling around the warm kitchen,

laughing and teasing, exchanging jokes and soapy dishes, she felt something give, deep inside her. A surge of warmth blossomed up from her belly and she knew, with a sudden certainty, that these were her people. She realized that this was the family that she'd never truly had. A family of her choosing. People who had accepted and cared for her, despite her strangeness and awkward ways. Could it really be, though? She hadn't known them all that long.

Time, m'inion, came a beloved, remembered voice inside her head. Aunt Calla. *Time is just a notion. You've known them as long as you need. They are for you, and you are for them.*

Gripping the quilt tightly around herself, she stepped down the last stair and entered the kitchen.

"Something smells lovely," she said, smiling.

Five faces turned to look at her, surprise and delight on all of them. There was a pushing of chairs and rearranging of cutlery and she was ushered to the seat nearest the stove. A cup of tea was placed in her hands and worried frowns creased foreheads.

Should she be up and about already? How was she feeling? A glass of water and three aspirin appeared at her elbow and Angus placed scrabbling paws against the side of her leg. Laughing, she reached down and helped him up onto her lap, wrapping the quilt around both of them.

"I'm fine, really," she said, her eyes bright. "You're all fussing."

"Of course we are, lamb," said Feargus, cupping his hands around her pale face. "You gave us a terrible fright. Don't ever do that again. Wandering off into the dreamlands, keeping company with rogue faeries. I'll not have it. Promise?"

Trudy lowered her eyes briefly then looked back at him,

smiling.

"Now why would I promise such a thing? Didn't I have the most delightful chat with him? He was a model of good behaviour. Gave me tea and everything."

Her friends stared at her, disbelieving for a moment then burst into laughter. The kitchen echoed with it, with the love and companionship, as bowls of soup were ladled out and passed around. Trudy hugged Angus close to her and buried her nose in his wiry fur, breathing in the scent of him. He smelled of the moors and salt air, of peat smoke and hearty vegetable soup. He smelled of home.

Mrs. Glenbogie carried her bowl of soup to the table, a small smile playing on her lips. She sat, opposite Trudy, watching with careful eyes as Trudy and Frances bent heads together to look at something in Trudy's hand. *The light one and the dark one,* mused the old woman. Glancing over at Cliona, she added, *with fire to bind them.*

Shaking off the worrying thoughts that followed, she reached for a lump of freshly baked bread. *Whatever's going on,* she thought, *it can wait until we've had ourselves a hot meal.*

Chapter 13

"I hadn't thought to be summoned like this again," said the blue-skinned faery with a hint of amusement in his bright green eyes.

The old woman laughed, a wheezing chuckle, and gestured to him to sit down. The wind had abated slightly, and the pelting rain diminished to a steady mizzle. The two sat opposite one another - on a tree stump and a boulder - at the top of the cliff where Cliona had sung the wind to her over a year before.

"I see you're managing easily," remarked Mrs.Glenbogie, "to be close to the sea."

Skelly nodded.

"Aye, it's not like it was the last time we spoke so close to the shore."

She pursed her lips and scrutinized his features. There were still traces of strain around his eyes and every so often he winced and shifted uncomfortably, but it was far from the agonies of their last meeting when she and Cliona's grandmother, then still young girls, had bound the lord of the sea to their aid against the storm.

"'Tis the lass, is it? Our Trudy?"

Skelly nodded and looked away, avoiding her gaze.

"It's alright, you daft git. As I told the rest of them, we've no right to judge the things you've done, seeing as we've done the same our own selves."

She grinned at the last and he caught her eye and smiled back. He nodded toward the piece of sea glass she held in her hand.

"I see you're keeping the magic safe," he said, tilting his head to one side.

"I have. Just as we promised we would that day. We keep our promises."

If he was supposed to take a deeper meaning from the last part of that, he didn't show it.

"And you brought me here because you just fancied a chat, then?"

Mrs. Glenbogie cackled.

"Something like that, aye," she said, suddenly sobering. "I need you to tell me something, Skelly. No tricks and no talking in circles, just the truth."

He spread his hands wide and adopted a look of hurt bewilderment.

"Now, then," he said. "You know as well as I do, that I cannae but tell the truth."

Mrs. Glenbogie snorted.

"Aye, and I also know that you are, and always will be, a shifty wee shite and I don't trust you any further than I could throw you."

Skelly scowled and crossed his arms.

"Oh, don't go into a sulk!" she exclaimed. "I've no' got the time for stroking your fragile ego so let's just get on with things, shall we?"

"Certainly," he replied in clipped tones. "How may I be of

service?"

Mrs. Glenbogie shook her head and straightened up on her tree stump seat.

"Right, then," she said. "Are you and that creature Cernach working together?"

Skelly's eyes widened. He ought not to be surprised that the old woman knew about Cernach. What surprised him more was that Cernach had allowed the knowledge of him to be held in her memory. Or else she'd found a way to do it herself. Not for the first time, he mused on the way his kind often underestimated the humans.

"I don't see how that's any of your concern," he answered. "I'm allowed to keep company with my own kind, am I not?"

"Well considering you're supposed to be sworn enemies, it raises a few eyebrows to think of the two of you so chummy."

Skelly's lips tightened.

Eileen held tightly to the sea glass in one hand and to a pouch that hung from her neck with the other.

"Answer the question, *faery*!" she commanded.

"We," said Skelly, struggling visibly, squirming on the edge of the boulder. "We have exchanged civil conversation, yes."

"Are you planning to use the girl against Lira in some way?"

Skelly's eyes widened.

"What do you know about…"

"Never mind that," she interrupted. "Answer the question."

"It's not what you think and certainly not that straight-forward," he said, shaking his head as if to dislodge the compulsion she was clearly wielding against him. "It would take all of them working together and even if they could, she would still have to choose…"

He broke off abruptly, clutching his head with both hands,

moaning.

"What're you doing to me, you wicked auld harpie?" he asked, trying to stand only to fall to his knees.

Mrs. Glenbogie reached out a hand to steady him. She gripped his shoulder tightly, his blue-green skin was hot to her touch.

"It isn't me, laddie! What's wrong?"

Shuddering he tried again to stand.

"You've got to let me go," he whispered. "It's her, she's close by. I can feel her,"

"Who's close by? Who's doing this? Surely, not…"

"Please…."

Skelly slumped sideways and lay motionless on the heather.

Suddenly the wind gave a mighty shriek, tearing at the scrubby trees, lashing the branches into a frenzy. One of them whipped at the side of Mrs. Glenbogie's face, sending her reeling.

She righted herself and started back toward the inert form of Skelly, muttering the words of the sending to release him from the thrall of her compulsion.

"Don't waste your time, old woman," said an imperious voice.

Suddenly, standing between Eileen and Skelly was a tall, elegant woman. Her long hair, as black as the deepest part of the sea, was unmoving in the swirling wind. She wore the bones of whales tied into a necklace and her dress shimmered with the iridescent scales of fish. Beside her, stood a massive black horse, streaming with sea water, red eyes flashing and its long, powerful neck snaking towards Skelly.

Eileen struggled to her feet and was buffeted by a fresh gust of icy wind.

"You'll be her, then?" she asked. "The one that's done all this?" she gestured out toward the pounding sea and the gathering black of rain. "Lira."

The woman laughed. It wasn't a pleasant sound - like the damp, squelching, sound of dead things moving under water.

"I am. And now, finally, I can see the punishment through to its end," she raised a long, sinewy arm. "Thank you, my dear, feckless mortal, for bringing him here. The magic he raised earlier wasn't quite enough to grant me access, but this has done the trick. So very convenient! And here I thought he'd be clever enough to keep far from my shores so soon after that last feeble effort."

She turned to face Skelly and began to sing a high, keening, song. The wind whipped ever higher, and the rain began to lash down, pelting them with icy needles.

Mrs. Glenbogie lurched, staggering against the force of the wind. She began a calling of her own, pulling the pouch from around her neck as she inched closer to the back of the strange woman. The wind shrieked and thrashed, and the old woman wavered and tilted.

Summoning the last of her strength she flung the pouch at the back of the sea queen's head and shouted.

"*D'síoraí grá!*"

"*For love everlasting!*"

The last she remembered was an agonizing scream, the sting of the rain and everything exploding into stars.

* * *

Frances and Cliona had walked Trudy back to her flat. They

walked on either side of her, each linking one of her arms in a show of support - both literal and metaphorical. Arriving at the painted yellow door, the three women and the dog stood huddled in the narrow overhang while Trudy fumbled with her keys.

"Now, get yourself up to bed and we'll see you tomorrow, yeah? Come over to our Frances' croft and we'll have a session. There's nothing that can't be fixed over a plate of curry and a bottle of wine," said Cliona with firm insistence. "I feel like we can sort this all out between us, don't you?"

"Do you need help getting up the stairs?" asked Frances, knowing Trudy was thoroughly overwhelmed by Cliona's enthusiasm. She'd been quiet during their meal but seemed happy enough and none the worse for wear for her ordeal. By unspoken agreement, no-one had pressed her for further details of her time with Skelly. She knew from experience, however, that conversations with the faery lord often needed processing long after they were over, and she suspected that was doubly the case with Trudy.

Trudy shook her head, grateful but wordless, as she was bundled through the entryway.

The two women watched through the mottled glass of the door as she made her way up the stairs, clutching the banister for support. Satisfied that she'd made it safely, they took simultaneous deep breaths then burst into nervous laughter. Angus whined, his bottom wriggling as he tried to insert himself into their attention. He could sense the nerves trilling underneath the light-hearted chatter.

"Come on," said Cliona, tugging Frances' elbow. "Let's get on, otherwise poor Angus will be soaked."

"He has his slicker on," said Frances, grinning down at the

little dog. She'd sent away for a bright yellow doggy raincoat, once she'd realized the rain on Glencarragh was even more persistent than on the mainland. He had protested at first but now thought himself quite a dandy, trotting along with complete immunity from the drenching downpours, although he drew the line at wading in puddles.

Cliona giggled.

"True, but it doesn't stop his tummy from getting wet."

Linking arms, the two set off in the direction of Cliona's house. From there, Frances would continue on up the cliff path before turning away from the sea and inward across the moor to her little shepherd's croft. It was a route they'd taken countless times since they'd first met Trudy, months ago.

"Did you ever imagine, when we met her, that she was connected in all of this," asked Cliona, gesturing with a hand in the direction of the village. "You know, with Skelly and the curse and all the rest of it."

Frances shrugged.

"Not at the time. But now, with the benefit of hindsight, I can see how maybe there were clues."

"Oh?"

"Sure, I mean her stone for one. You obviously sensed something about it."

"Not exactly Well, I thought maybe it was *something*. But I didn't think *she* knew. Most people don't. I mean, how often do people find themselves pocketing a stone that's taken their fancy." She shrugged. "And anyway, my particular specialty is sea glass and for all I can tell, this is just a stone. A pretty one, sure, but not glass." She paused, pursing her lips thoughtfully as she looked off in the direction of the sea. "Then again, if our theory about it being glamoured has some weight to it, then that changes things, doesn't it? And if it really *is* sea glass, I wonder about its significance. Because it has to mean something, or else why go to the bother of the glamour? I simply can't see it being a random occurrence, nothing ever is around here. We're all in service to the magic in some way or another."

"As Skelly is so fond of reminding us," said Frances with a sigh.

Cliona rolled her eyes but smiled.

"Same with your paintings, right?"

Frances nodded, shifting her own gaze out to the sea. Her paintings and their magic weren't something she wanted to think about just now.

"Do you really think it's sea glass then, after all? And a particularly important bit?" asked Frances, after they'd walked for a spell, each lost in her own thoughts.

"How do you mean?"

"Well, I was just thinking, you know how your gran and Mrs.G found Skelly's glass and so were able to summon him?"

Cliona's eyes widened. She came to a stop, tugging Frances to a halt beside her.

"Bloody hell! Do you think Trudy's stone, glass, whatever, belongs to someone with some power?"

"Don't get carried away," warned Frances, holding up a cautioning hand. "It's just a theory, it may be nothing."

"But that would explain it, wouldn't it? It would explain why Skelly is so interested in our Trudy. And it would explain why the glass is glamoured, wouldn't it?"

Cliona's eyes were bright, and her hair whipped in a frenzy around her face. She clutched Frances arm.

"We have to find out," she said. "This could be something

really huge. Surely Mrs. Glenbogie will know." Cliona's voice raised in pitch and her words tumbled out in a torrent of possibilities. "Maybe we could bind this person, whoever it is, like Gran and Mrs. G bound Skelly. We could have another one of the rotten bastards in our pocket."

Frances barked a laugh.

"Quite literally," she said, grinning.

Cliona threw her head back and laughed with her. Then, linking her arm in Frances' again, the two women marched off again in the pouring rain, a glimmer of hope brightening the dismal grey air between them.

Chapter 14

Feargus sidestepped the cats who were twining themselves around his legs as he stood at the back door.

"Be off with you," he said, half-heartedly. "I've not got a thing for you. Anyway, I'm fairly certain you've been fed."

"Aye, they have," came a voice from behind him. "But they're not above trying to con another meal out of a likely punter."

"Eileen!" exclaimed Feargus, turning around. "Good heavens! What on earth's happened to you? Are you alright?"

Mrs. Glenbogie flapped a hand, waving away his attention.

"Tis naught but a bit of a scratch," she said. "I'm more bothered by the tear in my good coat."

She gestured toward the elbow of her raincoat which was torn almost up to the shoulder. She had a long scratch over one cheek and was limping slightly.

"Come on," she said. "Let's go in and warm up, shall we? I don't know that it'll ever stop raining, the way things are going." She fumbled with the door handle.

"Good lord, woman!" said Feargus. "Your hand!"

"Oh, give over, you daft man! I've had much worse in my day."

"That may be so, you silly old bat. But that was when you

were years younger. Can't you leave the gadding about the moors to the young lasses, now?"

Mrs. Glenbogie pushed through the door and led Feargus through the passage and into the kitchen, shedding her torn coat as she went.

"Light the stove, will you?" she said. "I'll just go and change out of my wet things."

Feargus busied himself in the kitchen, lighting the stove and filling the kettle, muttering as he went about his tasks.

"You know, folk'll start wondering if they hear you talking to yourself like that. There isn't even a cat indoors to pretend with," said the old woman as she came back into the kitchen. She'd changed into a pair of purple sweatpants and a mottled green cardigan that had probably been old half a century before.

"Aye, and folk'll start talking when they see you dressed like a bag-lady, shuffling about in bedroom slippers with a herd of cats trailing behind you." retorted Feargus.

The pair of them broke into laughter.

"Ah, Feargus! Don't you know they've been talking about me for years?" she cackled.

He pulled her chair closer to the Aga and set her down, handing her a steaming mug of tea.

"True enough, I suppose," he said, sitting down opposite. "Now, are you going to tell me how you scratched your face and tore your coat?"

Eileen sighed heavily and wrapped her knobbed fingers around her mug.

"You'd never believe me if I told you," she said, avoiding his sharp gaze.

"Try me," he said, shuffling his chair closer and reaching

over to tap her purple-clad knee. "I'm not the ridiculous git everyone thinks I am, you know."

"I know, pet," said Eileen, a warm smile crinkling the corners of her eyes. "You weren't the toast of London theatre for nowt, were you?"

Feargus grinned wickedly.

"It's served me well," he replied, affecting a modest pose.

"That it has, you devious rascal. Now then, before I tell you where I've been, why don't you tell me how long you've been chummy with that fellow Cernach?"

She raised an eyebrow at the look of surprise on his face.

"That *is* what he's calling himself these days, isn't it?"

"Eileen Glenbogie, you old minx," laughed Feargus, clapping his hand to his thigh, sloshing tea over his other hand. "How did you…oh, never mind! Right! I'll tell my tale, and then you tell yours. Deal?"

Eileen nodded primly and settled herself back in her chair. It had been a lucky guess, but she'd take it.

"Deal."

Feargus took a mouthful of tea and closed his eyes for a moment. When he opened them, Mrs.G was watching him, her face expectant.

"There's not a whole lot to tell, really," he said, shrugging his rounded shoulders. "I actually haven't seen him in years — the last time was when I was touring with a theatre company around the west of England. He turned up in Shropshire, then again, further south. He's had as hard a time of it as your Skelly, you know. They've both suffered in their own way. Cernach possibly less so, as he's at least had the freedom to wander where he chooses."

Feargus grinned at the look of mock surprise on Mrs.

Glenbogie's face.

"Ah, surely you weren't fooled by me, lass. You must have had an inkling I wasn't entirely unfamiliar with the ways of Faery," He held his hands up, spread wide to mime the headline, "The Legend of Glencarragh!" He boomed in a showman's voice. "An ancient tale of love and betrayal set against the backdrop of a storm-cursed Scottish island." As soon as I saw one of the tourist brochures in a theatre in Birmingham, I knew where I'd end up. Of course, I'd only ever heard Cernach's side of the story. An ill-fated love affair with a princess of the sea or some such. What can I say?" He shrugged again and placed his hand on his chest. "It appealed to my romantic heart."

"And you never thought to let on that you'd had dealings with Cernach?"

"I'd hardly call them dealings."

"Well, I never," exclaimed Eileen. "I knew you weren't the wide-eyed innocent everyone else thought you were, but I would never have guessed at how much you already knew."

She leaned forward, scrutinizing the carefully schooled features of the old actor. He might've been fifty or he might've been seventy - it was hard to tell in a given moment. Decades of training in classical theatre and his natural penchant for intrigue made him a hard man to judge. A good heart, though. Eileen had always known that of him and so all else was happily left to the mystery. Until now, anyway.

"How long have you known him, then?" she asked, her curiosity satisfied, and her suspicions confirmed.

Feargus shrugged and glanced away.

"Since I was a young lad. I think I first met him when I was seventeen. Again, it was while I was traveling with a theatre group - in Devon, I think - sort of a transient, arrive-in-the-night troupe. We just turned up on village greens and put out the hat." He grinned at the memory. "Those were the good old days, I can tell you. Lots to be learned when you're playing for your porridge, as it were."

"That follows, I suppose," muttered Eileen. "His folk all like a bit of the fine arts, don't they?"

"It was the music that drew him, I think," said Feargus. "We had this very talented young fellow that played the pan pipes," he waved a hand at Eileen. "I know, I know. Very cliche I suppose. But there was more than one night where, if you squinted your eyes just right, just outside the light cast by the fires we'd lit, that you might see them. Just the outline, mind you. They'd sort of ease in and out. But they were there. And when Cernach showed himself to me - well, I didn't need much convincing. I always had a leaning toward that sort of thing. Hence, my decision to retire here, on your lovely island. What better way to spend my golden years than mingling with the faery people?"

"Hmm, so I imagine," said Eileen, not really paying attention. She gave a thoughtful glance at Feargus' down-turned face. "What did he want from you?"

Feargus looked up and frowned at the question.

"Nothing, really," he said, blithely. "It was almost like he just popped up for a bit of company. He's extraordinarily intelligent, if a bit full of himself."

"You don't say?" said Eileen, raising an eyebrow.

Feargus laughed.

"I'm not all that bad, am I?"

"Nay, pet. Carry on with your story."

"Nothing much more to tell. He'd appear from time to time,

always when I was with a touring company and we'd spend a few evenings together - good wine and good conversation - and then, without so much as a by-your-leave, he'd be gone. Until the next time when he'd stroll in like no time had passed at all.

"Do you suppose it's possible that maybe *he* sent *you* here?" asked Eileen.

Feargus paused, leaning across to put his mug on the edge of the table. He schooled his features into a thoughtful frown.

"I've often wondered if he had a hand in that. Wondered if maybe he'd planted the seed of it, guided me in this direction. But I don't recall him ever actually mentioning it directly, no. And really, to what end? I've no interest in the intrigue, I assure you, and no talents to contribute. He just told me his side of Skelly's exile story and left it at that."

"But you would think you might see him more often once you'd moved here."

"I suppose so," agreed Feargus. "He told me once that he's always drawn back to this place - that it's the one place where he feels like he can rest for a while. Which makes sense, all things considered. I am surprised that none of the lasses have ever come across him. It seems to me he'd have made himself known. Then again, with things as they stood between him and Skelly, perhaps it was better that he didn't. There was certainly no love lost between those two.

Eileen nodded; it was her turn to keep her face impassive. She let her gaze wander toward the window as the thoughts raced around her head.

"More tea?" asked Feargus, getting up and stretching.

"Ta very much, aye," she replied, frowning at his back as he turned to retrieve the teapot.

"Here you are," he said, holding out the teapot to refill her mug. "Now," he said as he sat down to face her again. "Since I've bared my truth to you, perhaps you'd be so kind as to bare yours to me? What in heaven's name happened to you?"

"As I said, 'tis nothing but a scratch," she held up her hand which was wrapped in a piece of clean linen. "I've put some of my salve on it, it'll be fine in no time."

"I'm sure it will and I'm sure I know you're avoiding the question. I'm more interested in where you've been and how you came to be injured in such a way," he held up a hand. "And don't tell me you were out foraging for nettles or parsnips or whatever it is you get up to out there in the hedgerows. Even you wouldn't be traipsing about doing that in this rain."

Suppressing a chuckle, Eileen set down her tea and folded her hands across her stomach and shook her head slowly.

"All the time you've lived on this island, Feargus O'Rourke, and you still don't know that 'tis not the season for the hedge-parsnips."

"Mrs. Glenbogie," said Feargus, warningly.

She held up her hands.

"Alright, alright. But I don't want any lectures on my behaviour. You all fancy me in my dotage but I've years left in me."

Feargus nodded, his eyes fixed expectantly on her face.

Eileen took a deep breath.

"I summoned Skelly."

She fixed Feargus with a warning look and he swallowed the indignant protest that was rising on his lips.

"I wanted to know what he was up to in regard to our Trudy. It just didn't seem right that all of a sudden he's taken an interest and rather than spend precious minutes speculating,

I thought I'd go straight to the source, as it were."

"And?"

Mrs.Glenbogie shrugged.

"We didn't get too far into things when Herself turned up."

"Herself?" Feargus goggled."What? You mean, Lira?"

He spoke the name of the faery queen in a hushed whisper. She was, after all, the root of all of their troubles.

Eileen nodded.

"Aye, the very one."

"But what on earth was she doing there? I thought there was some sort of, I don't know, truce-ground?"

"I wish I had the answer to that question," said Mrs.G, frowning deeply. "It troubles me to no end. She was aiming to finish him off, you know. I worry that she's somehow got stronger over the years."

"Finish him off?" Feargus spluttered. "Skelly, you mean?"

Mrs Glenbogie nodded.

"Sweet Mary…"

"…Star of the Sea!" finished Eileen with a chuckle.

Feargus shook his head in disbelief.

"So, what happened then?"

"Och, I had to look after him, didn't I? She's an arrogant piece, that one, so I used it to my advantage. She ought not to have dismissed an old woman so lightly."

Feargus smiled at the set of her jaw.

"Just so you don't think I go into these things lightly," she explained. "I always take a bit of insurance with me if I'm going to have dealings with any of his lot."

"Oh, and what is the nature of this insurance, then?"

"I make myself up a charm and carry it on my person."

Feargus gave her a studied look.

"And you're not going to tell me what's in it, are you?"

She shook her head then placed a finger at the side of her nose.

"Trade secrets, you understand."

Feargus chuckled.

"What did you do next? Did you have to call down the heavens or sing up a gust of wind to blow her back into the sea or what?"

Mrs. Glenbogie laughed, a cackle of genuine glee.

"No, laddie. I just threw it at the back of her head."

Feargus slumped back in his chair, shaking his head in disbelief.

"You threw the charm at the back of her head?" He repeated, passing a hand across his face, before clasping it to his forehead.

"Have you no notion of who she is? What she's capable of?" he asked.

Mrs. Glenbogie snorted. She eased herself off her chair and walked stiffly to the kitchen sink. She poured the dregs of her tea down the drain and turned to face an incredulous Feargus.

"I'm supposing that to be one of those rhetorical questions?" she remarked wryly. "Of course I bloody know who she is and what she's capable of! What was I supposed to do? Just let her do away with the wee shite?"

Feargus shrugged.

"Would it've been so bad? I mean, really…."

"Feargus! You can't mean that! What about the lasses, then? What do you suppose would happen to the lasses if aught happened to Skelly? Did that ever cross through your thick skull?"

Feargus blushed and looked down at his hands. He knotted

his fingers together and shook his head.

"Of course," he said, softly. "What *would* happen, do you think?"

"I've no idea, pet," answered Mrs. Glenbogie wearily. "Mebbe nothing. Mebbe we'd all be free of this whole nonsense altogether. Mebbe I should've let her kill him."

Feargus got up and walked over to stand in front of the old woman.

The strain of her adventure had aged her visibly, despite her bravado. She trembled where she stood and her skin was pale and haggard.

"Come here, you silly old bird," he said, reaching out to fold her into a gentle embrace. "Of course you couldn't let her kill him. Not knowing how it would affect the girls. Or the island. For all we know, he's the only thing standing between us and being swallowed by her hateful sea. You did what you always do - the very thing that keeps everyone safe."

"Aye," said Mrs. Glenbogie, her voice muffled by the thick fabric of Feargus' shirt. "Then why do I feel like I've made it all the worse?"

Feargus stepped back and guided her back to her chair by the stove.

"Oh, I don't know," he said with a wicked smile. "Maybe because you've no doubt incurred the personal wrath of an extremely vengeful sea-witch?"

Eileen laughed, then, loudly and deeply until the laughter turned to tears and she wept long and hard for how close they'd come to losing everything.

Chapter 15

"Knock, knock!" sang Frances, as she opened the door of the cottage. "I come bearing biscuits.". Angus squeezed past and flung himself on the figure standing at the large, scrubbed oak table. "And a somewhat damp and smelly dog," added, Frances glancing apologetically at the muddy paw prints that followed the little dog as he capered about the kitchen.

Cliona laughed, waving a hand in dismissal.

"Not to worry," she said, bending down to make an appropriate fuss of the ecstatic terrier. "The cleaning lady hasn't been yet."

"Ha!" said Frances, setting the mesh shopping bag onto the bench and glancing around at the clutter of chaos in the little cottage. "I thought it was her week off. I'll put the kettle on, will I?"

"No point in having biscuits without tea," said Cliona, rummaging in the bag. "Oh good, you got Garabaldi."

"Naturally."

"Did you bring anything for Angus, only I haven't filled up his treat jar. I wasn't expecting visitors."

"Are you ever?" said Frances, pulling a wrapped bundle from her coat pocket. "Here, I got him a marrow bone, but he mustn't get it until we sit down. Wasn't the whole point of you setting up camp here to keep the riff-raff from disturbing your genius?"

"If it was, it didn't work, did it?" retorted Cliona with a grin.

"Again, I say 'ha'," said Frances, setting the kettle on the hob. "Seriously, though, how are you managing?"

Frances gave her friend a meaningful look which Cliona did her best to avoid. Sympathy and understanding only served to bring her perilously close to tears and she was doing her utmost to avoid that state of affairs.

She shrugged and gestured with her hand to encompass the piles of fabric and half-pinned patterns. Racks of assorted clothing stood haphazardly along the edge of the kitchen and Morag's former jam cupboard had been transformed into yarn storage.

"Organized chaos at this point. I'm trying to get a bunch of stuff ready for the Solstice Festival but it's proving to be a bit tricky. I haven't quite got everything moved from the house yet, so I end up needing something and it's not here…"

Her voice faltered briefly, and she swallowed hard. She cast a furtive look at Frances who was leaning against the bench with her arms folded. Her blond hair was piled on top of her head in a lopsided ponytail and there was a streak of green paint across the collar of her t-shirt. She wore a much-darned mustard-yellow cardigan with large sagging pockets from which an ink-stained cloth and a fat charcoal pencil protruded. Cliona suppressed a smile, Frances had refused all offers of fashion guidance, claiming herself to be quite content to continue on in her distracted-by-the-muse style.

"You know what I meant," said Frances, her voice soft and

gentle, "And stop looking at me like you want to give me a make-over. You couldn't possibly do better than this perfect cardigan."

Cliona snorted, grateful for the kind deflection that Frances was offering. The whistling of the kettle gave her something to do rather than face her friend directly when she spoke.

"It's hard," she admitted, "much harder than I thought. I keep thinking I can hear her talking and the smell of the jam cupboard undoes me every time I go into it. The herbs...." She shook her head as she spooned tea into the pot. "They're infused into the wood, I suppose. Anyway, it's lovely and awful all at the same time. Just as I knew it would be."

Cliona's grandmother had left the little cottage to her only granddaughter after her death just over a year ago, but it had only been in the last few weeks that Cliona had decided to use the little house as her studio.

"I couldn't possibly have moved in," she'd told Frances when her friend had questioned her about it. "I couldn't have left mam all alone with my da, not so soon after losing Ewan as well. She needed me at home and I still wasn't sure what I was doing with myself."

Frances had left the discussion there, but she knew it had more to do with Cliona's guilt over the loss of Ewan and her perceived failure as a wind singer than her family's expectations. The two women had spent an emotional few days transporting all of Cliona's fabric and her sewing and designing gear into the little cottage, trying to turn something so beloved and familiar into a place for Cliona to work. It had proven very difficult, so resistant was Cliona to changing anything about the space that her gran had lived in for most of her life.

"Give it time," said Frances, accepting a mug of tea as the two women and Angus settled themselves into the armchairs by the kitchen fireplace. "It's bound to take some getting used to and besides, there's no timeline on grief, right?"

Cliona nodded, burying her face in the steam from the fragrant brew. She cleared her throat and smiled.

"Are you doing a table for the Fair? Or are you still being hounded by Harpy McShane to, what was it? 'Add a few bits of things' to hers?"

Frances winced and shook her head.

"Don't remind me," she said, "It's getting to the point where I'm afraid to go in the shop. The woman is relentless. Besides, the Fair is ages away, I can't possibly be expected to make a decision this early."

"Oh, I don't know," said Cliona, mischief sparkling in her green eyes. "It's expected to be a pretty big affair this year, you know. Now that we've got all those devoted bird and seal-watchers that are smitten with the place. Not to mention you've a wild group of devoted patrons now. *And* it's the last ferry from the mainland until after the holidays so it's bound to mean the hordes descend."

"Oh, shut up," said Frances, good-naturedly, passing Cliona the plate of biscuits, "Stop trying to antagonize me. Anyway, we've got far more juicy things to talk about than some far-off arts and crafts fair. What about our Trudy, then?"

Cliona let out a low whistle which made Angus leap up from his place on the hearth rug and run, barking madly, to the door. Frances rolled her eyes.

"Will you ever learn?"

"Is it my fault that your dog is overly excitable and dubiously behaved?"

"That sounds appropriately familiar," mused Frances as they waited for the little dog to realize there was nothing happening. "I almost miss the constant criticism of my dog-guardianship."

"Do you, though?" said Cliona, grimacing. "I'd have thought it was the best day of your life knowing your terms of service had been satisfied. How long has it been now?"

Frances shrugged, avoiding Cliona's eyes and focusing her attention on the crackling fire. "Not long, a couple of months or so? I hardly noticed, to be honest. He was certainly right; a year and a day passes by more quickly than you might imagine. Besides nothing's official and I still have a strong sense of him, so things haven't really changed all that much. I imagine he hasn't really thought of it. He's left me alone for a good while, and had done even before the time was technically up."

"Good of him," muttered Cliona. "I suppose he'd already been plotting his move onto Trudy by then."

Frances looked up, sharply.

"Do you really think so?"

Cliona groaned.

"Who can possibly know with that lot?" she said, her voice rising in indignation. "For all we know, this has been planned for years. Didn't Skelly tell you at the beginning that there were going to be three of us?"

Frances nodded. "Well, yes but I hadn't interpreted it to mean we were supposed to be some sort of team. Surely my part has already played out. And what about Trudy? What can he possibly have in mind for her?"

"Heaven knows," said Cliona, rubbing a hand across her face. "The poor wee thing is hardly suited for the drama and intrigue of the faery contingent. I imagine he just picked on her because she was the least likely to be able to resist his charms."

"Oh, I don't know about that, Clee," said Frances, doubtfully. "I wouldn't underestimate Trudy. I think there's far more to her than we know."

"You're kind and generous to a fault, Frances Blackburn," said Cliona with a wry smile. "Poor Trudy is about as fit for the sort of malarky that Skelly and his like serve up as is poor old Hetty Rowbottom."

Hetty Rowbottom was the village's eldest resident. At 98 years old she spent most of her day sitting by the fire in the pub, drinking large brandies and telling anyone who would bother to listen about the many ways her rheumatism made it impossible for her to get around like she used to.

Frances chuckled, imagining Hetty as she looked, tottering the few steps from her chair beside the fire to the waiting car of whoever's turn it was to run her home.

"Well, I happen to disagree. I think…"

But what Frances thought was drowned out by Angus' loud, excited bark and his mad dash to the door.

"Again?" wailed Cliona. "Foolish creature, there's nothing there. Honestly, you really ought to take him to dog classes or something."

"On Glencarragh? And which dog classes would those be?" said Frances, crossly. She got up and went to the door, shushing Angus as she went. "Look, silly dog, there's no-one there." Just to make a point, she flung open the kitchen door, then staggered back in surprise as Trudy's raised hand almost rapped her on the face.

"Oh!" said Trudy, blanching visibly. "I'm ever so sorry. Did I hit you?"

Frances suppressed a mild flash of irritation, for which she immediately berated herself, before taking a deep breath and saying, brightly,

"Of course not! Here's Cliona, falsely accusing Angus of all manner of things and he was right after all. Come in, come in. We're just having tea; I'll get you a cup."

Frances walked over to fetch a clean mug and gave Cliona a smug grin as she went. Cliona pretended not to notice as she got up and attempted to clear a space at the table for Trudy.

"Sorry, love," she said, gathering up a stack of fabric swatches. "I'm still trying to get myself organized and it's clearly not going well. Here, hold these a sec."

Trudy smiled, holding out her hands to receive the pile of linen, grateful to have something to do. Walking into a pre-existing gathering was one of her least favourite things, even when it was the two people she felt understood her best. Or, at least, accepted her at face value.

"No need to apologize," she said, as Cliona directed her to set the pile of fabric on one of the recently vacated chairs by the fire. "I imagine it must be hard for you to be here without your gran. Her feeling must be very much in the place."

Cliona paused, in mid-stack, looking at Trudy with a mixture of confusion and sadness. Her friend was such an odd combination; sometimes she seemed so oblivious to the goings-on around her, and sometimes she was so acutely perceptive as to be a bit eerie.

"Yes, actually," she said, finally, clearing her throat. "She's very much still here. It's why I haven't wanted to move any of the furniture around, you see."

"Of course," said Trudy, looking around at the strange jumble of Morag's old wooden furniture and the slightly more modern incursions belonging to Cliona. Her eyes rested on the silvery laptop that perched precariously on a tower of neatly folded t-shirts and she only just stopped herself from wincing. But not before Cliona noticed.

"I know," she said, ruefully. "Gran will be spinning knowing that's in here. She never did have time for modern technology, as you can see,"

She gestured around the little cottage which seemed to have been frozen in time. The old Aga and the oil lamps being the more obvious hold-outs.

"I think it's lovely," murmured Trudy, running her fingers along the edge of the jam cupboard, "it reminds me a lot of my Aunt Calla's cottage. I wonder…"

She shook her head.

"Anyway, sorry to intrude on your teatime but I wanted to thank you both for looking after me, you know, after my little…excursion yesterday."

Frances handed her a mug and ushered her to the kitchen table where they all sat down.

"Good heavens, no need to thank us. How are you coping, are you feeling alright?"

Trudy shrugged, taking a sip of the tea. She closed her eyes and inhaled deeply.

"Ah, that's lovely. You do make a lovely cup of tea, Fran."

"Flattery will get you everywhere," said Cliona, pushing the plate of biscuits towards her, "but don't evade the question. How are you managing?"

"I'm fine, absolutely," she said, truthfully. "I mean, I feel a bit wiped out, but it was a bit of a day yesterday so that's to be expected."

"True," agreed Frances. "It's not every day one gets whisked away to the land of Faery by a selkie-boy."

Cliona snorted.

"Something like that." She leaned across the table and gave Trudy's hand a quick pat. "Don't feel like you have to make light of this, we take it all very seriously you know. I mean, we never hear from Skelly unless something horrible is about to happen so don't hold back on our account. I think I can speak for us all when I say we'd rather know what we're up against."

Trudy felt a wave of heat rising from belly, flushing her cheeks. She offered up a quick smile.

"Well, actually, now that you mention it. There was something I forgot to tell you yesterday."

"Oh, good lord," groaned Cliona, putting a hand to her forehead in a dramatic gesture. "I knew it."

"Hush, Clee," said Frances, "don't be so dramatic, you'll frighten poor Trudy." She gave Trudy an encouraging smile. "What is it, pet?"

"Well," started Trudy, eyes down, running her forefinger around the edge of her mug. She had to be careful not to reveal too much. There was still a lot of what Skelly had told her that she wanted to sort through before she shared it with the girls. One thing she was sure he was right about, was that they'd never consider letting her do what was being asked of her, nor, if she was to be honest, was she sure *she* wanted to do it. The only other option was to find another way and Skelly had been predictably unhelpful in that regard.

"Well?" prodded Cliona, ignoring the glare from Frances.

"Yes, sorry," said Trudy, "I'm just trying to untangle everything, it was all so strange, you see." She looked up at Frances, seeing the look of genuine concern in her eyes as she gave

Trudy her full and patient attention. Trudy felt a stab of guilt, followed quickly by a surge of rebellion. It wasn't fair, she would have to say something. She, Trudy, would want to know.

"There's two things, actually," she continued, looking up at the expectant faces. "Firstly, Skelly told me that between us we might be able to figure out a way to break Lira's curse for good."

"What?" exploded Cliona, slamming the palm of her hand down on the table and making them all jump. "What sort of bomb is that to drop? And we *might* be able to figure it out? Arrogant little…"

"Cliona," soothed Frances, seeing the look of alarm on Trudy's face. "There's no need to get yourself worked up, let Trudy finish. Obviously, that's something we need to come back to, but what else was there, Trude?"

Trudy let her eyes slide away from Frances', she couldn't bear to see the kindness in them, knowing what she might be doing with the next bit of information.

"Moss," she whispered, her voice barely audible. "I think I saw Moss."

"You'd better explain this a bit better," said Cliona, glancing worriedly at Frances.

All of the colour had drained from Frances' face and she sat slumped in her chair.

"What do you mean you *think* you saw him?"

Trudy felt her heart hammering in her chest. Maybe this had been a mistake. After all, she wasn't sure, was she?

"It's just, I had a feeling that it was him," she stammered. "Only he's not quite like Frances has described him," she looked over at Frances, willing her to look up. "I mean, he seemed, I don't know, wild almost, and he stayed in the corners, in the shadows."

"Oh my god!" exclaimed Cliona. "Is Skelly keeping him *prisoner*?" She whirled to face Frances. "Is that his solution to your not being bound to him anymore? Of all the horrible, underhanded..."

"No, Clee," said Frances in a quiet voice. "Skelly wouldn't do that."

"How can you be so sure? Again, I ask you, we have no idea what he's capable of really, do we? Why does everyone insist on believing he's some kind of benevolent victim here? We have no idea where his loyalties lie, if he even has any. And now he's hinting at some idea that we can break Lira's curse while at the same time he's holding Moss hostage so we'll do what he wants."

"No," protested Trudy. "No, it's not like that at all. I didn't get the feeling that Moss, if it even *was* him...oh, maybe I ought never to have said anything. I just wanted Frances to know...I mean, I would want to know if there was even a little hope...I'm so sorry. I never know if I'm doing the right thing. I just wanted to do something nice, you've both been so good and lovely...."

Her eyes filled with tears, her face crumpled and flaming. Angus whined and tried to climb up onto her lap.

Cliona let out a sigh of exasperation.

"Oh, for heaven's sake, Trudy, stop crying."

"Cliona!" said Frances, shocked. "That's so unnecessary. Have a little feeling, would you?"

Cliona cupped the heels of her hands to her eyes.

"Sorry, sorry. I'm sorry Trudy, I'm a beast, I know. You know I don't mean any harm. I'm just frustrated, that's all.

Whenever Skelly rears his ugly blue-haired head I find myself bordering on frantic hysteria imagining what horrors await us."

Trudy sniffled, accepting the handkerchief that Frances was offering.

"You don't need to apologize, I'm the one who ought to be…"

"No," said Frances, firmly. "Cliona did indeed need to apologize, and you don't need to do anything other than to take a deep breath, have a sip of tea and tell us everything that happened. Don't leave anything out."

Trudy pushed back a strand of hair and took a deep sip of her tea, breathing deeply, as she'd been instructed. Angus had made his way onto her lap. He was perched precariously across her legs but she found the weight of him to be comforting so she let her hand rest on the wiry fur of his back.

"Oh," she said, forcing a brightness into her voice. "There was one other thing I forgot to tell you that also happened yesterday; I got sacked."

Chapter 16

Skelly studied the flames in the hearth. Centuries earthbound had taught him a few of the gifts of land-walkers, fire-scrying being one of them.

"What is it?" asked Cernach from his own chair by the fire. A fragrant plume of smoke curled from the clay pipe he held between his teeth, wreathing his head with a scent of moss and oak leaves.

"Your one is coming," said Skelly. "He just crossed through. Did you tell him…"

"No," interrupted Cernach. "I didn't."

The crackling of the fire filled the silence between them. The golden-red light of the early evening had given way to the darker tones of twilight. Outside, an owl called. The distant sea was a steady, murmuring presence.

Cernach stood up and went to stand by the window that faced across the moor.

"He accepted my company for what it was, when I was able to offer it. He demanded nothing of me, and I saw no reason to demand more of him."

Skelly laughed.

"Are you meaning that to be some sort of an accusation?"

"No, I'm not."

Cernach turned to face him, tamping out his pipe against the window frame. "Did it sound like one?"

Skelly shrugged.

"Guilty conscience, I suppose," he said. "Hard to imagine, aye?"

He grinned widely, no trace of animosity in his bright green eyes.

Cernach threw his head back and laughed his earthy laugh.

"In you? Most certainly, my friend."

He sighed heavily.

"The centuries are long when you've no hearth to call your own, Skelly. You, at least, have been able to fashion yourself something of an existence out of what you were left with."

He gestured to the tiny cottage and to the tattered and patched overcoat hung on a peg by the door.

"I've just done what I had to do," said Skelly defensively. "And I haven't got the freedom you have; I cannae go where I'd rather be. I wouldn't call being stuck here in the In-Between much of a life!"

"But you're *not* stuck, Skelly," said Cernach, gently. "You've got all three of them now, you need only…."

"No!" interrupted Skelly, his voice a harsh whisper. "I won't be responsible for it. Don't you see? Hasn't there been enough grief over this?"

"He's right, Cernach," said a voice from the doorway.

The two turned to see Feargus standing, dripping rain onto the doormat.

Cernach smiled warmly and held out his hands.

"Feargus! My old friend! So good to see you. Won't you come in?"

Feargus smiled thinly, tilting his head to the side.

"Och! You old fox! Didn't you teach me your own self?" he grinned at the brown-skinned man who grinned back.

Feargus glanced at Skelly who sighed and raised his eyes to the ceiling.

"Feargus, is it?" he said, wearily. "Won't you come and sit by my fire?"

The visitor bowed deeply.

"Thank you, kind sir. I accept your invitation and will gladly cross your threshold for the benefit of warmth and companionship."

"So be welcome," muttered Skelly, in the formal way.

"Excellent!" exclaimed Cernach, moving another chair close to the fire. "I think the occasion calls for the finest of brews!" He glanced expectantly at Feargus, who looked back at him with wide-eyed innocence.

Cernach's face fell in disappointment.

Feargus chuckled and pulled a large, dusty bottle from the pocket of his raincoat.

"Made with honey drawn of an ancient hive, infused with the flowers of the sacred thorn," he frowned and looked up, as if trying to remember something.

"The summer of '06?" asked Cernach, raising an eyebrow.

"The very one!" said Feargus triumphantly.

"How long, really, have you two been chummy then?" asked Skelly, suspiciously. He peered closely at Feargus, whose outline glimmered very slightly, then drew back in shock.

"You crafty auld bastard!" he swore. "Both of you!"

Feargus and Cernach roared with laughter.

The creature who called himself Feargus swept a courtly bow.

"Manannán mac Lír, at your service, m'lord. And may your

days be as bright as all the stars of the sea."

"What's your part in all this, then?" asked Skelly, when wine had been poured and the three sat ranged around the fire.

Feargus shook his head.

"I haven't got *any* part to play in this, dear boy," he said, settling back into his chair, hands and wine resting lightly on his ample middle. "I gave up meddling quite some time ago. You see, I'm convinced that the way forward for our kind is to simply and quietly assimilate into the mortal world and that's precisely what I've done." He nodded towards Cernach, who was watching him with a wry smile. "If not for Cernach inserting himself into my days from time to time, I daresay I would have extricated myself entirely."

Skelly snorted.

"All right for some, I suppose," he muttered.

"Not at all," replied Feargus, his gaze on the flickering fire. "It's simply a matter of deciding it shall be so and getting on with it." He let his eyes shift to Skelly for a moment and gestured at the worn corduroy trousers and knitted vest. "It seems to me you're halfway there yourself."

Skelly glowered, "It's just…"

"Easier?" offered Feargus, raising a shapely eyebrow. "Yes, I found it to be so after a while and then, once I decided to leave all the nonsense behind, it served me far better to allow the change to become more or less permanent."

"I was going to say, 'practical,'" said Skelly, his voice rising. "And not all of us have the luxury of leaving all the nonsense, as you put it, behind, do we?"

"Now, now," soothed Cernach, with a smile. "Let's keep our

heads."

Skelly shot him a menacing look but sank into a sullen silence. He leaned back in his own chair and took a long drink from his cup.

"Anyway," said Feargus, "let's go back to your original question, shall we? Officially, I have no part in your little feud, nor do I wish to acquire one. However, my comrade here prevailed upon my better nature to assist him in the retrieval of a certain lost item that you had requested?" He left the end of the sentence hanging in the air and regarded Skelly with an innocent look.

Skelly's eyes darted towards the kitchen, where sounds of quiet movement could be heard. He looked at Cernach who bowed his head slightly and held up his hands and shrugged.

"I, alone, do not have access to Deep Faery. I needed the help of a Guardian to get me through the door, as it were."

"But you said the lasses had raised enough magic…"

Cernach shrugged again.

"Indeed, which is why I was able to break the bonds that held your wee *bodach*, but I had to get there first, hadn't I?"

"And why are you telling me this?" said Skelly, jutting out his whiskered jaw.

"Simply to underline the point that I have no desire to get involved further," said Feargus, with a firm glance at both of them. "I feel I've done my good deed of the day, as it were, and that I'm here simply as a friend from the old days, enjoying a cup of good wine in…" he glanced at the two faces regarding him and felt a nudge of something he preferred to ignore, "in good company," he finished, raising his cup to them before raising it to his lips.

"You'll leave the lasses at the mercy of Lira, then? You've

no inclination to intervene on their behalf? Only, I got the impression they think of you as a friend. I expect ingratiating yourself into the mortal world would have the effect of these kinds of deep friendships developing, aye?"

Feargus stiffened slightly and swirled the amber liquid in his glass. Without looking at either of them, he spoke in a soft voice.

"As I have clearly stated, what argument any of you have with my sister, is none of my concern."

* * *

"These are lovely, Frances," said Trudy, reaching out with her fingers to gently trace the outline of the canvases that lay stacked against the wall of the cottage. "You've really caught the feeling of the sea, you know? I'm sure I can almost hear the sound of the waves."

Frances smiled. "I can't seem to help painting the sea…" she began, then broke off, giggling. "I wonder why that is?"

Cliona snorted one of her trademark snorts.

"Have you any fresh ginger?" she asked, opening cupboard doors and sticking her head inside. "Honestly Frances, your kitchen organization is an absolute shamble. I forgot to pick some up at the grocer's and I can't make my curry without fresh ginger..

"Of course you can't," said Frances, rolling her eyes at Trudy who just grinned.

"Have you ever known an authentic Gaelic curry to not have fresh ginger?" she asked Trudy pointedly. "Perish the thought."

"Funny, funny, funny," retorted Cliona. "I've never heard any complaints while you're both hoovering down a giant plateful."

Angus uttered a short bark. Cliona looked down at him and scowled with mock ferocity.

"You either, Mister," she said. "I daresay you'd turn up your nose and refuse to lick the plates if I didn't put the ginger in."

"It's in that basket hanging near the window. The one with the garlic in it."

"Right! Got it! Carry on with the art appreciation session. I'll be with you in a quick mo' once this is simmering. Wine?"

Ignoring Trudy's protests, Cliona filled her glass from a dubious-looking bottle of red wine. "Don't look at me like that," she said, adopting an air of innocence. "Feargus will never know. I got it from the back. He never looks at the ones in the back. Here, Frances. You're going to need this." She added a generous glug to Frances' glass and then retreated back to the Aga from where the delicious scent of a fragrant masala curry was wafting.

Trudy and Frances sat themselves down on the weathered, but gloriously comfortable tartan sofa. A gift from Frances' great friend, Sophie, it was one of the few things she'd brought with her from her old life. When asked why they'd paid the eye-watering cost to ship it across on the ferry, she could only say that it was to remind her of a time when she thought her life was in irreparable ruins and how the simple kindness of her friend had made her feel less of a failure. Angus promptly jumped up between them, scattering their papers and sloshing wine from their glasses.

"Angus!" they chorused together.

"Menace of a dog!" exclaimed Frances. "Honestly! I don't

know why I put up with him!"

Trudy grinned and reached out to tousle the terrier's ears. "He's alright," she said. "He just likes to be a part of things, that's all. Who can blame a creature for that?"

"Sure, whether he's invited or not! Anyway, let's get on, will we? I've got another stack of sketches and watercolors over in the other cupboard, but I think these are the ones to start with."

Before they'd left Cliona's studio, Trudy had told them what little Skelly had hinted at in regard to them finding a way to break Lira's storm-curse.

"He insisted he couldn't give me any direct information," Trudy had told them. "He said it would be a violation of some sort of law and that it was up to us to sort it out for ourselves."

"Typical," Cliona had snorted. "Funny how those laws of theirs have such convenient interpretations sometimes. So what did he say then?"

Trudy had smiled a nervous, apologetic smile. Suddenly it didn't seem like much of a clue at all.

"He said to look in Frances' paintings."

"What are they?" asked Trudy, taking up one of the stiff sheets of watercolor paper. "I've never seen anything like them."

"They're merrin," called Cliona from the kitchen. "They're sea elementals. What Skelly used to be, you know, before The Fall."

Frances chuckled.

"Yes, that's as best we know. I started seeing them a few

months ago - on one of my many trips down to the seaside. You know, at the behest of Skelly."

"Oh," said Trudy, "You actually *see* them, then? The faery people, I mean?" she asked. "I mean, they're just here, in the world, same as you."

Frances nodded.

"Sure. They're as commonplace to me as birds in the hedgerow. Well, they were at one point, anyway. Although I admit, it's better now. The numbers are definitely higher. Still, that could just be Glencarragh and not because of anything I'm doing. I'm beginning to doubt…"

She flapped the hand that wasn't holding her wineglass, dismissing that line of unhelpful thought.

"You know the story about that, though. Simple, unadorned answer is: yes. Some of them are bold, others I have to pay closer attention to see."

Trudy nodded as she listened, chewing her lip. This was one of those times where she wasn't sure if speaking up would be a good idea.

"What is it, Trudy?" asked Frances, gently, recognizing the turmoil of inner wrangling on Trudy's expression. "I'm fine if you want to ask another question."

"No, I haven't really got a question," replied Trudy, focusing on trying to smooth down the wiry hair on Angus' ruff. "More of a contribution. I want to tell you both something, but I'm worried you'll be cross with me for not mentioning it sooner."

"Ohh! Are you going to spill the beans on your rendezvous with Skelly, then? Finally tell us exactly what happened? Because, darling Trudy, I can read you like a book and you're definitely not telling us everything," said Cliona, plonking herself down on the arm of the sofa, a large goblet of wine in her hand. She was red-faced from standing over the boiling pot of rice; her hair was damp and clung to her forehead. "Do tell. We're all ears and trust me, nothing you could say would shock us at this point."

Frances shot Cliona a warning look. Of the two of them, Cliona was less patient with Trudy's awkward ways. Not for lack of compassion or understanding, but for the simple reason that her various oddities didn't matter to Cliona, who, in turn, found it hard to understand why it still mattered to Trudy. She couldn't grasp that Trudy wasn't used to such unconditional acceptance. It wasn't everyone who had Cliona's apparently miraculous ability to see everything so very clearly. It also didn't help that her sense of humour was often laced with sarcasm which was something that Trudy often found difficult to judge.

Cliona caught the look.

"Don't get all up at me," she said, with mock indignation. "I know, I know, I'm not using the proper words. I'll try to be clearer." She smiled and looked at Trudy whose face was creased with worry and confusion. Cliona's smile faltered for a brief moment as she thought for the thousandth time how terrible things must have been for Trudy that she'd become so guarded, even among friends who'd only ever treated her with love and kindness. She lay a hand on Trudy's shoulder, giving it a quick squeeze. "What I meant to say was that we couldn't possibly be cross with you. There's not a hurtful bone in your body and not the slightest chance you'd ever do or say anything with ill-intent. Now, tell us what you want us to hear. We're listening."

Trudy's eyes filled with tears, blinking furiously she put her hand on top of Cliona's and gave it a brief pat, nodding her thanks.

"There, look what you've done, Cliona," said Frances, her tone light and joking. She passed Trudy a hanky. "Got her all upset before she even starts speaking."

Cliona stuck out her tongue and leaned in to give Trudy a sideways hug.

"It wasn't me, it's the fumes from the curry. It's just that powerful."

The three broke off into giggles and the tension eased.

After the laughter died down, Trudy wiped her eyes and blew her nose. Angus burrowed himself under her arm and rested his head on her lap. She felt her shoulders loosen at the gesture. Angus always managed to help her feel better. She buried her fingers in his wiry fur, grounding herself in his warm presence.

"Right. I suppose there's no clever way to start this, so I'll just come out and tell you what happened, shall I?"

Frances nodded, encouragingly and Cliona smiled.

Trudy blew out a deep breath and focused on the feel of Angus beneath her fingers. Now would not be a good time for her to slip to the In-Between, even though that was what every cell in her body was screaming at her to do.

I'm safe here, she told herself. *I'm safe and I am loved.*

"Apparently, according to Skelly, all of the times I thought I was daydreaming, it was actually real. Same when I sort of space-out, like I do sometimes, if you'd ever noticed."

Frances glared at Cliona, a silent threat against the quip that she knew was likely on Cliona's tongue. Cliona simply raised an innocent eyebrow and turned her attention back to Trudy.

"Well," continued Trudy, "when I do that, it's actually me slipping between the worlds."

Frances stared at Trudy for a moment, a thousand questions flitting through her mind.

"But what does that actually mean?" she said, finally. "I'm sorry Trudy, but I don't quite understand when you say you 'slip between the worlds.'"

Trudy frowned, feeling her anxiety rising again. Cliona reached out again and put her hand on Trudy's arm.

"Take your time, pet. It's nothing to do with how you're telling us, it's just us being a bit thick, right?"

Trudy smiled, gratefully.

"Okay, let me try again," she said, taking a sip of her wine. The taste of it startled her. She had quick flashes of oaken casks and jasmine-scented summer breezes. Frowning, she looked at the glass. It was her first sip, surely it wasn't hitting her that hard. She pushed the sensation away and tried to focus on her explanation. She turned to Frances.

"You know how you just said that you see the faery people flitting about in our world - in our surroundings?"

Frances nodded.

"Right, well what happens with me, apparently, is that *I* can go into *their* world, rather than them coming into ours. Or at least that happens sometimes,"

She broke off, squinting her eyes closed.

"Not always, because obviously I'm still physically here. Oh dear, it doesn't make any sense, does it? It seemed perfectly clear when Skelly explained it."

Cliona grunted.

"Aye, I suppose it would have. He has a way of making things seem so obvious," she muttered. "Do you not think he was just telling you what you wanted to hear? I mean, sure, haven't we all got a wardrobe we slip through when life gets us down?

Frances gave her another glare and turned to Trudy.

"But when you were away with Skelly, just recently, you were still actually *in* Feargus' room. We could all see you. But you were clearly not there. And Skelly told me you were with him."

All three exchanged confused looks.

"Good grief," said Cliona with a grin. "I can see it's going to be a long night."

Chapter 17

The fire in the Aga had long dwindled to coals and the pots and saucepans from the meal were stacked haphazardly by the sink. In the living room, the assortment of candles were melted down to stumps and nubs and Angus lay snoring by the fire that Frances had lit in the grate several hours before. The three girls sat staring at the flames.

"Do you really not remember painting it, then?" asked Trudy, looking at the small watercolour that they'd propped up against an empty wine bottle. After her rather muddled confession, that none of them seemed to understand, they'd decided it would be easier to focus on the immediate task of looking for clues in Frances' paintings.

"Honestly, no," sighed Frances. "But that's not uncommon, you know. There's more than a few of these," she gestured to the various stacks and piles littered around the room. "that I've absolutely no recollection of having done. Especially the small ones. They're sort of over before I realize I'm doing them."

She shrugged an apology.

"And you don't go back and look at them?"

Frances shook her head.

"No. Most of the time I just wrap them up and take them in to Dorothy."

"What about the others?"

Frances squirmed in her seat.

"Skelly tells me which ones to take to Dorothy and which ones to send to the mainland."

"Ha!" said Cliona. "He's an art critic, too, is he?"

"Cliona," frowned Trudy. "I think that's unfair."

Cliona groaned.

"Don't you start defending him. For god's sake, you've hardly even met him. You've no idea what he's really like."

"And don't you ever get tired of raking muck all over everything?" snapped Trudy, surprising all of them. "Why do you have to be so hostile all the time?"

"Oh! Now look who's developing a backbone? Bit of Skelly rubbing off, is it?"

"Cliona!" said Frances. "That's not fair. Not at all." She gave Trudy a worried look, but the other girls' face was an expressionless mask.

Cliona glanced down, biting her lip.

"You're right. I'm sorry Trudy. I don't mean to be such a beast. I just find it all so very frustrating and I'm not very good at being frustrated. What are we supposed to be looking at? What sort of clues are we supposed to find? Honestly, I wish that stupid faery had been a bit more clear on the whole thing."

Trudy managed a small smile, burying the hurt and confusion that Cliona had raised in her.

"I'm sorry, too. I know I'm still new at all this and I ought not to be acting as though I have any notion whatsoever about what any of it means," she glanced at her two friends seated on either side of her. "You two are so matter-of-fact about it all. It's so commonplace here - this idea of faeries and selkies and ancient feuds. You all discuss it like you're discussing the weather or what's for tea. It's always just been stories to me. Or, at least I thought they were stories, the result of an overactive imagination"

Frances put her arm around Trudy and gave a squeeze.

"But it isn't just stories to you, though is it? Not really."

"How do you mean?"

"Well, and please forgive me if I'm getting this wrong and I hope you'll pardon me for giving any credence to Cliona's earlier, unfeeling remark."

Cliona scowled but there was no malice in it.

"But," continued Frances, "I've been thinking about what you said earlier, and I wonder if maybe you slipping between worlds as you call it, is sort of a defense mechanism. I mean, from what you've told us, you had an absolute horror-show of a childhood. All of the bullying and then your family basically just ignoring your…situation, not getting you any help you might have needed."

Trudy felt her chest tighten. She fought to control the cascade of memories that always hovered just below the surface of her conscious mind.

"So you see," continued Frances. "It all makes perfect sense. You have this innate ability to pass into the In-Between, and so what perhaps started out as the natural inclinations of a small child, turned into an escape for you, when things got difficult. Do you remember when you started doing this daydreaming stuff?"

Trudy sniffled. "As long as I can remember," she said. "I think maybe it was tolerated when I was little. Like you said, adults expect small children to be imaginative and make up fantastic stories and things. But when you get older, well, it's not so charming, I suppose."

Frances nodded, encouraging Trudy to accept the idea.

"And now, the fact that Skelly tracked you down - sent one of his own people to bring you to him - doesn't that strike you as a bit extreme? He wanted me for my paintings, but he didn't do anything more than drink tea and eat my lemon drizzle."

Cliona laughed.

"At least there was a bit of courtship there," she said with a grin. "He just turned up in my head one day!"

"It seems to me that you're very much connected to Glencarragh. He must feel you have some contribution to make here. An important one. The trouble is, because of this whole curse thing and the madly noble notion they have about not directly getting involved…"

"Which we all know is a load of bollocks because he just manipulates us instead of telling us what we need to know," interrupted Cliona, returning Frances' glare.

"What I was trying to say before I was interrupted, is that from what you've told us, I wonder if maybe he wanted you to know something, but he can't actually come out and say it, for whatever reason. And now we just have to sort out what that is. This painting is obviously our clue."

Trudy felt a stab of guilt. No, she wouldn't think about it. She picked up the painting again and studied it.

"Do you really think this is supposed to be me, then?" she asked.

Frances took the painting from her and pursed her lips.

"Well, I'm not sure who the man is - it isn't Skelly and it isn't one of the faery creatures I've ever seen."

"He's a bit dishy, don' t you think?" interrupted Cliona, elbowing Trudy with a wink.

Trudy blushed.

"He is, you're right. Too bad I've no recollection of ever having met him."

"But it's definitely you that I painted. Only not you. Sort of you if you were a forest nymph or tree sprite or something. But definitely you."

Trudy laughed loudly.

"That's about as far from me as I could ever imagine," she said, her voice fading to a whisper.

Cliona and Frances exchanged a glance.

"Oh, pet," said Cliona, leaning in to press against Trudy's side. "You do yourself no justice, you know."

Trudy smiled; her eyes bright with unshed tears.

"And you can tell a tall tale when the fancy suits you, Cliona Stewart. It's no secret I'm the odd one out here," She looked at her two friends. "Look at the pair of you - the Valkyrie and the fire maiden. And then there's me - mousey and prone to weeping!"

She grinned at the looks on their faces.

"It's alright - you needn't look so scandalized," she said. "I'm many things but I'm not deaf, or stupid. I know what Feargus and Iain have been saying."

"Bloody men!" fumed Cliona. "They've got absolutely no bloody idea!"

"Cliona's right," said Frances. "You should've seen me when I first met Skelly. I was a blithering mess. I was completely directionless, absolutely miserable. I was trying to convince myself that I was deliriously happy arranging geometric shapes into repeating patterns. Robot daisies, Moss and I used to call them. Living in that mouldy old studio, about to get evicted by the evil landlord." She shook her head, chuckling softly. Then her smile faded. "And then I lost Moss and I finally realized that what Skelly was telling me was true."

"And me," said Cliona. "I hadn't half a clue what I was about. Gathering bits of sea glass like I was still five years old, without any idea what it was for. And you don't need me to tell you again how the wind singing went, do you? My supposed 'gift'? There's me, scattered off in all four directions with the bloody wind. If it hadn't been for Skelly….."

"We'd be much worse off than we are now," finished Frances, quietly.

The three girls looked at each other solemnly.

"Oh, bloody hell," said Cliona.

They sat in silence for a while, each of them with their own thoughts.

At last, Cliona got up to retrieve another bottle of wine. At Frances' questioning glance she scowled.

"He never looks at the back shelf!"

Trudy grinned. "He's not going to have anything to look at the way we're going!"

"Well, we need to fortify ourselves, don't we?"

"You're right," said Trudy. "It's going to take more than one bottle for us to sort this all out."

"Exactly," said Frances, heading off to the kitchen. After a bit of rummaging and slamming of cupboard doors, she came back. In her hands she carried a cake tin and three plates.

"Not to mention a slice or three of a nice lemon drizzle!"

* * *

"There's something else I feel like I want to tell you," said Trudy, her cheeks flushed from the wine and the heat of the fire. "but I don't want you to be disappointed in me." Angus had burrowed himself under the quilt, which she'd draped across her legs, and she stroked the lump where his head was, absently drawing courage from his presence.

Cliona raised an eyebrow. She propped herself up on one elbow from the pile of cushions where she was sprawled by the hearth.

"Oh aye?" she said, grinning. "You going to confess to having carnal knowledge of the dishy fellow in the painting?"

Trudy shifted uncomfortably on the sofa, nudging an unresponsive Angus along so she could stretch out her legs.

She decided to ignore Cliona's remark.

She shrugged, half in apology, "It's just that I feel like meeting Skelly wasn't such a terrible thing." She paused, trying to choose her words carefully. "I mean, for the two of you, your lives were sort of in a mess when he came along and he only made them messier before they got a bit better. But for me, in a strange way, he's eased a giant weight that's been hanging over me my whole life."

Frances leaned in towards her friend as Trudy reached out to gently pat her arm.

"Listening to Skelly explain what I can do, then hearing your theory about why I slide into my daydreams makes so much sense."

She paused again, struggling.

"It means I'm not such a freak after all. Well," she broke off, laughing softly. "I'm still a bit of a freak, but not in the way I thought I was. Does that make sense?"

Cliona blinked rapidly. She wasn't going to cry. She

absolutely was not going to cry. She knew, though, something of what Trudy was feeling.

"I suppose what I'm trying to say, is that I want you both to know that I'm totally okay with it all. I'm going to do whatever it is that I'm needed to do because I finally feel like I'm maybe not so much the wishy-washy weakling that everyone thinks I am. That *I* thought I was. I feel…well, useful now. You know, being a part of this with you all. It doesn't really matter now, where I end up, because I know I've been part of something really quite special. Everything I've ever wished for, really. Since I was little."

Trudy stopped, biting her lip and frowning down at the ruby liquid in her glass. It was the colour of rosehips and the fiery blush of a midsummer's dawn. The flames from the fire reflected in the wine, strangely human shapes that danced and shifted. Ghostly memories of the last revelers of that midsummer night when the wine had first been served. She wrenched herself back to the present moment.

She hadn't intended to say any of those things, and so the voicing of it was the final realization of its truth. Out loud, at least. In her heart, she knew she'd come to it sooner.

Frances eyes shone and Cliona cleared her throat loudly.

Trudy sighed aloud and fussed over smoothing the quilt. Now that the words were out, she felt both relief and terror at what they might mean. Clearing her throat, she pushed a strand of hair from her face and forced a laugh.

"Oh, I don't know, maybe it's all quite ridiculous of me, but I feel like all roads have led here, you know? I mean, I've been a tremendous disappointment to most people in my life. All I wanted was to get back to Glencarragh and that meant such a lot of drifting about, moving from place to place and job to job, never settling. But not in that forgivable, romantic, bohemian sort of way, though, right? People think me more of a flighty weakling whose awkward behaviour makes it impossible for her to keep a job rather than a free-spirited *vagaboundeuse* or something fashionable like that. And even here, when I finally, against all odds get here to Glencarragh, it turned out that I might not even be able to hold onto that..."

"No!" interrupted Cliona, "We've already been over this. You absolutely cannot leave Glencarragh. We will find you a job so don't even think about what those silly creatures at the tea shop are saying. Besides, didn't you just hear what you said yourself? You're needed here."

Trudy nodded, smiling a watery smile.

"I think you're right, Cliona. I actually believe that my being here *matters*. I feel like I might finally make a difference after all, that I even have something to offer. I think I just meant that knowing I belong here makes it easier to think I might have to leave."

She looked at the faces of the women who had become her first real friends. She knew then, without a shadow of a doubt that she was making the right choice. For now, anyway.

"Och, Trudy pet," said Cliona, wrapping an arm around her thin shoulders. "Haven't you always had something to offer the world? Isn't just your being here, with us, enough to make it a better place?

Trudy smiled and leaned into Cliona.

"Perhaps," she said, letting her friend take the seriousness out of it all. "But sometimes it's nice to have someone else point it out to you."

"Skelly?" Said Cliona, with a grimace.

"Yes," said Trudy grinning more widely. "Skelly."

Chapter 18

The morning sun slanted through the windows of the cottage. The room had gone chilly as the fire dwindled in the hearth.

Angus roused himself from his corner of the tartan sofa - he'd been wedged at the feet of Cliona who had slumped sideways against Trudy, who was curled up in a tight ball in the opposite corner. At some point, blankets had been slung haphazardly over the two sleeping women and Angus had deemed it his duty to watch over them as they slept.

"Traitor!" Frances had whispered in mock severity as she'd turned off the lamp and crawled into her own bed.

He jumped down off the sofa and padded over to the tiny, adjacent bedroom where his mistress lay with one arm drooping over the side of the bed. He nudged her dangling fingers until she muttered at him to go away. Which he didn't. It was perilously close to breakfast and he wasn't used to having Frances sleep past the time when she ought to be thinking about opening a tin of food for him.

Whining softly, he jumped onto the bed and wriggled in beside her.

"You'd best get up," called Cliona from the kitchen, where she was sleepily filling the kettle and stacking the glasses and plates from the night's activity. "I don't suppose he ever lets you have a lie-in?"

Frances chuckled, swinging her legs over the bed and sliding her feet into her slippers. Angus bounced down off the bed and began to trot in excited circles.

"Not likely," she replied. "I never have to worry about oversleeping." She pulled a woolen jumper on over her pajamas as she scuffed into the kitchen. Taking a ceramic bowl and a tin of dog food from the cupboard, she began to assemble Angus' breakfast, nose wrinkling at the smell of the food.

"Are you making tea or coffee?" she asked.

"Either or both," replied Cliona. "I fancy a coffee first thing myself, but I'll make a pot of tea as well."

"Lovely. I like a morning coffee as well, but I think Trudy only drinks tea."

At the mention of her name, the two women looked over at the still-sleeping form of their friend.

"She really does seem to be managing alright, don't you think?" asked Cliona, worriedly. "It's an awful lot she's been through. And to think, on top of it all, she's been sacked. I can hardly believe it."

"Yes," agreed Frances. "All things considered, she's doing amazingly well."

Frances reached out and touched Cliona on the arm.

"She's stronger than she looks," she said. "The thing about Skelly is that I don't think he would've approached her if he didn't think she could manage."

Cliona nodded.

"I know," she said. She turned back to look at Frances. "It's funny, I've never thought of him as any kind of benevolent presence. He was too much in the awfulness of that time, you know? But, in his own way, he *has* been good for me, I see that now. If I hadn't had to stay on Glencarragh, I never would have started my herb course and I'm almost ready to open my little shop. I hadn't thought to be working for myself until years down the road. I mean, don't get me wrong. I still think he's a self-serving bastard and the fact he'd load all of this on Trudy, no matter how strong she is, only proves that. My gran told me he was alright, and I absolutely didn't believe her at the time, but I suppose she knew more about him than I did." She glanced over at the sleeping form of Trudy. "I just wish I knew what it was exactly that he wants with her that made him go to such an effort. I mean, why bother revealing all that about her daydreams? It's not like it really changes anything for her. I really worry about what might be coming, Fran."

Frances finished scooping the food into Angus' bowl and put it on the floor where he proceeded to devour it, the clink of his collar against the ceramic beating in time to his slurping.

"Are you getting Storm feelings?" asked Frances, not really wanting to hear the answer.

Cliona shrugged, not really wanting to give her one.

"Vaguely. But that's been sort of a steady undercurrent of feeling ever since the last one. I'm trying not to read too much into it."

"It's true what you're saying, though," said Frances, thoughtfully, changing the subject back. "If it wasn't for the horrible loss of your Ewan and then your da being so withdrawn and not wanting to sell the boat and everything…"

Cliona flinched but nodded.

"I know. I thought the world was coming to an end but after all is said and done, me and Mam are bringing in more for the family than the fishing ever did. Between the knitting and my little art postcards we're doing okay. Plus, I've sold quite a few patterns online and the shop, like I said, won't be far behind. And now the boat's been sold. Best thing we could've done, getting rid of that bloody boat. In a horribly twisted way, everything has worked out exactly as I hoped it would years ago."

Frances took two clean mugs from the cupboard and rooted around in the fridge for the bottle of milk.

"How is your da these days?" she asked.

"Much better, actually," said Cliona. "He's taking a computer class down at the village hall with an eye to taking over my online orders. He says we need to move into the cyber age and start selling the socks and jumpers online as well. Mostly I think he just wants to cut Dorothy out of the profits. And he's been looking to license my postcards. 'Scenes from the Wild Shores'. He's got it all planned out, apparently!"

Frances laughed. "Goodness! Isn't he forward thinking? That's terrific, though. It's good to know he's coping better It'll be easier on your mum, I bet. Mind you, Feargus and Dorothy won't be happy to share in the bounty of your work."

Cliona snorted a laugh. "Right! Shall we wake up sleeping beauty there and get ourselves off to Mrs. Glenbogie's?" she said. "I'm dead curious to hear what she has to say about finding our Trudy in that painting. Maybe she can see more in it than we can. I know I'm baffled by it. Perhaps we should pack up a selection of the other ones we set aside and get her to have a look. She's been keeping company with the faery population of Glencarragh far longer than we have, maybe she'll see something we haven't."

"Good idea," said Frances. "I think I have a sketchbook from around that time somewhere in the cupboard, as well. I'll dig it out."

As she rummaged in the bottom drawer of an old oak bureau, there was a loud crash as a stack of paintings slid from where they were haphazardly piled. The noise was enough to elicit a grunt from the vicinity of the sofa. Trudy popped up her head then tried to fend off an ecstatic Angus who felt the duration of breakfast to be too long a parting. She ran a hand through her sleep-tousled hair.

"You really need a better organization system, Frances. No wonder it took us so long find anything in all that chaos."

"I rather think it had more to do with the amount of Feargus' good wine consumed than my poor organization," replied Frances dryly.

Trudy giggled.

"I fear you might be right," she glanced over towards the kitchen. "Any chance of a cuppa?" she asked.

Frances shot Cliona a meaningful look. Cliona grinned.

"Get off your arse and get it yourself," she called to Trudy, laughing.

Trudy hesitated, then her face broke into a wide grin. She flung off the blanket and got to her feet.

"Don't much care for the service in this hotel," she said as she made her way into the kitchen.

* * *

Mrs. Glenbogie took one look at the three girls and put the kettle on to boil.

"Been pilfering from the back of the shelf, have we?" she

said, with a wry grin.

Cliona stuck out her tongue before leaning over to give Mrs. G a firm hug.

"Tea and a round of hot, buttered toast," she exclaimed, seeing the loaf of freshly sliced bread sitting next to the toaster. "Mrs. G, you are a brick."

"Cure for what ails you," said Eileen, smiling at them. "And it looks to me you might be a bit delicate. Good night, then?"

Trudy smiled, shyly.

"I actually don't feel badly at all. I didn't have as much to drink as the other two."

Frances playfully slapped at her arm.

"Tattling on us, now!"

Trudy smiled wider and shrugged.

"One of us had to keep a clear head," said Cliona, coming to Trudy's rescue. "Not that we accomplished very much, sorry Mrs. G,"

She collected mugs from the open shelving beside the stove. "And it had nothing to do with the wine," she added.

"Well, it was a good try," said Mrs.Glenbogie, sitting down at the table. "We've not got a lot to go on and it seemed a good idea at the time." Frances and Cliona carried on with the tea and toast while Trudy sat, awkwardly, beside Eileen.

"Can I be of help?" she asked, finally. "Only, I never know quite what to do. I don't want to be in the way...."

Her voice trailed off, disappointed. The confidence of camaraderie she'd felt back at Frances' croft seemed to have deserted her.

"No, no," said Mrs. Glenbogie, patting her hand. "leave them to it. It's too small a space to have three people moving around and it's hardly a three-course meal they're making.

Now, tell me what you *did* find."

Trudy picked up the canvas satchel into which Frances had tucked the painting in question, plus a couple more for good measure. She pulled them out, along with the thick, leather-bound sketch book that Frances had finally unearthed from the drawer.

Mrs. Glenbogie spotted the one with the Trudy-like figure in it immediately. She took it from Trudy's hands, her eyes shining.

"Well, look at that!" she exclaimed. "If it isn't the image of you, lass."

She turned to Frances who was just setting down a plate, piled high with hot toast running with rivulets of butter.

"Did you not know you had this?"

Frances shook her head.

"It must have been ages ago. And, like I told the girls, I don't always remember what I've been painting." She shrugged. "I can't explain it, really. It's just what happens with some of them. Like the one Cliona saw in Dorothy's shop that time, the one that made her come and find me." She broke off as she and Cliona looked at one another, eyes wide and mouths open as the same thought occurred to them at once.

Frances leaned over and pointed at the figure beside the Trudy-person.

"That's him!' she exclaimed. "I can't believe I didn't twig on last night. Look, Cliona."

Cliona nodded in agreement, her mouth full of toast.

"Must've been the wine," she mumbled through the crumbs.

Trudy leaned in closer.

"It's the same fellow from the painting of Skelly and the one with the antlers, in the sky over the wild ocean scene. He's the one with the antlers. Only without the antlers."

"But who is he, though?" asked Cliona, with a sigh of exasperation. She took the painting from Mrs.Glenbogie's hand and walked to the kitchen window for better light. Trudy followed.

"It looks like she's holding something out to the dishy fellow," said Cliona, squinting. "Honestly, Fran, why don't you paint on those giant canvases anymore? I almost need a magnifying glass."

"What you need is glasses," said Trudy, elbowing Cliona with a smile. "I've seen that look on children's faces that are sitting too far back in the classroom. They always end up with glasses."

"Don't tell her that," joked Frances as a round of toast popped. "Her precious vanity won't allow for glasses."

"Never you mind," retorted Cliona, huffily, handing the painting to Trudy and sitting down at the table with a dramatic sigh. "Besides, I would absolutely love to wear a pair of glasses, as long as the frames were suitably eccentric. Maybe I'd have a pair like Harpy McShane's and put them on a string."

"Sure, only yours would as least be functional and not just decorative," said Frances, sneaking a crust of toast under the table to Angus where he was waiting patiently. "Trudy, come and get some toast before it goes soggy. Cliona has put far too much butter on it. Trudy?"

Trudy remained standing at the window, the thick water-colour paper trembling slightly in her shaking hand. She looked again at the open hand of her look-alike in the painting, not daring to believe what she was seeing. Cupped in the long, delicate fingers was a small, mottled blue-green piece of sea glass, barely visible. Trudy swallowed hard.

"Trudy? You alright over there?"

"What? Oh, yes. Sorry, I was just trying to see what might be in the painting but maybe I need glasses too, because I can't see anything. Is the tea ready?"

Trudy clumsily tucked the painting underneath the pile on the corner of the table and set about busying herself with the milk and sugar, trying desperately to quell the feeling of rising panic. The chatter of the table continued around her as she sorted through what it might mean. Could the man in the painting have something to do with the talking fox? And how was it that the glass in the painting looked exactly like the sea glass she took from the beach all those years ago? She felt a twinge of pain behind her eyes and an involuntary swimming sensation that usually prefaced a slip into her imagination. She dug her nails into the palms of her hands, forcing herself into the room.

She looked back towards the pile of paintings, her vision blurring slightly. What was it she'd been looking at? She felt her attention wavering and the shimmering feeling in her brain returned. Maybe she should speak to Skelly about it all of this. Maybe now that they'd found the painting, he'd help them. *No, you need to stay grounded,* she reminded herself. *Let the girls help you solve this properly. Stop trying to hide.*

The soft warmth of Mrs.Glenbogie's hand on her own brought her back from her racing thoughts. She turned to look into the kindly eyes of the old woman.

"Is everything alright, lamb?" asked Eileen, her brow furrowing in concern. "Only you seem to be getting yourself all het up over there."

Trudy shot a guilty glance in the direction of Cliona and Frances who had their heads bowed over the sketchbook, before bringing her gaze back to Mrs. Glenbogie. She swallowed again and pasted a bright smile on her face.

"No, I'm fine, really. I'm just feeling a bit wobbly, that's all. I suppose maybe I had more of that lovely wine than I thought," she gave a little laugh, immediately recognizing how false it sounded. She looked at Eileen who stared back for a moment, an unreadable expression flitting over her face before she smiled kindly and patted Trudy's hand.

"Aye, well. Don't you let that pair of tearaways be a bad influence on you. Here, have another slice of toast. It'll soak up any of the extra alcohol."

Trudy smiled her thanks and obediently set to nibbling on a corner of toast, willing herself to remain calm and unflustered.

Mrs. Glenbogie leaned across the table and pulled the painting out from the stack where Trudy had tried to hide it. She gave Trudy a considered stare.

"We'll have another look at this painting once you've all filled your bellies. I get the feeling that mebbe you know more than you're letting on, even if you don't realize it."

Chapter 19

Mrs. Glenbogie pursed her lips, frowning thoughtfully. The plates had been cleared away and a fresh pot of tea stood on the trivet. She looked at Trudy.

"On your various travels," she said, ignoring the crimson flush that rose to Trudy's cheeks, "have you ever seen a fellow that resembles this?". She pointed at the watercolour. "Plus or minus a version with antlers, I don't doubt."

Trudy smiled nervously and shook her head.

"No, I'm fairly sure I'd remember meeting someone quite that..."

"Dishy?" offered Cliona with a grin.

Trudy blushed.

"I was going to say 'striking'."

"Either way, he's rather unforgettable-looking. I can't imagine why we didn't clue into it last night," said Frances, pouring a fresh mug of tea for Mrs. Glenbogie. "And honestly, we weren't that tipsy, I can assure you."

Cliona nodded in agreement. "It's true, Mrs. G. We weren't quite so sozzled that we wouldn't remember the other painting, the one of Skelly and him. I mean, really, it was the one that started it all, it's how I knew that Frances was here."

She reached out and gave Frances' hand a quick squeeze. Frances returned the gesture with a small smile.

Mrs. Glenbogie took a sip of her tea, sighing in delight.

"You do make a lovely cuppa, pet," she said to Frances who beamed. "Now don't trouble yourselves wondering why you didn't recognize him. I daresay he did that on purpose. You can't be blamed. He's a shifty bugger. Well, they all are, but him more than the rest."

Cliona frowned.

"You mean you know who he is?" she asked. "Why didn't you tell us?"

Mrs. Glenbogie grimaced.

"For the same reason you didn't recognize him in the second painting, *or* remember the first one, and why Trudy is so befuddled as well: *I* didn't remember. I don't always remember, myself. And it's naught to do with my aged brain, either, you cheeky minx," she gave a glare of mock severity to Cliona who suppressed a grin.

Trudy felt her brain revving into high speed and it wasn't a pleasant feeling. The muddled nature of all of this was becoming far too difficult; she found it increasingly hard to hold onto the unknowns.

"Please, Mrs.Glenbogie," she said, her voice quiet and strained. "Can you explain what you mean?"

Eileen looked at Trudy's pale, face and saw the struggle etched in her features. *Poor wee lamb*, she thought. *It's all too much for her.* She patted Trudy on the hand again.

"Aye, that I will. Sorry for all of the mystery, lass. I know it's hard for you to take in."

Trudy nodded, her eyes downcast. She busied herself staring at the painting in question: her look-alike and the powerful, antlered man. She still found it unsettling to see the suggestion of her own face on a creature far more beguiling and ethereal.

It was her as a faery, Frances had said, and Trudy found herself enjoying the idea immensely. She let the thought of it calm her. She felt the familiar, welcoming warmth and tingle wash over her, as Mrs.Glenbogie's voice faded into the background. *I'll only go for a moment,* she thought, dreamily. But then she was jolted back to the present by the pressure of Angus' paws against her thigh and his head nudging under her hand.

Good boy, Angus, she thought, reluctantly letting the tingling warmth recede as she smoothed his wiry head. *How right you are. I'm meant to be here, in this kitchen.* She looked around at the other three women, sipping tea as they frowned down at the painting. *For now, at least.*

"He goes by the name of Cernach," Eileen was saying. "And at the beginning of it all, and all of the time since, he's a forest god. One of the very oldest."

"Well that explains the dashing good looks," muttered Cliona, shaking her head. "Bloody hell."

Eileen gave her a disapproving look but carried on.

"More importantly, it was him who fell in love with the merrin-girl and charmed her out of the sea. Which, as you know, was the beginning of this whole mess for Glencarragh, with the storms and whatnot."

"Wait a minute," said Frances, leaning over to look at the painting. She pointed a finger at the image of Cernach.

"Are you meaning to tell me that this…person…is the one who married Skelly's daughter?"

Eileen sighed. "After a fashion, aye."

"And made Lira curse them all and cast them out of the sea? Including Skelly?"

Eileen nodded.

"But if he was a god, then couldn't he have done something to stop all that?" asked Trudy, "I mean, aren't they supposed to be all-powerful? Especially if he's so ancient."

"There was nothing to stop, really," explained Frances. "From what I know, the union between him and the merrin-girl didn't work out. At the end of the year and a day, she chose to go back to the sea. So, he would have lost her anyway. It wasn't until she actually tried to return to the sea that Lira went batty. And I'm sure he felt no obligation to Skelly or the rest of the merrin. And who knows, maybe he blamed them for his bride wanting to go back to the sea."

"Also bear in mind," added Cliona. "We've only ever had Skelly's side of the story in all of this. So take that as you will."

"There's a thought among certain factions," said Mrs. Glenbogie with a stern look towards Cliona, "that Cernach struck a deal with Lira at the time of the cursing. But what that could be, I can't imagine. He lost plenty when he lost the love of his life and it stands to reason he'd be bitter and angry. 'Tis only speculation anyway. And besides, forest god or no, lack of obligation or no, he was bound to comply with more universal laws, of the faery variety, that is."

Cliona grunted but said nothing.

"So why can't any of us remember seeing him?" asked Frances, wanting to steer the conversation away from Skelly and any associated conspiracy theories.

Mrs.Glenbogie shrugged.

"That's how he likes it, I suppose. It's part-glamour, part-sorcery. If you were to meet him, you'd not remember it, not if he didn't want you to. Or you might remember, but not in the exact way. He's a shape-shifter so you never can be sure who, or, what, you're seeing. I suppose it makes it easier for him to come and go as he pleases. I'd say that the only thing that's consistent about him, is that he's a right scheming bastard."

"Tsk, tsk," said Cliona, reaching for the sugar bowl, "Language, Mrs.G. Language."

Mrs.Glenbogie reached over to swat at Cliona who pulled back quickly, laughing.

Trudy stared at the painting, trying to force it into telling her something. There had to be more of a clue in it. She thought back to a few moments ago, right before she'd started to drift, when she thought she'd seen something. What was it she'd seen? As the banter continued around the table, Trudy narrowed her focus.

The sounds of conversation faded slightly into the background as she examined each figure closely. Soon, the song of the ocean sang in her ears and she could smell the salt in the breeze that was lifting the ends of her hair. The two figures stood before her, apparently engaged in conversation. Her look-alike held up a piece of sea glass, mottled through with blue and green. Trudy slipped her hand into her pocket, feeling for her own stone. She somehow knew that it was the same one. The man leaned in closer, examining the contents of faery-Trudy's hand. He reached out to take it, but faery-Trudy closed her fingers over it and pulled it back. He bowed his head.

"Trudy?"

The concern in Frances voice jolted her out of her vision.

Is that what it was, she wondered, absently, *a vision?*

She gave herself a mental shake and pulled her stone out of her pocket, placing it on the table. She glanced around at the mild concern, noticing, with a twinge of unfamiliar irritation, the added suggestion of pity. She'd learned to recognize that look a long time ago. She took a deep, steadying breath.

"If you look very closely, you can see she has a piece of sea glass in her hand," said Trudy, pushing the painting to the middle of the table. "I think, although I don't know how, that it's the same as my stone."

"What? The worry stone you carry about with you?" asked Cliona, incredulous. She darted a quick glance at Frances whose eyes were wide. She squinted at the painting. "Are you sure? How can you have seen something that small? I mean, I *suppose* it could be a piece of glass in her hand. But it could just as easily be a smudge of paint."

Mrs.Glenbogie reached out for Trudy's stone.

"May I?" she asked.

Trudy nodded.

Eileen picked up the stone, turning it over in her knobbled fingers. She closed her eyes and took a deep, breath.

"Aye," she said, exhaling sharply. "It could very well be a bit of glass, alright."

Cliona raised a quizzical eyebrow but refrained from saying anything, despite a rising tide of excitement

"How then did it come to be a stone?" asked Frances, carefully avoiding Cliona's gaze. The waves of impatience were rolling off her. "Trudy has told us the story a few times. She found it on the beach when she was visiting Glencarragh as a child. She met a talking fox, didn't you?" Frances turned to Trudy and smiled.

Trudy blushed.

Mrs.Glenbogie let out a small groan.

"A talking fox, lass?"

"Well, yes. I mean, I thought so at the time, I was quite young, you see. But then I realized it was just one of my daydreams," she faltered. "Then again, since they're not daydreams then…"

She put a hand to her head, closing her eyes tightly.

"I'm sorry, I don't know what to say now. I'm feeling very muddled."

Trudy's heart pounded in her ears. She wasn't good at telling lies. Even half-truths were beyond her ability most of the time. But she didn't want her friends to know what she'd done, what Skelly had told her she'd done, the promise she'd unwittingly made and what were the possible consequences. Talking about her stone came worryingly close to all of that.

Frances came around the table and put an arm around her friend, rubbing her shoulder soothingly.

"Don't fret, Trudy. This is confusing for all of us. I think," she looked at Eileen who nodded. "I think we've all been tricked very badly here."

Trudy looked up, eyes wide.

"Do you think I tricked you?" she said, tears threatening. "Because I would never want to do that on purpose. I would never want anyone to feel I wasn't being truthful. It's just there are things that are too awful to mention and…"

Trudy burst into wracking sobs.

Frances and Eileen exchanged worried glances and simultaneously silenced Cliona with meaningful glares. Frances set about comforting Trudy while Mrs.Glenbogie pushed away from the table and disappeared into her back room. She emerged a few minutes later, carrying something wrapped in cloth. Sitting back down at the table, she began to unwrap the little bundle, revealing a small wooden bowl.

"Is that one of Iain's?" asked Cliona, reaching out to touch the knobbly-smooth surface of the bowl. Not wanting to let an opportunity pass by, Iain had started collecting large pieces of driftwood from the beaches and turning them on his father's lathe into platters and bowls, which were then dutifully sent to Dorothy for sale to eager tourists. But this wood wasn't the usual grey-brown of the Glencarragh driftwood.

Mrs. Glenbogie nodded.

"Aye, it is. I took myself out and found a particular type of wood, from a particular place and had him make it into a wee bowl for me."

Cliona opened her mouth but didn't ask the question that was burning on her lips. There were things about Mrs.Glenbogie that weren't mentioned out loud. They were quietly accepted and appreciated, but not often discussed.

"Aye, and I can smell the smoke of the wheels turning in your minds," said Eileen, without looking at the girls. She pulled a small bottle of water from the pocket of her cardigan and poured it into the bowl. Trudy's sobs had subsided to quiet, shuddering sniffles. "But we haven't time to get into the details of my wicked ways. What matters is we get to the bottom of the mystery at hand. Now, this wee bowl is going to help us with that. May I place your stone into it, lass?"

Trudy nodded, tear-stained face suddenly curious.

"I imagine some of you'll be fit to burst with questions at this point, but suffice it to say, this isn't an ordinary bowl and what's in it, isn't water out of the tap, aye?"

Cliona squirmed in her seat but remained silent. Frances smiled at her, knowing the level of torture she must be experiencing. First their theory about the glamoured stone being proven and now this. Trudy blew her nose on Frances' offered hanky and pushed her hair back behind her ears. The three sat in enraptured silence as Mrs. Glenbogie stared into the small, wooden bowl.

Finally, she spoke.

"Just what I thought," she said. "And plenty I hadn't. As you might have guessed," she looked steadily at Frances and Cliona who flicked their eyes away. "This isn't an ordinary pebble from the beach. It's just like what Trudy saw in the painting. It's a piece of sea glass."

Frances peered into the bowl, but only saw the mottled grey of Trudy's stone.

"But why does it look like that?" she pointed her finger towards the bowl, then sat back, understanding dawning on her face. "I mean, it's a glamour of course but who would want to put a glamour on a piece of sea glass?"

Cliona rolled her eyes.

"Oh boy, I simply can't imagine," she said, sarcasm dripping from her words.

Mrs. Glenbogie shook her head.

"No, it wasn't Himself as did that."

"How can you possibly know that, Mrs.G? Surely you wouldn't take his word for it?"

"I don't need to, pet. It doesn't have the mark of him on it. At least, not in the way of the glamour."

Cliona let out a sigh of frustration.

"Okay, for those of us who aren't the magical brain-trust, can you kindly explain?"

Mrs.Glenbogie gave her a withering glance but nodded.

"What I think I'm seeing here, as I said, is a piece of sea glass. Not only that, it's far more powerful than the usual variety of selkie-glass. On par, if you like, with the piece that your gran and I stumbled across all those years ago."

She paused for dramatic effect and was pleased to see the looking of dawning recognition on both Frances and Cliona's faces. Trudy, as she would expect, was still a vision of misery. And who could blame the poor mite?

Eileen fished into the bowl and pulled out the stone, for that was what it still resembled and held it, dripping, between her thumb and forefinger.

"This glass, I believe, belongs to none other than Fia, Skelly's daughter."

Cliona sucked air in through her teeth, whistling.

"Well!" she said. "We hadn't expected that!"

"What do you mean, you hadn't expected it?" asked Eileen with a frown.

Frances and Cliona exchanged a guilty look.

"Well," said Frances, "Cliona and I had developed a bit of a theory, pure speculation you understand, but we didn't want to bring it up because we hadn't any proof…"

"You should've said," said Trudy, accusingly. "It would've made looking for clues in the paintings a lot easier, don't you think?"

"I don't think we thought of that," said Cliona, with a sheepish grin. "Did we, Fran? And, to be honest, I'd forgotten all about it until just now."

Frances sighed.

"So had I. Your antlered friend again, I presume?"

Mrs. Glenbogie gave a wry smile.

"Likely, lass. His magic is a bit more far-reaching it seems. Anyroad, back to what we do know, in case we end up not knowing it before long."

"Right," said Frances, "So, the glass belongs to Skelly's daughter…maybe I should write this down…"

"And Skelly, as we know," prompted Eileen.

"Was Lira's consort," finished Cliona, shaking her head. "No wonder someone wanted this glamoured. Anyone who knew what it was could do a fair bit of mischief."

"But how?" asked Trudy, finding her voice at last.

"Because," explained Frances, "anyone with the know-how, can, theoretically, call the creature attached to the glass to them." She paused, turning it over in her mind, carefully following the trail of logic, trying to commit it to her memory. Her face cleared, her eyes brightening. She looked to Mrs.Glenbogie for confirmation. The gentle nod gave her everything she needed to know. "And if you can call the creature to you…"

"You can bind the bastard," finished Cliona, her face shining. "Just like we said, Fran. We've got her, don't you see?"

"But how?" said Frances turning to Eileen. "Didn't the daughter perish in the…well, the exile. Didn't she sacrifice herself so that the rest of them could carry on as selkies rather than be obliterated?"

Mrs. Glenbogie nodded.

"So the story goes. Which is supposedly what sent that nasty piece, Lira, completely off her rocker. Her own daughter turned against her at the last. And I wonder sometimes if she didn't have a bit of help in that."

"Noooo," wailed Cliona. "I'd forgotten about that. Damn it! So it's pointless then, isn't it?" She groaned, resting her elbows on the table, gripping handfuls of her hair. "How much do I despise these creatures, let me count the ways. This is just another way to rub our noses in it. Dangle the carrot and then yank it away."

Trudy sat quietly. She knew the answer. Or, at least, she thought she did. It could mean the world to all of them if she was right. It would mean the world to her. It was an answer to all of their worries. But who was she to put something like that forth? What did she know? Angus whined softly, nudging under her elbow. She smiled an inward smile. Maybe this was the choice she was meant to make.

"I think I know the answer," she said, and so told them.

Chapter 20

The rain ran in steady, beading rivulets down the glass, blurring the view out over the rooftops. The quiet, steady patter made a pleasant change from the aggressive lashing attack that had woken Trudy from a restless sleep. She stood, half-seeing, mug in hand, letting her thoughts drift over the events of the previous days.

When she'd suggested that using her stone - Fia's stone, she reminded herself - to bind Lira, pointing out the connecting bond of motherhood, her friends had been dubious at first. Cliona, by her very nature, automatically doubted anything to do with their nemesis. Not all mother-child bonds were strong, Frances had gently reminded her, as if she, Trudy, needed reminding of *that*, and Mrs. Glenbogie had just sat, staring into the fire, an unreadable expression on her face. After working through those initial doubts, however, an animated discussion had ensued as they'd turned over the possibilities, eventually coming to the conclusion that it was definitely worth a try and what did they have to lose? All of that had been decided, however, without further input from Trudy.

She gave a small sigh and sipped her coffee. She actually preferred coffee first thing, but everyone assumed she was exclusively a tea-drinker and she didn't like to risk upsetting people by correcting them. The apologetic bluster of people realizing their wrong assumptions made her deeply uncomfortable. And it's not as if she didn't enjoy tea. Just not first thing.

She let her gaze wander to the cluster of plants that lived on the wide windowsill, letting her fingers trail over them, checking the soil, wiping dust from broad, waxy leaves. Wherever she'd lived, she'd always made space for having houseplants. She would have rather had an outdoor garden but living in a series of flats hadn't allowed for that, so she made do and found taking care of their often finicky needs to be immensely rewarding. Sometimes, people brought her their desperate cases, plants on the brink of expiring and she'd nursed them back to health. There'd been more than a few supermarket rescues too, the marked-down-for-quick-sale specimens for which charging any money at all was a crime itself. But she had a soft spot for those neglected, unwanted creatures and couldn't walk past a rack of anything wilted or yellowing without placing it tenderly into her basket.

Her fingers rested on the crinkling leaves of a fern - needs misting, she thought, absently. Aunt Calla had taught her how to care for all kinds of plants, showing her how they could talk to her through her fingers, telling her what they might need or what they didn't want.

"I always wanted a cat," she said, aloud, ostensibly to the fern. "Mother said I wouldn't be responsible enough to care for one, you know. She said I was too flighty, that I would forget to feed it when I was in one of my moods, as she liked to call them."

Trudy looked at the collection of thriving greenery on the

windowsill, then out at the grey morning and found herself coming to a decision.

"The only thing more ridiculous than her saying that, was me believing it. And speaking of believing…."

She crossed over to the telephone that sat on the small table that stood on the wall opposite the balding, corduroy sofa that Feargus had found for her at an estate sale. It was a dreary olive green, but Cliona had made her some brightly coloured cushions which had livened it up considerably. Cliona, she reflected with a wry smile, had livened everything up considerably. Her impatience and quick-temper, the mercurial moods that blew in and blew over as quickly as a Glencarragh storm had unsettled Trudy immensely at first, and, if she were honest, they still did. But she'd learned from Cliona that people could be annoyed with you and still love you. That the two states weren't mutually exclusive.

Her fingers drummed on the table for a brief moment. Cliona wouldn't hesitate, she thought, imagining her red-haired friend standing over her, arms folded as she told Trudy how silly she was being while at the same time having dropped everything to offer her moral support in whatever was the nerve-wracking task of the moment. She smiled, picked up the receiver and dialed.

"Trudy!" shrilled the voice down the line. "Is everything alright? I haven't forgotten a birthday or something, have I?"

"No, mum," said Trudy with a tiny, suppressed sigh. "Everything's fine, I just wanted to ask you something."

There was the briefest of pauses before her mother responded.

"Yes, dear, what is it? Do be a pet and get to the point quickly, will you? I'm expecting a delivery any minute and I'll have to sign for it. Daddy's off to the club as usual. It's his morning, as you know."

"Yes, yes, of course," stuttered Trudy, her well-collected thoughts suddenly in disarray as she faced possibly annoying her mother. She took a steadying breath.

"I wanted to ask you about when we spent the summers here, on Glencarragh,"

"Oh, that. Honestly, that was all your father. They were his relatives, after all. I thought it the most odious little place. And that sister of his…. hateful woman, as I'm sure you remember, dear."

"Yes, yes, Aunty Ivy. She really was quite horrid, wasn't she? Only, I was wanting to ask about Aunt Calla."

She held her breath and closed her eyes.

"Who's that, darling, did you say? The connection must be terrible. I suspect they haven't updated their phone lines since they were first put in."

"Aunt Calla," repeated Trudy, "Who you used to send me to stay with so I wouldn't upset Aunt Ivy."

There was a significant pause this time.

"Mum? Are you still there?"

"Yes, yes, sorry darling. I was just thinking of something else entirely. Now, how are you doing, really, petal? Your father and I worry, you being all alone up there on that wretched island. Surely you would be happier coming back down to civilization?"

Trudy fought down a rising irritation. This was so typical of her mother, ignoring the things that she didn't want to cope with.

"Please, mum. Tell me about Aunt Calla."

"Trudy, darling. I do wish you'd get your head out of the

clouds. There is no such person as this Aunt Calla, at least not beyond your wild imagination. Was she one of your pretend friends, then?"

"What?"

"Yes, dear. I decided it was the best option to send you off to play every day - to get you out from under Aunt Ivy's feet, you see. It was best for everyone. I packed you a little lunch and sent you out right after breakfast and you would come in just as it was getting dark and have the lovely supper I'd set aside and warmed up for you. You were quite happy with the arrangement, I assure you. You came home with such stories and, given the circumstances, I let you get on with it. It really was quite safe, you see, the island had absolutely no criminal element, which is about all it had to recommend it. Let me tell you, it was quite a relief to me when that awful woman finally moved herself to the mainland...."

Trudy was only half-listening after that. Her tongue cleaved to the top of her mouth and her scalp prickled. The knot of snakes who lived in her belly and who had been settled for so long, suddenly took up their squirming and writhing, leaving her feel faintly sick.

"...there's the door. I really must go. Don't forget what I said, and do consider coming back from that awful place, will you? Kisses!"

Placing the receiver gently onto the cradle, Trudy let herself slide slowly down the wall until she was sitting on the floor beside the table.

I'll let myself cry for five minutes, she told herself, as the tears slid down her cheeks. *Five minutes should be long enough to grieve for someone that never existed.*

* * *

Trudy sat on the floor for quite some time. The shock of learning the truth about Aunt Calla had become a vague echo in the back of her mind, replaced by a sort of numbness that left her thoughts drifting aimlessly and a pervading chill that emanated from her chest. The faint queasiness remained.

Idly, she wondered if she ought to phone someone - Frances would be the better choice, she'd be less likely to try and find a bright side and she knew what it was like to love someone that nobody else thought was real. Trudy choked back a sob and dug her nails into her palms. She was not going to cry anymore. Pulling herself together, she got to her feet and smoothed down her hair and her skirt. Slowly and methodically, she retrieved her coffee cup from where she'd left it on the windowsill, pausing to run her fingers over the bamboo that Iain had brought her after visiting his sister on the mainland. It was supposed to be lucky, he'd told her, lucky that he'd found it because his sister, bless her heart, had three healthy children but no skill with plants and the poor thing had dried out completely. He'd convinced his sister to let him have it so *she'd* be lucky to not have its demise on her conscience because he knew just the person to revive it. Sure enough, a few days of water and quiet murmured encouragement and it was again thriving. It's all any creature needs, Trudy had told Iain when she showed him the glossy new leaves on the bamboo, a bit of care and encouragement.

"Aunt Calla taught me that," Trudy whispered to the bamboo. "'A bit of care and encouragement brings out the natural strength of a thing', she would say, 'Everything has the power to heal itself, given the right circumstance.'"

She poured the dregs of her coffee into the sink and washed and dried the mug, letting the familiar action soothe her ragged nerves. Somewhere between putting the mug back in the cupboard and draping the tea towel over the oven handle she came to a decision. She wanted answers and she knew just where she was going to get them.

** * **

The further she walked from the village, the lighter the rain became. What had started out as a stuttering downpour had now faded into a gentle mizzle. The clouds hung dark and low over the moorland and a ribbon of fog snaked across the horizon. The comforting smell of damp earth combined with the occasional breath of salt from the sea filled Trudy's lungs and with each breath she felt the tension leaving her body. Her chest expanded with every breath of Glencarragh that she breathed in and with every exhale, she let go of the niggling worries that crowded her mind.

"Whatever else happens," she said, aloud to the sullen sky, "I'm not leaving here. I won't. I'm going to sort this out." The only answer was a sudden gust that blew a fresh spray of rain into her face. She grinned and threw back her head, sticking out her tongue. She spotted a bird overhead, riding the thermals, hardly needing to flap its wings as the wind carried it along.

"Are you trying to catch flies?" said a familiar voice, startling her out of her rapt observation. "Only standing there with your mouth hanging open isn't the most alluring of comportments."

"You!" breathed Trudy, her eyes wide as the fox approached, his brush held at a jaunty angle. He sat down, several feet away and regarded her with curiosity.

"Yes, it is I," he replied, his black eyes twinkling as he slightly inclined his head. "Well met, Bright One." He paused, frowning slightly before adding, "Yes, I'm very much here and very much real. As are you. As are many things that many people would conveniently and, dare I say, comfortably, deny. There's an alarming lack of effort these days, don't you find?"

"But, how?"

"Now, now. Let's try and get that mouth closed, shall we? You're gawping like a landed salmon…and," he tilted his head and showed an alarming set of sharp, white teeth, "…I'm ever so fond of salmon. It would be terrible if I got confused and tried to eat you, don't you think?"

Trudy felt a wave of unease pass through her before she noticed the merry glint in the fox's eye.

"Come on, come on!" he said, leaping to his feet and bounding off across the heather. He looked back over his shoulder. "Allow me to be your escort. I have a fairly good idea where you might be going."

"Why on earth should I trust you?" said Trudy, wanting to follow him as she really hadn't an exact idea where she was going, only that she knew she would get there eventually. "You and I don't really have a history based on honesty now, do we?"

The fox smiled again, toothily before bowing his head. The air around him shimmered and then he was gone. Trudy blinked and spun around, certain that he would pop up some-where else but he seemed to have disappeared. Shrugging, she set off again, unsure if she was relieved or disappointed that the fox had gone. Just then she saw a figure approaching; it was a tall, elegantly dressed man with black hair and skin the colour of fallen leaves. He wore a frock coat and a froth of lace at his collar, looking every bit the character from a period drama. He had deep-set eyes and a wide, laughing mouth, his hair combed back from a high, widow's peak. Trudy felt her skin flush and her mouth go slightly dry as her eyes slid, involuntarily away from his face.

"I thought perhaps we could try again," murmured the man, as he offered his arm. "Perhaps this is more to your liking?" He waved a hand down at himself, tilting his head in a familiar gesture. Trudy nodded, but said nothing as she placed her hand in the crook of his elbow. "Appearance is everything and nothing, don't you find?" asked the forest god, twirling a silver-topped cane that she hadn't noticed until that moment. "My esteemed colleague says I'm too much a dandy, but I rather like this style of dress. It suits my roguish manner, wouldn't you say?"

"It certainly says something," replied Trudy, finding her voice. She kept her gaze out towards the horizon, willing the little cottage to come into view.

"Indeed," said Cernach, regarding her with an amused smile. "I think you'll find it easier to get where you're going if you focus less on the target itself."

Trudy suppressed a snort, covering her mouth with her free hand as she recognized a touch of Cliona in her reaction. Smiling inwardly, she replied, "Do you mean I ought to focus on the journey, then, and not the destination?"

Cernach frowned.

"Have I said something to amuse you?"

Trudy shook her head, clamping her lips together tightly.

"Not really," she said. "Only it sounded a bit like one of those tiresome things that people like to say when life gets difficult and all you really want is them to understand that you're struggling."

"Ah, I see."

Trudy doubted that he did but was glad for the distraction. They were walking far more slowly than she would have preferred. A leisurely stroll across the moor was likely to allow her the opportunity to change her mind over the whole thing.

"Can I get there on my own?" she asked, finding the silence awkward. She was painfully aware of his presence beside her. He was handsome enough to be thoroughly disconcerting and the fact of what he was only made it worse. How was one meant to behave in the company of a forest god, anyway? A powerful one at that, if Mrs. Glenbogie had her facts right.

"You can indeed, child," he said, with laughter in his voice. "But surely you know that by now?"

Trudy shook her head.

"I can't say I know much of anything for certain at this point. Apparently, my entire childhood was one long fever dream."

Cernach threw back his head and laughed. Trudy tried not to flinch at the sound.

"Is that what you think, Bright One?" he said, turning to look at her. Trudy looked down at the heather. She shrugged.

"It's becoming apparent, yes," she said.

"And yet, here you are," he said, casting his arm wide and gesturing at the expanse of undulating moor with his silver-topped cane. She noticed then that the carving at the top was the head of a fox. "Surely that means you don't truly believe everything you've been told?"

"I suppose not." She pulled her gaze from the heather and forced herself to look into his face. His eyes met hers and for a moment there was a sadness in them, which was quickly replaced with the twinkling merriment. She had the sudden thought that he was probably very exhausting to be around for any length of time. Looking at him became increasingly uncomfortable so she let her eyes go back to the horizon. They were approaching a small rise and she willed the cottage to be on the other side of it.

"I suppose I want to prove to myself what I do believe," she said.

"And that is?"

"That something that felt so very real - that *feels* so very real - simply has to be so. That maybe people just say things to make themselves feel better and that maybe it's time I…"

She faltered, unsure of what exactly she thought it was time for. Except, she admitted with some reluctance, it was something she'd been coming to know for quite a while.

Cernach waited.

Trudy cleared her throat.

"I think that perhaps it's time I took control of my situation," she said, smiling widely as they crested the rise and the little cottage came into view. She stopped walking and took her hand from Cernach's elbow. Taking a deep breath, she turned to face him and bobbed a small curtsey, bowing her head.

"Thank you for your escort, my lord," she said, glancing over at the cottage. A curl of smoke spiraled from the chimney. "I can manage on my own from here."

Without anything further, Trudy set off down the hill.

"Yes, Bright One," said the forest god. "I do believe you can."

Chapter 21

For all of her bravado in front of Cernach, Trudy felt her courage wavering, the closer she got to the little croft on the hill. At one point she paused in her advance, stopping to take in the strange perfectness of the scene ahead. The weather-beaten grey stone was much the same as many of the buildings on Glencarragh and the familiarity of it was both comfort and confusion. Surely a cottage of faery build would be made of something more…what, sparkling? Trudy laughed at herself; child-Trudy had never questioned such things, why start now? A raven cronked overhead and she looked up, shielding her eyes from the bright sun.

"I'm going, I'm going," she muttered towards the circling figure. "Don't you have some other mischief to attend to?"

"I see that talking aloud to oneself is a common affliction," said a voice from somewhere in the region of her knees. "I had always thought it peculiar to my mistress."

Trudy gave a little gasp of delight and stepped back, eyes shining. She clasped her hands in front of her mouth and took a steadying breath.

"Hello. It's Moss, isn't it?" she asked, in a soft voice. He was much improved in appearance since the last time she'd seen him, but his large eyes still shifted warily as she looked at her.

"I've heard so much about you."

The little brownie stiffened slightly, pulling himself up to his full, two feet or so of height.

"Idle gossip, I shouldn't wonder," he said, primly, smoothing his hands down his neatly mended and pressed tunic. He had a large bag slung across himself which bulged with greenery of some kind. "I assume you are planning to visit the sheep farmer?"

He spoke the last two words as if he'd just smelled something fairly unpleasant.

"The sheep…farmer?" repeated Trudy, blinking.

Moss ignored her and started walking in the direction of the cottage.

"I would have rather had some notice," he was saying over his shoulder. "As much as my usual standard isn't appreciated around here, I do like to preserve some modicum of decency and a kettle already on the hob would be the very least…"

Trudy stared, open-mouthed at the retreating figure. The last time she'd seen him - well, she'd hardly really seen him at all - he'd been scurrying about in the shadows like a wounded animal. Surely the effects of all that had befallen him in Deep Faery wouldn't have mended themselves so soon? Trudy thought of Frances, and the look of pain and regret on her face when Trudy had told them she thought she'd seen Moss in Skelly's cottage. Imagine if Moss were fully restored? The idea of it filled her with renewed determination and she set off after him, hurrying to try and catch up.

"You may as well come in," called Moss from the dark interior as she approached the door. "He's not here but he will be. Just as soon as he knows you are."

Trudy peered through the door, letting her eyes adjust to

the change of light. The windows of the croft were small but had been cleaned to a gleaming brightness, letting in as much of the day's sunshine as was possible. Still, though, it was quite dim, and several oil lamps gleamed, casting a soft glow around the simple, spare interior.

"Ought I not wait to be formally invited in?" she asked, remembering the last time she'd been there.

"Only if you fancy standing out there 'til he gets back," came the reply.

"Can't you…"

"No, I bloody well can't."

Trudy gaped, unsure of what to do next.

"For Pan's sake, stop standing there gawping like a fish and just come in," said Moss, appearing in the doorway, brandishing a large wooden spoon. "That lot are all full of their airs and graces, pretending like they keep to the old customs of courtesy and hearth-welcome when everyone knows they're just plotting the next way they can do each other over."

The little man stood, nostrils flared and large brown eyes glaring. He wore a Liberty print apron over his tunic and Trudy felt her eyes settling on that, rather than face his obvious irritation. Frances had made him that apron.

Moss followed her gaze and his shoulders sagged just a little. He passed a hand across his eyes and sighed.

"Just come in, will you? I've got the kettle on and I'm just mixing up a batch of blackberry biscuits. They're last season's berries but they've kept well." He tilted his head, as if waiting for something.

Trudy's thoughts raced ahead of her. She really didn't want to get off on the wrong foot with Moss.

"Of course," she stammered, "A fine and expert hand in preserving the harvest makes all the difference, doesn't it?"

A smile twitched at the corners of the brownie's mouth and his eyes gleamed. Nodding stiffly, he gestured with his wooden spoon and Trudy stepped through the doorway into the cottage, feeling like she'd just passed an important test.

* * *

A short while later and Trudy was back outside, enjoying the warm sunshine. She and Moss had carried a small table and a couple of chairs through the back door of the cottage and set them up with a view of the sea.

"It's far too lovely to be indoors, don't you think?" she'd asked him, chewing her lip. "And you're making such a delightful spread, it seems like something which ought to be enjoyed as a picnic tea," she added, smiling.

Moss had pondered that briefly and nodded.

"Indeed," he said, rummaging a drawer and producing a blue-checked tablecloth. "I see you have far more of a sense of these things than the sheep farmer. It will be most pleasant to provide for someone with a scrap of taste and refinement for a change. I miss…"

He stopped abruptly and cleared his throat.

"Would you be so kind as to assist me in taking out the furniture?"

"Will he be much longer, do you think?" asked Trudy, nibbling on her third blackberry biscuit. They were the most delicious thing she'd ever eaten. Crunchy on the outside, soft and chewy in the middle and the dried blackberries offered a sweet-tart tingle that delighted her taste buds. The first one had been halfway to her mouth when she remembered something her Aunt Calla had told her about eating faery-offered food. Moss had seen the look of suspicion on her face and his withering glare was enough to keep the biscuit moving. "Only, I feel as if I've been here for hours and I don't want to out-stay my welcome."

Moss smiled, pouring them both another cup of tea.

"As I'm sure you know," he said, passing her the milk jug. "Time moves a little differently here. You've been here exactly as long as you need to be."

Trudy smiled, accepting the fresh tea. She closed her eyes briefly, feeling the gentle, salt-scented breeze wafting over her sun-warmed skin.

"Perhaps," she murmured, opening one eye. "But you didn't answer my question."

Moss clapped his hands together in genuine delight.

"Excellent! You're catching on. Now, when any of them starts on with their flowery nonsense, you'll be quick to pull them up. And, to answer your question, I think you'll find that he's just coming through…"

"Having a tea party, are we?"

Trudy gave Moss a quick look, and he gave a subtle nod as he rose to take his leave. Taking a deep, steadying breath, she placed her teacup down with a slow, deliberate movement before turning to face the voice.

"Hello, Skelly," she said, smiling. "I've been waiting for you."

"How long have you been waiting?" he asked, dusting the crumbs from his second blackberry biscuit from his beard.

Trudy remembered Frances telling her that he had a weakness for cakes and biscuits. She leaned over the table and took the last one from the plate, quietly enjoying the look of surprise on his face.

"As long as I needed to," she replied. A clatter of dishes came from inside the cottage and she pressed her lips together firmly to suppress the threatening smile.

Skelly's eyes shifted to the back door of the cottage and then back to Trudy.

"I see our friend has been giving you some pointers," he said, tilting his head. "Are you feeling like you needed them, then?"

Trudy shrugged, aiming for nonchalance.

"I have some occasional difficulties with social situations," she said. "And it seems there's a whole other set of rules when dealing with persons of a magical nature. Rules of which I have clearly not been sufficiently informed. So, when in Rome, as they say. Moss was simply clarifying some basic courtesies and such."

"Oh, aye. And do you feel able to tell me, then, why it is I'm finding you sitting drinking my tea and eating my biscuits on this fine day?"

Trudy looked him squarely in the face.

"I'm here for some answers."

He quirked a substantial eyebrow.

"And I won't be leaving until I get them."

"Well, then," Skelly sighed and leaned back in his chair. I suppose we'd better have another pot of tea, hadn't we?"

"My Aunt Calla," said Trudy, without further introduction. "I want you to tell me the truth," she held up a hand, "and not some distorted faery version of it, either. The actual truth."

"Did you speak with your mother, then? Like I said."

"I did."

"And?"

"And she said exactly what you knew she'd say - that it was all just a figment of my imagination and that I was sent off to play every day just to get me out from under everyone's feet. My father has one sister and that's Aunt Ivy."

"Then why are you asking me?"

Trudy bit down on her lip and dug her fingernails into her palms. She would not get upset. She would not cry. She swallowed.

"Because I don't believe her. I don't believe that anything that felt so real - as real as you and I are sitting here drinking tea in this apparently non-existent place - could be just something I made up."

"Well then it isn't, is it?" said Skelly waving a dismissive hand. "That's your answer."

"No!" shouted Trudy, banging the flat of her hand onto the table, making the empty biscuit plate jump. Skelly's eyes widened briefly, then narrowed, the emerald green of them glinting. "I want you to say it. I want you to say the words."

"I don't see as it matters," he replied, regarding her with slight wariness. "You ought never to depend on the words of another person over your own true knowledge of a thing. That's a road you don't want to go down. Just ask your one, Frances, about that."

Trudy choked back a clog of frustrated tears.

"It *does* matter," she said through gritted teeth. "Don't you understand? I've let people tell me my whole life - what to do, how to do it, what's the best thing for me. And you know what? I didn't mind. It meant things could be comfortable and peaceful and I didn't upset anyone and everyone could be happy and there were no cross words."

"What about you, though? Were you happy?" Moss leaned in the doorway, drying his hands on a lavender coloured tea towel. He glared at Skelly who scowled back.

Trudy took a deep, shuddering breath.

"Yes," she said. "For the most part, anyway. Enough that it didn't bother me all that much." She let her mind drift back to her houseplants that ought to have been a cat, before shoving that thought away. "It's important to me that things are simple and uncomplicated. It makes life, things…easier for me."

"Then I'll ask you again, lass," said Skelly, his voice soft, "What does it matter what I say? Isn't it the easier thing for you to believe what your mother has told you and get on with it, rather than get yourself all het up and come marching across the moor to find me?"

Trudy closed her eyes and spoke, her voice wobbled only slightly.

"But I don't believe it," she said, her voice firming. "I know what's real. And Aunt Calla was real."

She felt a hand on her arm. A pleasant, warm tingle radiated from the touch, flooding her with a kind of soothing calmness. She opened her eyes to look into Moss' large brown ones.

"Then trust yourself," he said, reaching up with a clean corner of his tea towel to dab at the tears that had trickled out from beneath her closed eyelids. "Trust yourself to know what is true."

* * *

"We know about my stone."

Trudy leaned against the trunk of a large chestnut tree. The fragrant candelabra blooms scented the air with sweet scent and the sun dappled through the wide, flat leaves. That it seemed oddly out of place in the middle of the otherwise treeless moor, blossoming in the wrong season, warranted no more than a passing notice on Trudy's part. There were bigger questions at hand.

"Oh, aye," grunted Skelly as he leaned on his walking stick, just out of the expanse of shade provided by the tree. He squinted up at the sky, which was blue and cloudless.

"We looked at Frances' paintings, like you said, and there was the one with..."she faltered a bit, remembering the young woman who everyone said resembled her, but who was Skelly's daughter, before continuing, "with a figure of a young woman standing with Cernach, or, who we assume is Cernach."

Skelly shifted position, turning his shoulders slightly so that she couldn't see his face.

"Aye, it would be Cernach, alright," he said, "And as you'd probably also guessed, the young lass would be my own wee girl."

He turned to face Trudy, a strange light in his eyes.

"You don't have to beat around the bush with it, it's been a long, long time."

He turned back to look out over the moor.

"And what did your meeting of the minds come up with then, after finding this painting?"

Trudy ignored the sarcasm in his tone.

"We're going to try and bind Lira," she said, "If we bind Lira, then we can..."

"No, you can bloody well not!" swore Skelly, rounding on her. The air shimmered and he stood, towering in his true form. He approached her, fists clenched and the tattoos on his forearms writhing wildly. Trudy resisted the urge to step away. Instead she pushed off from the tree and stood straight, facing him.

"Then why did you even suggest it?" she asked, meeting his brilliant green eyes. "Because you're the one who told us to look, so one must assume that's what you hoped we'd find. Didn't you say that I had to come to this willingly? Wasn't that your way of tricking me into coming up with my own idea? So then of course it would be my own will."

"Pan's hoary beard," he said, the air crackled with ozone and there was a strong smell of ocean swirling around them. "That's not at all what I intended. I should have known, though, with that lot helping. Or is it hindering? I suppose that was the fire-headed one's idea, was it?"

Trudy scowled.

"We came up with the idea together," she said, "It was me who recognized the stone and Mrs.Glenbogie who discovered what it really was and then we all came up with the solution together."

Skelly's eyes narrowed as he searched her face. She refused to look away, even though every cell of her was screaming with discomfort.

"Because it *is* a solution, isn't it?" she pressed him. "It's a way around me having to give myself over to the sea. If we bind Lira, we can force her to do what we ask, to stop the storms."

Skelly's shoulders sank and he passed a hand wearily over his face. He faced her as the sheep farmer, looking every bit a haggard old man.

"It's no solution, lass. It's a death sentence for you all."

"Well then why on earth would you send us on such a wild goose chase, then? Why would you even suggest that there was an alternative to my promise?"

Skelly stood, silent for some minutes, facing out toward the moor. A curlew cried, a barely visible speck in the sky and the coconut scent of gorse traveled on a light, dancing breeze. In the distance, Trudy could see Moss moving around in the little kitchen garden that he'd coaxed from the tangle of grass and heather.

"I just needed to know you're willing to try something," he said, finally. "You must know that I cannae interfere in this, not something between you and her."

"Her? You mean Lira? I never…"

"No, lassie, not Lira."

He turned to look at her again, something unreadable on his face.

"I don't understand, then," she said, "Who?"

Skelly sighed and his mouth quirked into a small smile.

"'Tis your Aunt Calla, so-called, we have to thank for all this," he said. "And she's no' someone any of us wish to cross."

Trudy's thoughts swirled in a wild, uncomprehending scramble. What on earth was he talking about now? She felt the all-too-familiar knot of panic gathering strength in her chest. Forcing herself to take a deep breath, she placed a hand against the trunk of the chestnut tree, letting the rough bark connect her to the quieter place in her mind.

"Lucky for you, lass," continued Skelly, "You've managed to win the favour of some folk who've got a bit of power of their own and between us, I think we've sorted out an answer."

"Oh?" said Trudy, faintly. "And what's that?"

Skelly grinned, his teeth impossibly white in the creased, sun-browned face. He bowed, slightly mocking and offered his arm.

"Walk with me?"

Trudy gave him a withering look.

"Is that a question or a command?" she said, placing her hand in the crook of his elbow. "I can never tell with you lot."

He walked her as far as the crest of the hill. In the time it took them to get from where they'd been standing to, what Trudy came to understand was, the boundary of the In-Between, Skelly had given her another option. They stood, wordless, at the border. Beyond, the sky was gun-metal grey and she could see the haze of rain falling in the distance. She looked back, and saw the little croft still bathed in sunlight and clear skies.

Chuckling, she gestured and said, "Bit of a stereotype, isn't it?"

Skelly grinned.

"Surely, you'd not deprive us of our little affectations?"

Trudy leaned into him for a moment, squeezed his arm and let go, standing sideways so that she could see both vistas. Back towards the cottage, the small figure of Moss still moved around the garden.

"Will he not come back?" she asked, without looking at Skelly.

"That's for him to say, not me," he replied, his chin resting on his hands as he leaned onto his stick. "He's come 'round, you can see that, but there's a shadow in him that wasn't there before he was taken."

"Oh," said Trudy, faintly uneasy at what sort of shadow might follow a person from the depths of Faery. "I suppose I wouldn't know as I've only just met him. Only he seems quite well."

"Aye, well and there's the matter of yon painter having been responsible for it all. He won't say but I think he's…"

Trudy rounded on him, eyes flashing.

"That's not fair! You can't blame Frances for the horrid and evil things *your* people did to him."

Skelly flinched and looked away.

"They're not *my* people," he muttered.

"Oh, for heaven's sake, stop splitting hairs," she said, waving a hand impatiently. "Do you know, I'm so fed up with the posturing and scheming. I'm beginning to doubt very much that any of you care about anything other than your own petty grievances. And I, for one, am deeply resentful at having been dragged into the middle of them."

Skelly stared, eyes wide. He straightened up, tucking his stick across himself into the crook of his elbow.

Trudy glanced one more time towards the croft, a faint look of regret crossing her features, before straightening her own shoulders. She inclined her head slightly.

"Thank you for your hospitality," she said. "And for speaking with me on these matters. I will reflect on what you've told me, and I trust that all will unfold as it should."

He followed her gaze to the horizon, where the sky had darkened another shade of grey.

"Aye, well. I wouldn't be reflecting too long."

When Trudy turned back to reply, she found she was alone.

Chapter 22

The three girls made their way down the uneven steps to the beach. The rickety wooden handrail provided some means of support, but it was still a treacherous descent.

"Isn't this a health and safety issue?" asked Trudy as she slipped for the third time on the rain-slick stairs.

"Och," said Cliona, laughing. "Only a mainlander such as yourself would make a comment like that! Didn't we all just learn to take our first steps going up and down this stairway? Besides, it keeps the tourists away from the best bits!"

Frances grinned back at Trudy who shook her head, clutching at the railing as she took a last grateful step onto the wet sand at the bottom.

The wind blew in fierce gusts, whipping their hair and billowing their jackets.

"This way!" shouted Cliona above the pounding of the surf. "It's over there — see the outcropping?" She pointed toward a cluster of large rocks that jutted out from the shore.

The sky was leaden and looming black, the threat of further rain imminent.

* * *

"It feels like it's been raining for weeks," Frances had complained earlier as they set off from the comforting warmth of Mrs. Glenbogie's kitchen.

"Aye, and it'll rain for weeks more if we don't get this mess sorted," said Mrs. Glenbogie, gently herding Trudy away from the others. She'd made a show of tucking in the flaps of Trudy's mackintosh.

She had paused in her fussing to fix Trudy with a piercing gaze. Her old eyes were unnaturally bright, and she'd made an effort to smile encouragingly into the pale, wan, face.

"You know, then, I expect, what's to be done, lass? *Truly*? He's told you properly?"

Trudy's eyes had widened and then she'd nodded, mutely, as Mrs. Glenbogie placed a hushing finger to her lips.

"And you know the true price of it? And that they cannae take anything you aren't willing to give, aye? This plan you three came up with could very well work. But it might not. And if it doesn't, you'll have to do your part."

Again, Trudy had nodded.

Mrs.Glenbogie had nodded as well and squeezed Trudy's elbow firmly.

"Right then. You've every blessing as is mine to offer and every gratitude of myself and those gone before me." She glanced meaningfully at Trudy's mackintosh pocket, from which a corner of diaphanous fabric protruded.

Trudy blushed and pushed it further in and gave her a watery smile.

Cliona had jostled her arm.

"Oh, for heaven's sake, Mrs. Glenbogie! We've only just mopped up the waterworks and now you've got her going again!"

The four women had laughed, a forced jollity in the undercurrent of the serious and solemn conversation that had ended in their gearing up to face the wind and rain.

"Now mind you keep watch over her, pet," Mrs. Glenbogie had said to Cliona as Trudy and Frances made their way to the back gate. "She's strong where it matters and she's got a power of her own, but she hasn't had the upbringing of it, aye? She still thinks she's something less of a person."

Cliona had nodded, grimly and then gave a wide smile.

"Don't worry, Mrs. G. Don't we have you and Gran on our team? What more could we ask for against a vindictive sea cow?"

Mrs. Glenbogie had chuckled as Cliona's bright red head disappeared around the door.

Sighing heavily, she'd reached down to stroke the damp fur of one of her newest hangers-on.

"Come on then, Mogs," she said. "Fancy keeping me company by the fire for a spell?"

The ginger cat had purred loudly and pushed past her through the open door.

* * *

It was when they'd shown her the painting that she started to put it all together. It seemed so far-flung and improbable, but she'd learned, over the years, not to question some things too closely. Even still, there was much she didn't fully understand, and she'd said as much to the girls. And then Trudy had handed over the stone.

They'd sat in her kitchen, two of them bright faced with the discovery, the other pale and drawn and unwilling to meet her eye.

So it's up to her then, Eileen had thought, a pang of grief for what had come to pass all those years ago and what it meant for them now. It was a desperate cruelty what Cernach had done to a lonely, frightened little girl. *'Tis a terrible burden for such a wee lass.*

She'd shaken her head. *Naught to be done for it,* she'd reminded herself. The choice wasn't hers to make. Besides, Skelly had managed to gather them all, to show them without telling them, to give the poor lass a different choice and that in and of itself was enough to warrant her respect. And her co-operation. It was their only chance.

"Right, then," she'd said, aloud, when Trudy had told them her idea and they'd talked their way into a plan. "I suppose this means we've work ahead of us, aye?"

"But will we be able to do it?" Frances had asked. "Can we really bind Lira with Trudy's glass? I mean, you bound Skelly, but it was *his* glass that you had. Will it be enough that it belongs to her daughter?"

"Well, we're going to bloody well try," said Cliona, standing up and making a show of clearing the tea things. She tried to quell the rising anxiety of knowing what lay ahead. Her last foray into singing the wind had ended horribly and despite numerous unpleasant training sessions with Skelly afterwards, she'd never been put properly to the test. "And if Mrs. Glenbogie thinks we can do it, then that's enough for me."

"Are you sure, Clee?" asked Frances, her face full of concern for her friend. "It's an awful lot to ask of you. I know how you feel about the wind singing. It's one thing to have to do it because of a storm and another to do it voluntarily."

Cliona gave her a grateful smile. She walked over and stood between the chairs where her friends sat. Putting a hand on both Frances' and Trudy's shoulders, she gave them a squeeze.

"This time will be different," she said, her voice catching. She gave Mrs. Glenbogie a meaningful look and Eileen nodded gently. "This time I'll have my sisters, with me. I love Iain dearly, but the poor soul was never really up for the task of coping with me. The small matter of a Y chromosome, am I right, Mrs.G?"

Mrs. Glenbogie smiled, her face creasing into a million lines, her eyes sparkling.

"That's the way, lass. You three are going to end this nonsense once and for all," she replied, silently muttering a plea for forgiveness as she spoke.

* * *

Cernach stood, overlooking the beach. The wind played with the lapels of his oilskin and ruffled his carefully combed black hair. Down below, three bright spots of colour moved over the wet sand as the girls made their way toward the outcropping of stones.

"*D'síoraí grá*", he murmured softly.

The air shimmered and a large black raven lifted off, calling raucously into the swirling wind, as it flew toward Skelly's cottage.

"For love everlasting"

"You know what they've planned, then?" asked Cernach as

they both stood now, watching the three women joining hands.

Skelly laughed, hollow and without mirth.

"Haven't I been leading the poor lasses by the nose all this time?" he asked, sourly.

"I suppose," replied Cernach. "But you can't compel them to anything that's truly against their own will."

"Aye. But they don't know that, do they?" said Skelly with a sigh. "They cast me as the villain long ago. And it suited me to let them get on with it. It'll make it easier in the end, aye?"

"Then you don't believe that they know the true nature of young Trudy's bargain?"

"Och! No!" said Skelly. "They'd never go through with this if they did. They care for her; they feel like they have to look after her. They wouldn't let her set foot near the bloody sea if they knew what was at stake."

Cernach smiled a smile of bitter sadness. "Well that's one thing we can all understand, isn't it?"

He glanced down again at the figures on the beach and sighed.

"And you offered her the other choice?"

The weathered face of the old shepherd stretched and smoothed as the glamour fell away. The tall, blue-skinned faery ran a long-fingered hand across his sharp-angled face. The bones and shells woven into the ropy strands of his hair clicked and clacked in the gathering wind.

It was Skelly's turn to sigh.

"The time comes when you set aside all else but for the peace of your heart. It's been too long, Cernach, and this is as good a place as any. If I can spare them the loss, I will."

They stood in silence for a moment, a moment that seemed

to stretch down the corridor of time from which they'd both traveled for so long.

"Will it work?" asked Cernach, softly.

"I don't know," said Skelly, turning to his fox-faced companion. "I truly don't know."

* * *

"There are those of us who think Cernach did a great wrong by you, tricking you into the bargain," Skelly had held up a staying hand. "No, let me explain it all, without you interrupting me with questions. And just so as we're clear, there are some questions even I'm not able to answer."

"If you're just going to expound further in a cryptic and confusing way, I'll thank you to not bother," Trudy had muttered, scowling.

Skelly narrowed his eyes briefly but ignored her comment.

"As I was saying, Cernach tricked you and that was possibly not the best way to go about things. But he is what he is and it's not for me to comment on his methods. His heart has been full of grief and revenge for a long, long time and revenge is a thing that blinds, aye? That said, you lasses have powerful allies whether you believe it or not, including Cernach, and between us all, there's a chance we can all get what we want out of this unfortunate predicament."

"Is that what this is to you? An unfortunate predicament?" Trudy felt a rare rise of temper.

Skelly kept talking.

"Don't come over with the judgements, lassie. I've heard it all afore now and it's not going to do us any good to drag it all up again. Anyway, I'm free now to tell you this because you've come willingly, and the truth of the situation is before us."

"And that is?"

"That you made a binding promise to give yourself over to the sea. You swore an oath to Cernach, a god of the forest under the eye and the blessing of the Old Mother. It's as binding a promise as there ever was, lass. To go against it could have consequences I don't know any of us can even imagine."

Trudy swallowed, knotting the fingers of her free hand in the fabric of her coat.

"However, there's a thing you need to know about the Old Mother, or your Aunt Calla, as she showed herself to you…"

"Why are you calling her Old Mother?" interrupted Trudy. "What does that even mean?"

Skelly waved off her question and carried on.

"…it's that she's as tired of Lira's foolishness as anyone. She cannae stand an imbalance in the order of things and our Lira is getting a little too big for her boots as far as we can all see. Mostly, she just lets things get on with themselves, but sometimes she'll put her hand in, if she thinks any of us are getting out of bounds."

Trudy snorted.

"Well that's the first thing that's made any sense," she said, giving Skelly a mocking smile. "She sounds like any mother with wayward children, as far as I can tell." She pursed her lips at Skelly's look of vague confusion. "Because that's what you all are acting like - spoiled, misbehaving children."

It was Skelly's turn to scowl.

"Do you want to hear what I have to say, or not? Because it's no skin off my back to see you walk into Lira's clutches.

In fact, it would suit me right down the ground. I'd get what I want, and I'd be rid of you aggravating lot. You'll find she's got a grand sense of justice about her."

Trudy paled slightly and took her hand from the crook of his elbow. She crossed her arms in front of herself and hugged tightly as she walked.

"That's exactly what I mean," she said, her voice quivering only slightly at the subtle threat. "I point out a simple truth and you lash out at me in a huff."

Skelly puffed a breath of air through pursed lips and scrubbed a hand across his forehead.

"Ah, but you're right, lassie. I'm sorry for it. Shall I continue?"

"Please do."

"Right. Now you'd have to go far, far back in the history of Glencarragh for the whole story - now that's a one for another day, and mebbe you'll have a look into that your own self," Skelly paused to give her a meaningful look before continuing, "but a gift of knowledge was made to someone who desperately needed it. And from that gift comes the way that you might trick Lira out of what she's owed at the same time as you keep the binding oath you made."

"Oh?"

Skelly turned to look at her, his face breaking into a broad grin as he swept an arm in a wide gesture.

"Do you suppose you'd like to live here, in the In-Between?"

Trudy frowned, trying to read the expression on his face. Was this some sort of trick? She felt her energy draining all of a sudden. The scheming and subterfuge that seemed as natural as breathing to the faery folk was thoroughly exhausting.

"Can you just speak plainly," she said, crossing her arms. "I'm afraid I haven't the energy to sift through all of the intrigue."

Skelly pursed his lips, regarding her with mild irritation.

"And don't go off in one of your huffs, either. I really can't be bothered."

"Right then," said Skelly, stiffly. "I'll speak as plainly as I can." He jabbed a gnarled finger towards her. "I've given you everything you need to know, as much as I'm able. The rest is up to you, the knowing of it is available to you, you just have to know where to look. As things are, I see that you have three choices. You can do exactly what Lira wants, you can do exactly what the lasses think will work, or you can find another way."

"But I…"

"I've told you everything you need to know," repeated Skelly. "Think hard on what I've said, on everything that's happened and, most of all, remember that you have friends."

Chapter 23

Trudy shivered violently inside her mackintosh. The slight drizzle had transformed into a steady splatter of cold rain that trickled unmercifully down the back of her neck from the sodden strands of her hair.

At least we're sheltered from that godforsaken wind, she thought grimly.

The three women stood huddled on the lee side of the rocky outcropping.

"Right," said Cliona. "This is where my gran and Mrs. Glenbogie summoned Skelly all those years ago. My gran always said that a binding like that leaves a trace of magic that ties the parties to it for always." She stopped to clear her throat. "Since Gran can't be here - in person - and as a wind singer of her line, I ought to be able to find the thread of the old spell." She looked at the pale, rain-slicked faces of her friends and nodded firmly, "I *will* find the thread."

Frances smiled weakly and reached out a cold hand to each of her companions.

"Together," she said. "The power of each of us is proven more when combined with the power of one another," she grinned. "Skelly taught us that one himself, didn't he?"

"Trudy?"

Cliona raised a questioning eyebrow to the shivering woman beside her. She glanced worriedly at Frances who shook her head imperceptibly.

"Yes, Cliona," said Trudy, squaring her shoulders. "I'm quite ready."

* * *

Feargus was just settling himself by the fire when the knock came at the door - sharp and insistent and not likely to go away if ignored.

He swore quietly, setting down his book and his tumbler of whiskey and slid his slippers onto his feet.

"Coming!" he called out to the persistent hammering. "Keep your bloody hair on," he muttered under his breath.

"Eileen!" he said, startled, as he opened the door onto driving rain.

The old woman stood, draped in oilskin from head to toe, rain streaming from the peak of her hat.

Feargus squinted past her into the unpleasantness of the afternoon.

"Is everything alright? Will you come in out of that horrible weather?" He stepped aside and waved his hand in the direction of the narrow passageway.

"Hadn't you ought to ask me if I'd like to sit by your fire?" asked Mrs. Glenbogie, scowling. "Or have you dispensed with the old formalities, like?"

Eyes widening in brief shock, he regained his composure and smiled widely.

"What gave me away, then?" he asked, tilting his head to

one side.

"Never mind that, you bloody trickster," retorted Mrs. Glenbogie. "Just get your sou'wester and follow me down to the beach. The lasses will have a need of you."

"Now, then, Mrs. G. Surely you must know I'm not…"

"You bloody well are!" shouted the old woman, brandishing her walking stick in his face. "Besides, 'tisn't just the lasses as will need you. It's your old cohorts as well — they've no idea how bad this could get if it all goes pear-shaped. I think we might have sorely underestimated that Lira creature" She gave Feargus a calculating look and added, "as well you may know."

"Now listen here," puffed Feargus as he struggled into a pair of bright yellow Wellingtons. "You can't expect me to interfere in this, Eileen. It's not the way things go on, you know that."

"Never mind trying to pull that one, Feargus," snapped Mrs. Glenbogie, handing him his rain hat and shoving him out the door into the pelting rain. "You're in this up to your shapely eyebrows, and you'd do well to remember from now on that I'm not fooled by you. Not anymore. I'm desperate ashamed that I hadn't cottoned on before now." She glanced sideways at him, as he fumbled with his keys, watching the expressions flitting across his face.

Having satisfied himself as to the security of the back door, Feargus grunted and shrugged down into his raincoat, scowling.

Mrs. Glenbogie smothered a grin and set off in the direction of the beach.

"Come on then, pet!" she called back. "We've an appointment with an old friend of yours!"

* * *

Cliona fumbled in the pocket of her coat, her cold fingers closing over the small pouch containing two pieces of sea glass - Skelly's and now, his daughter's.

Trying to keep the quiver out of her voice and the tremor from her hands, she fought down the rising nausea that signaled the influence of the wild magic that drove the wind. She glanced, worriedly at the sky. Was it possible that Lira knew what they were doing? Swallowing her fear, she reached out to Trudy.

Trudy's attempt at a smile was more of a grimace as she felt in her pocket for the cool, soothing softness of the faery-spun material in there. She gripped it tightly, screwing up her face against the imprecations of the wind, which, despite the shelter of the rocks, was managing to find its way amongst them.

"It's a Storm-wind," Cliona had explained to her frightened companions as, without warning, she'd slumped, groaning, against the rocks with her heel of her palms pressed into her eye sockets. "The wild magic pulls at me from somewhere deep inside - gives me a thumping headache and makes me want to hurl my guts out."

She'd grinned wickedly at the concern on their faces. "Fabulously romantic stuff, eh? Who wouldn't want to live among the fecking faeries, right? Isn't it all just glitter and unicorns pissing rainbows?"

Frances had subsided into hysterical giggles at the last bit and soon the three of them were leaning on one another, tears of laughter streaming down their rain-numbed faces.

Finally, wiping her face and squaring her shoulders against the pain, Cliona had insisted that they pull themselves together and get on with things. She hadn't told the other two just *how* badly she was feeling and how frightened. There was no sense of Skelly nearby and with her gran gone and Mrs. Glenbogie so far away back in the village, she felt terribly alone and not at all sure that they were doing the right thing. What was she thinking that with only one, utterly catastrophic wind-song under her belt, that she could try binding the powerful sea witch that had been laying waste to Glencarragh for centuries? Madness, utter madness.

Frances was having similar doubts. She, too, had only a vague sense of Skelly - which was unusual, being this close to the ocean. She reached out with her mind, cautiously, afraid to summon him too soon, but strangely anxious for his familiar presence. Her own binding was to have lasted a year and a day and, without ceremony or acknowledgement, that time was up. Could it be the bond between them was simply gone? Now would not be the best time for that to be the case.

Only Trudy was unperturbed by the rising of the wind. She found herself soothed by the rhythmic crash of the waves against the sand. The tempo increased and the wind began to hum in her ears, muffling the sound of her friends' voices. Slowly, a gentle warmth had begun to infuse her shivering body. Her thoughts began to drift; she fancied that she saw spots of light flashing across the surface of the grey-green sea, like the sun-dazzle of a bright summer day. Shapes flickered at the edges of her vision, the rainbow-glint of fish scales, the foam-flecked crest of a water-horse, the sleek, brown skin of a seal.

"Trudy!"

The sound had come from somewhere far away, a voice muffled by time and distance. She ignored it; she was suddenly tired of the enormous effort it took her to cope with the world around her. Instead, she found herself letting go of Frances' hand and stepping closer to the edge of the sea, trying to catch the images that flickered and danced there. Surely it would be so much easier just to do what was expected?

Suddenly, a sharp tug on her arm yanked her back. Once again, the rain was cold and sharp, and the wind shrieked.

"What were you doing?" Frances asked, her face creased in a frown. "You were a million miles away. Now is absolutely not the time to let yourself drift to the In-Between. We need you here, Trudy. Look at me!"

"I, I, don't know," Trudy stammered, shuddering. "I'm sorry. It, it just seemed to pull me, so."

"Right!" Cliona said, firmly, ushering Trudy back into their little circle. "That settles it; we have to get on with this thing before it all goes arse-end up. I've an awful feeling we're being watched, and I don't particularly fancy the idea one bit."

* * *

After her visit to Skelly, Trudy had spent most of the rest of the week in the stuffy, windowless, basement room that housed the Glencarragh Historical Society, poring through stacks of old ledgers and shipping manifests.

"Do you know what you're looking for, pet?" asked the kindly Mr. Jamison. He was the unofficial island historian and took great pride in the collection of moldering tomes in his care. "Only it might be easier to narrow down the search.

You must understand that much of what I've gathered here is of a rather, well, anecdotal nature. It's all a bit haphazard really, and it's mostly in my own head what's what and where," he glanced around the room with a wistful sigh. "I'd love a bit of proper shelving. Mebbe one of them glass cabinets for the more delicate bits."

Trudy had smiled, understanding precisely what the stacks of papers meant to the wizened little man. She immediately resolved to enlist Feargus and Iain in knocking up some shelves and procuring a nice glass cabinet. Providing she managed to come safely out the other side of her situation.

"Well, I can't say I know exactly what I'm looking for, but I do think I'll know it when I find it. I wonder, though, have you anything in the way of old folktales or legends of the area?"

Mr. Jamison beamed.

"Now isn't that the strangest thing?" he said, turning to open up a slightly battered cardboard box. "I've only just come into possession of this particular collection. Now and then, Feargus from the bookshop brings me items of interest. Grand fellow, he is, always has an eye out for treasures I might want."

Yes, indeed, thought Trudy, hiding a smile.

"Now, some of your more scholarly folk will see it as a bit of foolishness, like," continued Mr. Jamison, "but there's a great deal we can learn from the old stories, and more so from the very folk who'd lived them, as it were."

He pulled out a small, cloth-bound book and handed it to her.

"Here you are, it's a wee volume that was put together nigh on fifty years ago, I think. I was just a lad myself, but I do remember someone, and I can't remember rightly who, probably some toff from the University, coming here themselves to collect the stories from the old folk at the time. Might this do?"

"Oh, lovely, yes!" Said Trudy, eyes shining.

Mr. Jamison turned back to the same box and pulled out a large ledger.

"This might be of use, as well," he said, smoothing a wrinkled hand over the dusty leather cover. "This here is the ledger from our old village pub. They found it in the wall when they were doing the renovations."

His lovely kind eyes darkened a little and his voice became almost a whisper.

"There were some dark times on Glencarragh, my girl. Dark times indeed." He cleared his throat and gave her a thin smile. "Never mind me, here I am rabbiting on like an old fool," He placed the cardboard box next to her on the table. "You go on and have a rummage in there, Feargus knows his business so I'm sure there'll be something good in amongst the dusty bits. Now, then, what is it you're hoping to discover?"

Trudy smiled down at the book in her hands then back up at Mr. Jamison.

"Well, Mr. Jamison, I seem to have got myself into a little predicament and I believe," she tapped the cover of the book, "I believe the answer to how to get myself out of it is in here."

* * *

"Okay," said Cliona, shaking the large piece of smooth, blue-green glass and the mottled brown stone out onto the palm of her hand. "Glass? Check. Raging nausea? Check. Secret weapon?" she glanced at Trudy who lowered her eyes and nodded, "Check."

Taking a deep breath, Cliona cleared her throat and grinned at her two companions.

"Frances? Can you give me a middle C?"

It was as exhilarating as she remembered it.

She was the wind and the wind was her. The power and the infinity of it swept through her, tugging her in all four directions as the wind-song soared, pulled from the core of herself and from the timelessness of the wind itself.

Steady, lass, came a familiar voice inside her head. *You've got it, but just barely, now.*

We're here, Skelly, sent Frances, relieved, from somewhere close by. *Cliona? We've got you.*

The wind surged through Cliona, but, this time, anchored by the women around her, she held firm, singing it to herself, winding it around her like a garland, letting the gusts stream from her fingertips.

This is what it should be, she thought, drifting with the currents of air. *This is what freedom tastes like - salt and water and love.*

I'm okay, she sent outwards with the wind, tendrils of thought that wove into the minds of her friends.

From somewhere far away, she saw herself standing on the beach, head thrown back and arms stretched wide, her hands held tightly on either side. Her bright red hair flew wildly around her pale, drawn, face. Around her stood her friends - Trudy shuddering with cold, her soaking brown hair plastered to her face and Frances, paint-splattered jeans and anxious frown. Further away, vague and flickering on the cliff's edge, there was Skelly and a man she vaguely recognized. And then she saw Mrs. Glenbogie, stumbling down the crooked steps to the beach, Feargus right behind her, his bright yellow mackintosh a cheerful smudge against the black, rain-slicked edges of cliff face where the land ended and the sea began. Then, a voice - like the memory of a favourite song - sang itself into her awareness.

Gran! she breathed out with a rush of joy.

Aye, lass. Didn't I tell you I'd never be far off? Now then, my brave, clever girl, 'tis long past time we ended this, aye?

The wind shrieked and howled across the beach, drawing the salty spray of the foaming sea and spattering it across the faces of the people gathered in the lee of the rocks.

Cliona swayed from side to side as the force of the wind ran through her. It was definitely different this time, more powerful, but more controlled. She held tightly to the threads of consciousness from her friends — from Mrs. Glenbogie and most of all, her beloved gran.

"*Och, pet. You've barely a need of us auld women, aye?*" came the smiling voice of her gran. "*You've found your way with it now.*"

"*Didn't I tell you, eh?*" sent Mrs. Glenbogie. "*I knew you'd be proud of the lass...*'

"*If you've done with the mutual admiration society,*" snarled Skelly, his voice tight with strain, "*Can we get on with the business at hand?*"

Chapter 24

"Are you alright, Trudy?" asked Frances, aloud squeezing her hand tightly. There was a strange silence surrounding them, the howling of the wind reduced to a muffled roar.

Cliona stood tall, a look of fierce concentration on her face.

"I'm okay," said Trudy, eyes wide with wonder, "I can carry on, we won't have much time before…"

Suddenly a thundering crash battered against the shield of the wind.

Steady on, lass.

Mrs. Glenbogie was standing beside them now, just outside their circle. Feargus stood beside her, looking mutinous.

She glared at Feargus, who pretended not to notice. Reaching out, she rapped him sharply with her walking stick.

"Stop your sulking and help the lasses. Tell them what they need to know…. Now!" she said, poking the stick firmly between his ribs. "Before it's too late."

"What's going on?" asked Frances, glancing at Feargus who stared fixedly out to sea. "Why on earth is Feargus here?"

"There's something you ought to know before you start the binding," said Mrs. Glenbogie. "Something this lot wasn't planning on letting you in on." She gestured towards Trudy and Feargus.

Trudy started guiltily.

Frances blinked.

"Trudy? I thought we'd decided what we're doing. What haven't you said?"

"Leave the lass," grunted Skelly, suddenly appearing beside her. "She's to make her own choice in this."

"What do you mean? Cliona? Do you know what this is all about?"

Cliona moaned softly.

I can't concentrate with all this nattering...

I'll hold it, pet. You'd best have a word with your friends, sent her gran.

Nodding, Cliona hummed down her wind-song and staggered slightly as she regained her balance. Her face was strained and white as she looked from Mrs. Glenbogie to Trudy and Feargus.

"Tell them, lass," said Mrs. Glenbogie to Trudy. "It's only fair that they know what you've agreed to before they take a part in sending you to it. Because that's what will happen if the binding doesn't work. You'll have called her here and she won't leave quietly."

Trudy broke the circle, her hand trembling as she tried to push a wet strand of hair from her face.

"No you don't," said Cliona, reaching to grab her hand again. "Whatever he's talked you into, we're not letting you out of our sight for a second."

"He didn't talk me into anything," said Trudy, her eyes filling with tears. "I want to do this. I *have* to do this, don't you see?"

"Do what?" demanded Frances, leaning in to search Trudy's face.

"End the curse," said Skelly, moving to stand behind Trudy. "She's agreed to help end it forever."

"But how?" said Frances, eyes wild and her voice rising to a shriek. "Trudy, please! Tell us what's happening. You're frightening me."

Trudy gave Frances a small smile.

"I made a promise, you see," she explained. "I *knew*, I'd always known, that was the one thing I must never do. Aunt Calla made me say it every day before I went out exploring. She must have known that I might…" Trudy stared wildly at Skelly and Feargus. "Of course, she knew," her voice dropped to a whisper. Skelly shifted beside her, reaching out a steadying hand. The warmth of his touch calmed the trill of panic that was threatening. "Because all along she was the one who…" Trudy shook her head, that was knowledge she wasn't quite ready to deal with. "She understood me. She knew that traveling into the In-Between was the only way I could face being in the everyday world. I'd go mad, otherwise. You do see that, don't you?"

Her friends stared, uncomprehending, so she continued.

"So when I wanted to take the stone - and I really, really wanted it because it felt, I don't know, special somehow and I believed it would give me some sort of power over the people who bullied me and misunderstood me…" she broke off and sniffed, "I was only little,"

"Aye, and he took advantage of that, the rotten swine," said Mrs.Glenbogie, putting an arm around the shivering Trudy. "Go on, lass. Tell them the rest."

Trudy sniffed again, wiping the heels of her hands in her eyes.

"Basically, the fox told me that I could take the stone, but

I was to make a promise to the sea in return for it. That I would, one day, give something of myself to the sea the way the sea had given something of itself to me. Or something like that. The wording was strange and old-fashioned, and I didn't really understand it."

"Of course you didn't bloody understand it!" exploded Cliona, her face like thunder. "For crying out loud you were just a small child. What sort of monster would ask for a promise like that from a small child?"

She glared at Skelly who glared right back.

"It wasn't me," he said, holding up his hands. "I haven't the shape of a fox."

"But you're more than happy to reap the benefits of it, is that it?"

Skelly's glare faltered and he shifted his eyes away from Cliona's furious ones. She rounded on Mrs. Glenbogie and Feargus, who stood slightly off to the side looking distinctly uncomfortable.

"We have to stop this," said Cliona, her voice rising into panic. "We have to stop this whole thing, right now. All of it. There's no way we can risk our Trudy like this. And you," she pointed a finger at Feargus who had the good grace to look momentarily frightened, "what's your part in all of this anyway?"

Feargus hunched down in his mackintosh, hands thrust deep into the pockets.

"I have no part in this," he muttered, "but Mrs.Glenbogie insisted that I accompany her. A gentleman doesn't refuse a request for assistance."

"Oh, shut up with that nonsense," said Eileen, tapping him none-too-gently behind the knees with her walking stick.

"Right, let me get this straight," said Frances, finally finding her voice. She looked at Trudy, who stood shuddering miserably between Skelly and Mrs.Glenbogie. "You made a bargain with this fox character, who obviously was some glamoured form of a faery…" she paused, frowning. "Did we already talk about this? I feel like we ought to know this. Anyway, so you're meant to do what, give yourself to the sea in return for taking the stone, which was actually a piece of selkie glass?'

"A soul for a soul," murmured Skelly, gazing out at the roiling sea. He turned back to the group of staring, angry faces. "It's a way to break Lira's curse. A mortal child willingly offering itself to the sea. It's fair payment, so she thinks, for the loss of *her* child."

"Your child," reminded Mrs.Glenbogie. "Let's not forget that."

Skelly shrugged.

"She's long gone away now," he said, his eyes seeing far away from the shore. "There's no coming back from where she is. She's gone too far."

The catch in his voice made Trudy look at him. Her heart ached a little for what she heard.

"This doesn't make any logical sense," said Cliona, sputtering. "Surely haven't people flung themselves into the sea in despair? I mean, there was that poor soul a few years ago that just wandered in and never came out."

"Cliona," remonstrated Frances, shooting a worried look at Trudy. "Surely that's not what's meant," she looked to Skelly for confirmation and she shook his head.

"No, no, lass. That's not the case at all. Quite the opposite. The mortal that joins the sea, must do just that. Give over their land-dwelling life to *live* in the sea, as a selkie. That's why Lira thought it was a just punishment. And because it's not a bargain that would likely be taken up, I imagine she thought herself quite clever with setting it."

There was a collective exhalation in the group, none so big as Trudy's. She felt herself wobble slightly and Skelly gripped her elbow in support. He looked down at her, his eyes wide.

"Surely you didn't think you had to fling yourself to your death, lass?"

"Well, no-one ever said, directly," she replied, her voice quavering. "You all said I was bound to give myself to the sea. What was I supposed to think? I just followed the words."

"You utter bastard!" shouted Cliona, "I can't bloody believe you had her thinking she had to go and drown herself in the sea. You thoughtless, heartless, piece of…."

"Steady on, old girl," said Feargus, coming to Cliona's side, laying a hand on her shoulder. "There's no need to turn this into another fight. There's been enough of that, don't you think?"

Cliona tore her gaze away from Skelly, who stood unmoving under the torrent of her abuse, and directed it towards Feargus. Looking into his kindly blue eyes, *the blue of a summer sea,* she thought absently, she felt the anger drain out of her. He was right, there had been too much animosity already.

"I apologize," she muttered. "Not for what I said, you understand," she hurled another glare at Skelly, "but for how I said it. Mostly."

Frances smiled and squeezed Cliona's arm. She looked at Trudy who appeared to be standing slightly taller.

"What do you want to do, Trudy?" she asked. "We're forgetting that it's you who has the final say here because, if I heard correctly," she glanced at Skelly who avoided her eyes. "the person entering the sea needs to do so willingly."

"That's right, lass," said Mrs.Glenbogie. "You always have a choice and no silly promise will change that. They can't make you do anything."

"But what about the bargain I made with the fox?" asked Trudy. "I thought by doing that I'd given up my choice in the matter. I used my choice to take the stone, didn't I?"

Frances shook her head.

"It was a trick," she said. "A trick of the language. They have a habit of that."

Skelly still refused to look at her.

Trudy glanced around the circle, at the dear, strained, worried faces. She looked at Skelly who was the picture of discomfort and misery, then wider to the beach and the cliffs and the sea. She turned to face him, taking his hands in hers and forcing him to look. The familiar tingle from contact with him warmed through her, stealing away the bitter, driving cold. A summer sun beat down on them and the wind, softer now, rippled over the heather. Sheep dotted the moorland and the sky was a cloudless, expansive blue.

"You've made a home here," she said, looking towards the tiny cottage where the familiar curl of smoke spiraled from the chimney. "Somewhere to belong."

Skelly shifted and followed her gaze.

"Aye, it does well enough."

"I think it does more than that," she said, smiling. "I think that if I could find a place like this, a place in between, I'd be happy to spend my days. And you'll be pleased to know that, with the help of some true friends, I've found the way to make that happen. But you must promise *me*, something."

"What's that, *mo chara?*"

"That you won't tell the girls anything until it's over. Don't let them try and stop me. There won't be time to explain if this binding doesn't work…"

"It won't," interrupted Skelly.

"We need to let them try," said Trudy, squeezing his hands. "You know, compromise isn't always a bad thing."

"No, no 't'isn't," he agreed, regarding her with his sea-green eyes whose corners crinkled when he smiled.

Trudy laughed, then, a genuine laugh, not something she remembered doing since she was a small girl, roaming the shores of a long-ago beach.

Chapter 25

Four humans, one faery and a retired god of the sea stood in the shelter of the rain-slick rocks as the sea roared behind them. The sky was a roiling mass of thunderheads and sheets of rain lashed sideways. Despite the assault, arms were folded and faces fixed in either scowls or curiosity.

"She's the answer," said Skelly, a quiet power in his natural form, oblivious to the cold rain that ran in rivulets from his blue-green hair. "She's the bridge between the worlds, between the land and the sea. That's just the way of it. A bargain is a bargain."

He looked around at the bewildered, unbelieving faces.

"She's agreed to be bound to it, whether any of you like it or not. But," he paused, looking at Trudy who gave a slight nod. "if you stop standing around debating the subject, we might not have need of her promise at all."

Cliona frowned, arms folded across her chest. The wind spun her hair in a wild, red halo around her head.

"That's assuming we get it right and never mind that, what in the bloody hell just happened there? The two of you just slide off for a private conversation? Is there anything else we mere mortals need to know?"

"Cliona, please," said Frances, seeing the look of hurt cross Trudy's face. "Let's not do this now. Trudy, are you willing to try the binding at least?"

Trudy nodded. "Yes, absolutely."

"But if it doesn't work, you'll have to go," protested Cliona. "It's like Mrs. G said, if we call Lira and can't bind her, she'll unleash bloody hellfire on us. And you'll have to go…"

Trudy walked over and took Cliona into a tight hug.

"You'll manage," she whispered. "You're far more capable than you think. And don't worry about me, no matter what happens, I'm going to be just fine. Please trust me in this."

Trudy gave her a quick squeeze and stepped back, holding out her hands.

"Shall we?"

Suddenly there was a deafening shriek as the wind surged.

"Gran!"

Cliona staggered against Frances then stumbled into Trudy, knocking her from the circle.

"Hurry, everyone, I need you…."

Frances pulled Trudy back toward her and the three friends clasped hands tightly.

"All of you," groaned Cliona, the wind-song rising through her, buffeting her sideways. "I'm going to need all of you. Gran isn't managing…."

Skelly stepped in beside Trudy and pulled Feargus into the circle.

"Bugger off, Skelly," said Feargus, yanking himself free. "I told you…"

"Leave him," said a deep voice. Cernach materialized on the other side of Trudy, grasping her hand.

"Who the hell are you?" said Frances, shocked by the

appearance of the dark-haired stranger, but no-one bothered to answer.

"Oh no you don't," said Mrs. Glenbogie stepping forward, moving between him and Trudy, taking his other hand.

"Cannae trust any of you, you feckless bastards," she muttered. "I hope to God you know what you're doing."

"*Ah, rest your troubled mind, good lady,*" sent Cernach, with a wolfish grin. "'*Tis all well in hand.*"

"*Aye,*" she sent back. "*That's what I'm afraid of.*"

"What's happening?" shouted Trudy, her face a mask of terror as the storm surged with new ferocity. The wind and rain pummeled mercilessly; it was all they could do to remain on their feet. Cliona swayed with the effort of holding the wind, gripping tightly to the hands of her friends.

"I don't know how long I can do this," she moaned, faintly. "It's so much stronger than before...."

Steady pet, we're all here, came the lilting calm of her gran's voice.

"Feargus, you common shite," grunted Skelly. "It wouldn't kill you to at least keep us dry, would it? Give the lass a hand."

Feargus scowled. He remained outside the circle but seemed unbothered by the raging storm. His face twitched between concern and nonchalance before settling on concern. He saw the strain in Cliona's face and the wide-eyed terror in Trudy's and his shoulders slumped in a sigh.

"Very well," he said, and made a casual gesture with his hand.

Suddenly they were no longer being battered by the wind and rain. Frances blinked in surprise and Trudy stumbled at the sudden cessation of the need to stand against the gale.

Only Cliona remained straining with the effort of the wind-song.

"Feargus! What on earth?"

"Aye, Feargus. Now might be a grand moment to fill the lasses in, don't you think?" said Skelly, an amused smirk on his face.

"I don't think we've got time for that," murmured Cernach, nodding his head toward the shore.

"Pan's hairy…"

A scream tore from Cliona's throat as she broke the circle and pitched forward onto her knees.

"Bloody hell," swore Frances, clasping her hands to the sides of her head.

"Skelly!" shrieked Trudy before collapsing onto the wet sand.

"Trudy? Can you hear me?"

Cliona knelt on the sand with Trudy's head cradled in her lap. Trudy moaned softly and opened her eyes.

"What happened," she asked as Frances bent to help her sit up. Frances winced sharply as she straightened.

"Are you hurt, lass?" said Skelly reaching out to touch Frances. Frances flinched and pulled away. Skelly withdrew his hand.

"Sorry," said Frances hurriedly, "I didn't mean…it's just you're positively *humming* with that…whatever it is."

"Sorry lass. It's the storm…. the sea…"

"Can we forego the pleasantries?" asked Cernach in his smooth, rumbling voice. "May I remind you that we seem to have attracted some unwanted attention," he gestured again toward the water's edge.

His voice and manner were calm, but his face was taught with strain. Flickers of light and movement flashed around him, leaving the ghosting images of antlers and wings and pointed ears. Skelly looked at him sharply before turning back towards the rising problem.

Stepping out of the roiling surf was a tall, black creature resembling a horse. It was beautiful in a terrifying way – all bared-teeth and savage grace. As it crossed out of the water, the ocean streaming from its glistening coat, a statuesque woman with night-black hair and skin the color of kelp, slid gracefully from its back. The wind and rain came to an abrupt stop and an uneasy silence fell over the sea's edge.

"Lira," murmured Skelly.

"But we hadn't even started to summon her," said Frances, looking wildly from face to face.

"Shit," said Cliona, a look of utter exhaustion in her stance.

"Aye, 'tis a bit of an understatement, that," said Skelly with a small smile.

"What'll we do now?" whispered Trudy from where she remained sitting on the sand. "It's not going to work, is it?"

"What an astute observer you are, human thing. Such as you *are* human, that is." said Lira, her voice was the wet rasp of scales over pebbles. She scowled down at Trudy, disgust mingling briefly with wariness on her smooth features.

"Well done," she sneered at Skelly. "It seems you've managed a decent effort since last we…. *spoke*." Her smile revealed a row of sharp, pointed teeth. She inclined her head toward Mrs. Glenbogie who stood with her arms folded in front of her in a gesture of stubborn speculation. "Well met, old woman. Don't fancy you'll get off quite as easily as last time."

She glanced around at the gathering of friends.

"Indeed! What a charming reunion we have here! All friends together, yes? How perfect to know that we can be rid of you all in one sitting."

Feargus swore unintelligibly and spat on the sand at his feet.

"Really, *brother*," said Lira silkily, "I thought you'd long finished bothering yourself with the affairs of mortals. What brings you to my shores on such a fine day as this? Have you finally decided to return to us?"

"Brother?"

"Feargus!"

"What?"

The exclamations overlapped one another and served to jolt the gathered force out of their initial shock at seeing Lira materialize. Gradually, the implications of her unbidden arrival sank onto the group with a horrifying lurch.

Feargus sighed heavily.

"Sod off, Lira. You're wasting your time here. I have it on reliable information that they're more than capable of putting a stop to your ridiculous nonsense."

"Ridiculous nonsense?" Lira's face became a mask of fury. Behind her, the sea began to churn and foam. "How *dare* you?"

"Quite easily, as a matter of fact," said Feargus calmly. "Seeing as I've now, as you so conveniently reminded me, got myself embroiled in the affairs of mortals."

He walked toward her, placing himself between the gathered friends and the furious queen. Smiling broadly, he held out his hands in a gesture of expansive goodwill.

"What do you say, sister? Shall we just go our separate ways and pretend like none of this ever happened? Call it even?"

Lira's slanted eyes widened in disbelief, her mouth opened

in an 'oh' of outrage.

"What in the hell is he up to?" whispered Cliona to Mrs. Glenbogie. "Did you know about any of this?"

"Not as much as I thought," replied Mrs. Glenbogie, shaking her head in disbelief. She placed a hand on Cliona's. "Quietly now, gather them to you. I'm guessing he knows what he's doing. We won't have much time once he starts."

Lira shook with fury. The wind began to whine and hum. Cold, sharp, needles of rain started to fall.

Feargus cocked his head to one side. He tucked his hands deep into the pockets of his bright yellow mackintosh and shrugged.

"I don't see what the fuss is about. It all seems fairly straightforward to me."

He took another step toward Lira, glancing as he did towards Cernach who seemed to be shuddering in and out of view, flickering like a faulty television signal.

Lira followed his glance and sneered at Cernach, who was fading rapidly.

"I should've thought you'd know better than to stand so close to my realm, *forest* lord," she spat viciously.

"Aye, and I'd've thought you'd know the same," said Skelly, stepping forward to grab Trudy's hands, pulling her from the sand. At the same time Feargus pulled his hands free of his pockets and flung something high into the air.

He roared, a strange, guttural sound and began to chant, his voice booming across the empty beach.

By wave, by stone, by grain of the eternal sand,
By leaf, by bough, by cloud of the eternal sky,
Rise now, the water of life,
Rise now, the giver of dreams,

Rise now to hold fast the mystery,
Rise now to champion the lost.

Chapter 26

A thick, impenetrable fog rose suddenly from the sand, enveloping them in a damp, white cloud, obscuring Lira and the sea's edge from view.

From the other side of the wall of mist, Lira shrieked her rage. The whiteness muffled the sound and enclosed the friends in a silent circle.

"Right! We won't have long, she's a lot stronger than she used to be, even land-side."

Feargus held up a hand to silence the surprise and indignation.

"Never mind, if we pull this off there'll be plenty of time for explanations."

"And if we don't?" retorted Cliona.

"Then none of it matters," replied Mrs. Glenbogie.

"Bugger that," snapped Cliona. "I want to know what we're getting ourselves in for," she glanced up at the sky, currently obscured by the concealing mist, "and would someone please tell me who in the hell is holding the wind?"

Feargus waved away the question. "The wind is indifferent, it always has been. Lira calls it into a storm just as you call it into submission. Right now, you're somehow holding it between you. I imagine it's got something to do with those three," he gestured toward Skelly, Cernach and Trudy. "And the fact you're all here together."

"So now what?" asked Frances, worriedly.

"Now we finish what was started all those years ago," said Trudy, turning to smile at Cernach who bowed deeply. Trudy surprised herself and sank into a low curtsey.

"And how, precisely, will this be achieved?" demanded Cliona, fury and fear contorting her features. She was drained by the earlier efforts of trying to hold the wind and worried for what might be coming next. She looked anxiously at Trudy who seemed to be quite calm, happy, even. Cliona felt a wave of cold sweat prickle her scalp; she couldn't lose another one. She glared at Cernach, or tried to. She found her eyes sliding away from his face and decided he was entirely to blame for their situation. "And you, you hateful bastard," she rounded on him. "I have more than a few words to say to you about the way you've treated Trudy. Don't think you'll get away with that load of bollocks."

"It's alright, pet," said Mrs. Glenbogie, equally weary. "Keep a cool head. I've no notion as to what they might be up to, but I'm afraid we're going to have to trust them."

She turned to Trudy where she stood between Skelly and Cernach.

Smiling kindly, her eyes crinkled at the corners.

"How long will you go, *mo chroí?*"

"Well, I….um…" Trudy stammered, looking guiltily between Mrs. Glenbogie and her two friends.

"Go? Go where?" Frances' voice was panicked. "Trudy what are you doing? You are NOT stepping into that sea. I won't let you."

"It's alright, Frances. It's going to be alright, I promise," said

Trudy, smiling through her unshed tears. She looked at Skelly who nodded, closing his eyes. "It's not what you're thinking. We've got it all sorted, don't worry."

"Please," pleaded Frances, her voice breaking, looking around at the faces of her friends, "don't do this. Whatever it is. There must be another way." She whirled on Cernach and Skelly. "How could you be so cruel? You're asking too much of her."

Cernach bowed his head.

"I truly regret the terms of the situation, believe that. However, I think that you'll see it's not all as dire as you might imagine. I do believe my old foe and your dear friend have, between them, hatched a plot. Am I correct?"

Skelly remained silent, his eyes closed, Trudy beside him, her hands resting lightly on his arm. She blushed, shifting uncomfortably beneath the forest god's gaze.

She closed her eyes and let herself slip.

* * *

"Did you do it?' she asked. "Are you ready?"

They stood, side by side at the crest of the small hill that led down towards his cottage.

"Aye, and it's a grand, thing lass, so thank you for it. Truly. And as for you, I think you'll find it all as you remember."

Skelly turned to her, his eyes shining with unshed tears. He reached out and squeezed her hand, before letting it go to point over at the horizon. Two figures emerged from the cottage and were making their way towards Skelly and Trudy.

"Here they come."

It was Trudy's eyes turn to shine. She placed her hand in the crook of Skelly's elbow and hugged his arm tightly.

"I can't wait to see Frances' face!"

* * *

Mrs. Glenbogie lay a hand on Frances' arm.

"Leave her," she warned. "She's gone wandering, I think."

"What? Right now?" spluttered Cliona. "Good grief. I know this is stressful, but you'd think she had a better sense of when it was appropriate to go gadding off into fairyland than when we're all facing certain doom."

She waved a hand at the strange, shifting fog and the chorus of shrieking wind and shrieking sea queen on the other side of it.

Frances couldn't help but smile at her friend.

"Bit theatrical, no? Anyway, I think Mrs. G is right, Trudy gets a certain look to her when she's off and away. Skelly's there, too, isn't he?"

Mrs. Glenbogie nodded, gesturing towards the pair of them.

"I think our one is right," she shot Cernach a vaguely distasteful glance, "I think the pair of them are up to something. Trudy is the key to it all, do you see? I think we've underestimated the importance of that. We've underestimated *her*."

Cernach smiled, bowing his antlered head once again.

"Indeed, my good woman," he said, his eyes resting briefly on Trudy. "But no more than she underestimated herself. And don't dismiss the importance of the gathering here," he swept his arm over the damp, dripping group. "There's a great power in your comradeship and your collective desire to keep this drizzling lump of floating rock safe from harm."

"Drizzling lump of what?" began Cliona, indignant. "Listen here, you smarmy, deceitful …"

"I don't suppose we could resume the witty banter at a later time," interrupted Frances. "Only Lira seems to have renewed her ongoing objection to our drizzling lump." She nodded toward the outer edge of the mist, where the once muffled sound of the sea was getting louder.

"You're quite right, Frances my dear," said Feargus. "We simply do not have the luxury of genial conversation just now. We have one chance and one chance only to send my dear sister packing once this mist comes down and, as much as I would love to continue to be of assistance, it's down to the three of you."

Feargus glanced toward Skelly and the now perfectly solid outline of Cernach.

"Nice ruse, by the way, old chum," he murmured to Cernach who simply smiled and dipped the improbable rack of antlers which grew from his forehead.

"And you two, of course," pointing towards Frances and Cliona who was still regarding Cernach with frowning suspicion.

"Naturally," grimaced Skelly, opening his eyes. "Can we get on then? She's not getting any quieter out there." He glanced at Trudy and nodded softly.

"You can come out, now," she said, in the direction of the rocky outcropping.

Frances let out a strangled cry and dashed towards one of the emerging forms, coming to a startled stop when the little creature she'd known so well cried out at the sight of her and held up a warning hand. The selkie-boy lay a gentle hand on Moss' arm, muttering soothing noises.

"Moss? What's wrong? It's just me, Frances."

Her voice cracked and tears welled up to see the little brownie, standing close to the selkie-boy. His eyes were wide and frightened, his gaze darting between the figures on the beach and the wall of fog down at the shore.

He's had a terrible time of it, came Skelly's voice in her head. *He won't be able to manage in your world, not yet. Not for a while, maybe ever. We probably shouldn't have asked him to come, not with all this business going on, but we wanted you to know he was alright.*

How long? asked Frances, silently, her heart breaking all over again. She'd almost given up and now to see him, so familiar, and yet not, was almost worse than not knowing where he was.

Not long. He was in a far, far worse state when Cernach found him. He's done well, in the In-Between, back to himself in a lot of ways. It's different here, though. I'm sorry, lass, I didn't want to get your hopes up.

Frances realized, then, what he'd said.

We?

Trudy. It was Trudy who asked me to let her bring him to you. Just so you'd know that you'd all brought him back. Cernach couldn't have got to him without you. Don't fret, lass, we'll look after him.

Before she could question any further, her attention was caught by the flurry of activity among her friends. She turned back to the rocks, but Moss was gone. The selkie boy took her hand and she allowed him to lead her back to the group. She avoided everyone's eyes, not feeling able to bear what she'd see in them.

"Sorry to intrude, lass," said Feargus, gently, "but we must get on." Frances nodded, silently and took her place in the circle.

Feargus cleared his throat and turned to Cliona.

"Cliona, I believe you have the item in question?"

Cliona scowled at his mock politeness, but her gaze softened into worry as she looked between Frances and Trudy.

"What's to say you don't just drop us in it when we give it over?" she asked, passing the sea glass to Mrs Glenbogie. "You're a bit difficult to trust, you see."

"They won't," said Trudy.

"Why?"

"Because Skelly loves his people; he loves his home and he's been away from it too long. As for Cernach, he may live by a different set of rules than the rest of us, but he has honour and loyalty and that stands for something. We've all made sacrifices here - Frances, you lost Moss. Cliona, you've lost Ewan. We've all been asked for something more than we think we can give. But in the end, we've never been asked for more than we can offer or more than what we can survive together. That's something we have that Lira doesn't - friendship, loyalty, love. She can't understand any of that and that will be her undoing. We've a chance to send Skelly home and stop the storms for good. We have to at least try."

"And if it doesn't work? Are you supposed to just walk into the sea and disappear forever? Do you actually want to live like one of them?"

She gestured towards the selkie boy who stood behind Trudy. "What's he doing here, anyway? Going to escort you in?"

Trudy's heart ached for the grief already etched on Cliona's face.

"You're not going to lose me," she said, "Skelly has…well, we've sorted it."

"You keep saying that, but how can you trust him?"

"He'll keep his word," said Trudy.

"But how can you *know*?" said Cliona, her voice urgent.

"I just know," said Trudy. "Do you trust *me*?"

Cliona nodded.

"Then trust him."

"Now you're absolutely sure, lass?" asked Mrs. Glenbogie, taking the glass from Cliona and cupping her other hand around Trudy's damp, pale cheek.

Trudy nodded, mutely, not trusting herself to speak.

Mrs. Glenbogie smiled. "You're a brave wee girl, I'll say that. You always have been, even when you didn't think it. Just living amongst us must have tested you sorely."

Cliona made a choking sound behind her but held her tongue at Mrs. Glenbogie's sharp glance.

"Right then. Cliona - are you ready? When Feargus drops the mist then we need to be ready to meet that poxy sea cow. Your gran is here, and Skelly will lend us all that he can, won't you?"

She narrowed her eyes as Skelly shifted uncomfortably under her glare.

"Still, not as much as we'll need, right? So this is where the rest of you come in. We need to join the elements if we're to send her packing."

"Oh, Mrs. G, what do you *mean*?" asked Frances, shakily. "I'm sorry, but I don't understand." Her voice broke and she began to cry. "I'm sorry. I'm so sorry. I want to be helpful, but

I just feel so useless. Seeing Moss just reinforced how badly I've failed him. How can I..."

Trudy stepped across the circle and took Frances into her arms in a firm hug.

She whispered into her ear, "It's alright, Frances. It really is. And so will Moss be." she pulled back, tears in her own eyes. She smiled through them, "And falling to bits is my job, remember?" She turned to Cliona who grinned sheepishly.

Letting go of Frances and stepping back to the edge of the circle, Trudy spoke, her voice calm and clear. For the first time in her life she felt truly grounded.

"You're all exactly who and what you need to be — always remember that. Frances - you are fire - for the creative spark that makes beautiful paintings, that brings life and magic and memory to a mundane world. Cliona - you are air — for the wind-song and the fury of your temper, your fierce protective instinct for those you love best."

She turned to Skelly.

"You, of course, are water - a soul in exile - lost but never forgetting and never giving up."

She stood tall and squared her shoulders.

"I am earth. I am the anchor and the bridge between the worlds," she smiled shyly at Cernach. "I am the gift given freely."

Smiling around at them, she drank in each of their faces - all of them strained and worn with worry but firm with determination.

"And all of us together - we are spirit. We are love and friendship, loyalty and courage."

She reached out to take Skelly's hand on one side and Cernach's on the other. Cernach reached for Frances and

Mrs. Glenbogie took Frances' other hand.

"Are we ready?" asked Mrs. Glenbogie. They all nodded grimly, planting their feet in the wet sand.

She reached into her pocket with her free hand and pulled out Trudy's stone, the sea glass that held the soul of a daughter of the sea. Her voice strong and clear she said:

For the gift given freely,

For love everlasting.

Settling the glass in the palm of her hand, she reached for Skelly.

As the glass touched Skelly's skin a blinding streak of silver light shot from him - it jumped around the circle, lighting each person with a silver-blue glow. The wind began to roar more loudly, and the pounding of the waves crashed through the buffering sphere of the mist. Lira's shrieking howl pierced the muffled silence.

"Feargus!" shouted Cernach, staggering against the force of the rising wind. "Now!"

The mist fell and the sea roared in.

Chapter 27

Trudy stood on the edge of a calm sea. The waves lapped gently, the foam advancing and retreating in an eternal caress of the earth's edge. The sky shimmered crimson and white, a frosted confection of the sun's descent over wispy clouds.

"You'll be alright then?" asked the tall faery, his eyes bright with tears. The wind lifted the tangled knots of his blue-green hair, sending the shells clickety-clacking against one another like castanets. "You'll know what to do?"

"Of course, she will," said the dark-haired man who stood on the other side of her. "She's got the whole of Faery to bless her, hasn't she?"

"And her human friends," reminded Feargus, his hands tucked into the pocket of his tartan waistcoat. "I don't imagine you can underestimate the power of that lot," he said with a wry smile.

Trudy smiled at her three companions. She smoothed her hands down the cool, shimmering fabric that she'd draped around her neck like a scarf.

"I'll be fine," she said. "It's like coming home, remember? Besides, I'll see you again."

Looking out toward the horizon, she saw the brown-green

head of a seal bobbing in the undulating surface of the sea.

"He'll guide you through," said Skelly, "No matter what you see, and be warned, lass, she'll try and lure you away, especially once she realizes what we're doing. No matter what happens, know that he's right there beside you to keep you right."

Trudy nodded.

"I'm not frightened," she said, meaning it.

She took a step into the rippling surf and sighed.

Without looking back, she kept on walking.

The three watched as a second seal joined the first then disappeared under the surface.

"Lira will be furious," said Feargus, turning to Skelly. "You know she can't stand to be thwarted."

"Aye," said Skelly, with a grim smile. "I've some experience of that."

"It was honourably done," said Cernach, tilting his antlered head towards Skelly. "She has no fault to find in it."

Feargus snorted.

"Since when did Lira care about honour?" he asked, bitterness in his voice. "You can be sure there'll be retaliation of some kind or other."

Skelly shrugged.

"It was always going to be that way," he said, gazing out at the endless stretch of water. "So what does it matter in the details of it?"

Feargus placed a hand on Skelly's shoulder.

"It matters to the lasses and it matters to me. Trudy is a friend and beloved of us all. This was nobly done, Skelly."

Skelly grunted.

"It's him you want to thank," he said, jutting his jaw at Cernach, who had moved away to stand at the edge of the sea. "He's the one that told me how to work around it."

Feargus turned to look, frowning at the back of the tall, broad-shouldered man who was also an ancient god of the forest.

"Do you suppose he'd planned it this way? From the very beginning when he found the wee girl on the beach?"

He turned back to Skelly, who was staring impassively out to sea.

"And if he did, how could he know you'd be willing to go along with him? That you'd help her sort out what to do. Never mind what it means for you. The two of you were sworn enemies."

Feargus face held a bewildered admiration as he looked back over to Cernach who remained at the edge of the sea.

Skelly's gaze joined his, piercing green eyes glittering like sun on the water.

"He's had a long time to think about it, I suppose," he said, finally. "But I'm not fool enough to imagine he did it out of the goodness of his heart. That's just not his way."

Feargus burst into a roar of delighted laughter that boomed over the empty expanse of sea and sand.

Clapping a hand briefly on Skelly's shoulder again, he started to walk back up the beach. He took a few steps then turned back, still chuckling.

"Come on, laddie," he said, "They'll be waiting."

Chapter 28

The fire crackled and spat in the grate, casting a warm, red glow over the crowded kitchen.

They hadn't known what to do with themselves after it was over, but it was with unspoken agreement that they finally made their weary way back to Mrs. Glenbogie's cottage.

The room smelled of the sea and damp wool, overlaid with the earthy scent of a pot of strong tea brewing on the hob.

Cliona sat nearest the stove, wrapped in a quilt, her hands cradling a large mug. Frances shared a cushion on the floor with Angus, who tried to wriggle under the blanket of multi-coloured crocheted granny squares that she'd draped over her legs.

They hadn't spoken for a long time, not until Iain had burst through the back door with Angus, demanding answers and explanations. He was white-faced with worry and his hands shook as he poured hot water into the teapot.

"You've no idea how it was," he'd said when he'd been convinced to stop pacing around the kitchen. "The bloody wind was wild. People were all in a state, carrying on like it was the bleeding apocalypse. Not that you'd know different, the way the rain was lashing down in sheets. Utter bloody madness. I thought for certain we were in for another one of those bloody storms, and you lot nowhere to be found. I thought you'd gone and got yourselves washed into the sea, forchrissakes. And then it was all over. Like someone turned off a switch."

He raked a hand through his hair, his eyes still wide at the memory of it. His gaze swept over the huddled group, taking inventory.

"And where the hell is Trudy?"

"How many boats?" Cliona asked, ignoring the question.

"Only two, and not sunk, just badly damaged." Iain had replied. "Of course, it was the tourist boats - neither of their captains would believe me when I tried to warn them."

Cliona had snorted at that.

"I imagine they've a change of heart now?"

"I thought you'd finished the business? So, it doesn't much matter, does it?"

Iain had heaved a shaky sigh and slumped into one of the wooden chairs.

"Right, will you please tell me what in the name of all that's holy went on down on that bloody beach? And, more importantly where our Trudy is?"

"Bloody hell," breathed Iain, when the telling was over.

They sat in silence, listening to the crackle and pop of the fire and the tick-tock of the kitchen clock.

"She's gone to the sea?" he asked, after a while. "But how? How can she not be…"

Frances shook her head, her eyes still bright with tears. "She's living in the sea. Like a selkie, I suppose. At least, that's how I understand it."

"That's something of it, lass," said Mrs.Glenbogie, her voice soft. "Regardless, you can be sure she'll be looked after. Himself is a lot of things but he does keep his promises."

Iain blew out a long breath.

"And this…arrangement, will stop the storms?"

Frances nodded again.

"Yes, it was a loophole in the curse that banished Skelly. Or something like that."

Cliona snorted but said nothing. She was too tired for arguing. In the end, it had been all she could to keep the wind under control once Feargus had lowered the shield of fog. They'd never stood a chance.

"So why didn't your first plan work?" asked Iain, after chewing over the details for a minute. "It seems it should have."

Cliona tried to shrug but her shoulders were too heavy.

"Best I can guess, Lira is a heartless bitch and she couldn't care less that we had her daughter's glass?"

Frances chuckled softly.

"I think what Cliona is trying to say is that Lira has been filled with hate and vengeance for so long, she's forgotten the reason why. I think there's even a part of her that doesn't remember either her daughter or how much she loved her. I mean, she must have at some point, to unleash such a fury on all of those involved with taking Fia from the sea."

"Like I said, she's a heartless bitch."

A knock on the door startled all four of them and made Angus shoot up from his place on the floor, barking. It was his excited, welcoming bark.

"Who the bloody hell is that?" grumbled Mrs.Glenbogie,

to the delight of the three young people. "Iain, lad, spare my tired old bones, would you?"

As Iain went to answer the door, Cliona reached out from her chair by the stove and put her hand on Frances' head. Frances leaned back against her friend's legs response.

"Are you okay?" Cliona asked, gently. "I mean, it's more than losing Trudy for you, isn't it? Your wee Moss..." her voice trailed away.

"I'll be fine," said Frances, taking a shuddering breath. "I mean, I know, in my head that they're both okay and that's the most important thing. It'll just take my heart a bit of time to catch up."

She broke off, feeling another glut of tears rising in her throat. She took a sip of her tea to wash them back down again. She would have a proper cry once she was alone in her croft with Angus.

The sound of loud male voices drew her attention and before she could decide if they were arguing or not, Feargus appeared in the kitchen. Or, more accurately the god of the sea, and brother to their arch nemesis who just so happened to call himself Feargus.

"Are you sure this is a good idea, mate?" Iain was saying, as he followed Feargus into the kitchen. Having not seen what Feargus could do, he was having difficulty imagining his friend as anything other than a mildly eccentric, overly theatrical, owner of a used bookshop.

"Too late," he finished, somewhat unnecessarily as he saw the faces of the three women. Angus hadn't been apprised of the new information so was jumping up and down trying to get Feargus' attention and, hopefully, a biscuit from the selection he knew Feargus kept in his pocket.

"Ladies," said Feargus, bowing his head. He stood on the threshold of the kitchen, his hands folded in front of him, waiting.

"Och, man," said Mrs.Glenbogie, wearily, breaking the tension. "Come and sit by the bloody fire. But take your coat off, you're dripping all over my clean floor."

Feargus grinned widely and bowed more deeply before peeling off his wet mackintosh.

Frances smiled and got up from her cushion.

"Cup of tea, Feargus?"

He nodded gratefully and lowered himself into the chair furthest from the fire. And Cliona.

Cliona glowered at him before turning to Mrs.Glenbogie.

"I must say, Mrs.G. your language leaves much to be desired. I don't know what Gran would have to say about that."

They all erupted into a much-needed shout of laughter and allowed the business of getting tea and getting warm erase everything else from their minds.

After a while, when they were all settled and mundane, quiet conversation had eased the weight of what had happened, Frances turned to Feargus - because Feargus was who he'd always be to her.

"Can you please tell us what's happened to Trudy? I mean, truly happened?"

Feargus sighed and placed his mug on the table. He spread his fingers wide and placed them across his ample, tartan middle.

"It's not at all what you think," he said, slowly. He held up a hand, "Please, let me finish before you raise any objections about the way it all had to happen." He didn't look at Cliona when he said it, but everyone knew to whom he was talking. She subsided in her chair with a muttered curse.

"You only know what you were told, and that's how it had to be in order to make sure nothing went wrong."

Cliona took a deep breath in but said nothing.

"The terms of the curse were clear - and, as far as Lira was sure, unlikely to ever be challenged. What you probably don't know, and it's a story for another day, is that, in addition to the raising of storms, she's been trying for centuries to punish the mortal world by holding its lost ones to the sea. But, as in all things, it's not a gift unless it's given freely. And so far, that hasn't happened."

"Until Trudy," whispered Frances, knotting her fingers in the blanket around her shoulders.

Feargus nodded.

"Until Trudy. But," he raised a finger, "as you know, Trudy was more or less tricked into giving her promise."

This time Cliona couldn't help herself.

"Right, and that's not at all something that…well, you lot are known for," she said, her voice dripping with scorn.

Feargus looked at her, seeing the hurt she was unsuccessfully trying to hide with sarcasm.

"Ah, Cliona, lass. I'm exactly who you see me as. Do you not know that? Besides, none of us, no matter how powerful, can hold a glamour that is false. Because a glamour is exactly that, just a layer over the truth. And I, for one, made a choice to leave that world behind me. What you see, really is what you get. I am, for all intents and purposes, as human as any of you."

Cliona sniffed loudly and looked away from him.

"That may well be," she said, "but that's not what I'm talking about. I'm talking about that…man, whoever he is and we'll none of us remember, I'm sure. I know I can't."

Frances nodded her head, frowning.

"Me either. I mean, I know that he was there, but I can't really remember who he is or what he looked like."

Feargus snorted.

"Yes, well. That's Cernach for you. I suppose he's had his finger into so much intrigue over the years it's probably the wisest strategy. Cernach, however, was the one who pointed out the error of Lira's ways. A loophole within the loophole, if you like, in the terms of her curse."

Iain leaned forward, eyes gleaming.

"This sounds promising," he said, looking around at the women. Frances lifted her shoulders in a vague shrug and Cliona rolled her eyes. Mrs.Glenbogie sat in watchful silence, her hands wrapped around her third mug of tea. Iain's eyes widened at their lack of reaction. "What? You mean you weren't in on the plan at all?"

Feargus shook his head.

"No, lad. As I said before, it had to be kept quiet because Trudy was worried that she'd not be able to go through with it if you all found out. Poor lass was doubting herself all the way through. Ultimately, it had to be her choice, that was the thing and, as it turned out, she surprised us all."

Cliona sniffed loudly.

"You lot are wild fond of pretending any of us has a choice, aren't you?"

"Cliona," said Mrs. Glenbogie quietly. "That's enough, pet. There's no blame and no room for anger here in this. Trudy did make her choice and she made it freely. It wouldn't have worked otherwise, aren't you taking this in?"

"But," Cliona choked back a sob. "She's a selkie, a bloody seal! What if she gets eaten by a whale or caught in a fishing net or…"

Feargus held up a hand.

"If you'd let me finish the story, Cliona?"

He handed her a large, orange-spotted handkerchief. She glared at him briefly before accepting it, blowing her nose loudly then handing it back to him with a watery grin.

He grinned back, tucking the soggy hanky back into his waistcoat pocket.

"As I was saying," he continued, "Cernach pointed out the fact that although the terms of the curse required a mortal to freely give themselves over to the sea, it didn't specify for how long."

Iain's eyes widened and he rubbed his hands together, beaming.

"Oh, for heaven's sake, Iain," said Cliona, unable to stop herself from smiling at him. "Are you that desperate for excitement your life. You'd think this was the grand mystery of our time being solved."

"Well it is," replied Iain. "I've a great feeling about how this is going to end."

Feargus winked at him but continued.

"And Cernach has knowledge of things - and I cannot fathom how because he keeps it all very close to his chest, even from me and you would say we were of equal standing," he paused for a moment and puffed out his chest, eliciting another eye-roll from Cliona, this time one of indulgent affection. "So, all I can really tell you is that, with the right circumstances and with the right help, a mortal can pass safely through the sea to the faery realms."

"And that's where our Trudy went!" exclaimed Iain, thumping his fist onto the table making everyone jump. Angus leapt up, barking.

"Hush, Angus," said Frances. "Let me see if I'm understanding this, Feargus. You're saying that Trudy passed through the sea, then. She's not living in it?"

Feargus nodded, then shook his head, then nodded again.

"Right," he said, looking like his habitual muddled self, "Right on the not living in the sea bit."

"Then where the bloody hell is she?" said Cliona, wearily running a hand through her hair, leaving it in a wild state of curling profusion. "And Skelly? What does this mean for our favourite exile? Is he off into the waves himself now, pleasegodletitbeso."

Frances kicked Cliona under the table, but Cliona ignored her.

"As far as I know, Trudy is now happily ensconced in a wee cottage, apparently one of great historical importance to both Trudy and Glencarragh. And that's where she'll stay, safe and happy in the In-Between, for a year and a day."

"And then she'll be back? She'll come home after that?"

Frances's eyes shone, her hands clasped under her chin.

Feargus smiled, his eyes softening with affection for his friend.

"After a year and a day, she'll be free to choose again. Whether she wishes to stay in Faery or return to the mortal world."

Frances face fell. She knew, as well as everyone in the room, that what would seem an easy decision for most people, would be a difficult one for Trudy.

She cleared her throat.

"Do you really think she's happy, though? Did she make a choice that she was happy with?"

"Aye, pet. I do," said Mrs. Glenbogie, breaking her silence at last. "I think she was. She was a changed lass near the end of it. The only part of it that sent her wobbling was knowing she'd be upsetting you lot. Otherwise, I could see the light shining out of her with the knowing of it. This world can be a cruel, inhospitable place to folk like our Trudy. She'll be happy, of that I'm sure. So, don't worry yourselves. I'm sure between the three musketeers here," she shot Feargus a wry look, "they've set her up to get on just fine."

"How, though? Wait, does this mean that Skelly can't go back to the sea? I mean, if Lira knows she's been duped, I can't see her being happy about it." asked Frances. "Isn't that right, Feargus?"

"Yes, Feargus. Will sister-dearest be in a strop over this?"

Feargus ignored Cliona's good-natured jab. He reached across the table to pour himself another mug of tea. They all waited, with varying degrees of patience, as he spooned sugar, poured milk and stirred.

"Right, and that's the thing, isn't it? Even though the terms of the original curse have been adhered to, and so Skelly's exile ought to have ended the second Trudy walked into the sea…"

"Well, it certainly stopped the storm right quick," said Iain, interrupting. "So that bit worked anyway. And you might say that was the most important bit."

He sheepishly avoided the glare he could feel emanating from Frances and Mrs.Glenbogie.

Feargus nodded.

"Aye, but because of the rather creative interpretation of it all, I don't think we'd be wise to rest too easy on our laurels where my dear sister is concerned. You know yourselves, and I hardly recognized her, she's become a twisted creature, so full of hate and vengeance that she's forgotten why this all started in the first place. It's why your binding didn't work, Cliona. There's no love left in her at all. If there was ever any to begin with."

He paused, staring into the swirl of his tea. France lay a hand on his arm.

"I'm sorry, Feargus. That must be difficult for you."

Feargus gave her a sad smile.

"Not at all, lass. We were never close. Too different and besides, parentage can be a vague concept at our level. It's just a sad thing for the world when we forget the important things. Anyway," he gave his head a little shake, "There's no need to be maudlin. Trudy is safe and happy and we're free from the ravages of storms, for a good while, at least."

"You never answered the part about Skelly," said Cliona, regarding Feargus with mild suspicion.

"Ah, yes. Our venerable friend," said Feargus. "The short version is that, by pointing out this alternative approach to Trudy, he gave up his chance to return to the sea. The concession is that it won't any longer be an agony for him to be close to it, he can move about freely, if you like, but he can't go back and stay there. It's just too dangerous. For him and for Trudy. At least until we know what Lira will do next."

The room fell silent then, the only sound was the rumble of the Aga and Angus trying to arrange the floor cushion to his liking. The tail of the cat clock ticked in time as they each pondered the implications of what Feargus had just told them.

"You mean he gave it all up, then, for our Trudy?" asked Iain, a grudging respect creeping into his tone.

Feargus smiled, tilting his head towards Cliona.

"Indeed, like myself, he's well and truly of this world now. You wouldn't imagine him capable of such selflessness, would you now?"

Cliona snorted.

"Never in a million bloody years!"

"Och," said a voice, behind them. "No need for a million, lass. 'Tis only a few hundred by my count."

"Skelly!"

The figure of an old, patchwork, sheep farmer struggled through the kitchen door, fending off the ecstatic overtures of Angus. He stood, awkwardly on the threshold, his tweed cap in one hand, a brown-paper parcel in another. He reached over to hand a speechless Mrs. Glenbogie the parcel as she rose from her chair to meet him.

"Fancied we'd have a bit o' lemon drizzle, aye? To toast our wee lassie and put some things to rights." He remained standing inside the doorway, a question and a wariness on his creased face. "That's if I'm welcome among you."

Mrs.Glenbogie smiled, a twinkle sparkling in her eye. She bowed deeply from the waist.

"Skelly, my old friend. Won't you come and sit by my fire?"

The stunned silence lasted only moment longer before the kitchen erupted in activity. Cliona leapt up to refill the kettle and Iain retrieved another chair. He patted Skelly awkwardly on the shoulder as he passed him, and the old man nodded without lifting his gaze.

The warm kitchen filled with laughter, a welcome release of the tension and sorrow they'd not realized they were still holding.

Outside, the last remnants of rain dripped from the eaves and the raucous cry of a raven echoed through the rising dark.

"Oh, and Frances, lass?" said Skelly, as Angus ran in excited circles around his chair. Frances paused in her gathering of plates for the lemon drizzle. "Have you not yet learned to control that bloody dog?"

THE END

Epilogue

"You'll want to run a comb through that hair," said Moss, bustling past with a wicker basket full of elderflowers. "You've got company coming."

"What? Who could possibly..."

"Pip, pip!" called back the little brownie. "No time for dithering!"

Trudy sighed.

"He's the most awful tyrant," she confided in the hens, who clucked and muttered around her feet. "Here you are, that's the last of it for now, my darlings." Trudy threw a final handful of oats and cracked corn onto the grass where it was set upon with great, cackling delight. She wiped her hands down her apron front and sighed again, glancing around her as she did so. She was standing just outside the kitchen garden, on the other side of the stone wall that marked the boundary between it and the narrow band of moor that stood between the cottage and the cliff's edge. Looking in the other direction, she could see the wider expanse of moor that rose behind the cottage, a rolling carpet of purpling heather, dotted with sheep and yellow gorse. Whoever was visiting her, would be coming from that direction.

"Right," she said to the hens, who had since moved on

to more exciting fare, "I suppose I'd better make myself presentable."

The smell of something baking wafted from the open door of the cottage as she walked up the garden path. Trudy smiled to herself. Moss had certainly regained his sense of courtesy, or, as he called it, hearth-welcome. In the few weeks since she'd arrived in the In-Between, she hadn't been able to discover his secret of somehow always having a batch of something ready to fling into the oven at a moment's notice. The little brownie looked up from where he was placing the large white flowers into a pan of water.

"You'd better get a move on, my girl," he said, frowning. "He'll be here any minute."

"Who?" said Trudy, exasperated. "Who on earth would be coming here? I'm sure Skelly wouldn't have warranted such a fuss."

"No, indeed," said Moss, curling his lip. "And why must you be so contrary? I'm merely suggesting that you look like a feral pixie and it might be nicer to greet your guest looking less like you were dragged through a hedge backwards."

Trudy looked down at herself. She'd been down to the shore earlier that morning then had been working in the garden. There was sand clinging to the hem of her dress and a rim of dirt around her fingernails. She walked across the room to the large mirror that hung over the fireplace, and saw that her hair was, indeed, looking a bit windswept. She rubbed at the streak of soil on her forehead and grinned widely, "I happen to think I look bloody marvelous," she said.

"And I absolutely couldn't agree more, dear girl," boomed a voice from the doorway.

Trudy spun around.

"Feargus!" she shrieked and crossed the room in one happy bound, throwing herself into his waiting arms.

"You really do look well," he said, once they were seated outdoors with a pot of tea and what had turned out to be lavender shortbread. "The country life agrees with you," he added with a smile.

Trudy hugged herself, eyes shining.

"It really does, Feargus. It really does," she paused for moment, then asked, "how is everyone? They aren't too cross, I hope?"

Feargus chuckled.

"Cross? Good heavens, no. Why would they be cross? They were worried for you, and obviously upset that they won't be seeing you for a while, but no, never cross."

He reached for another biscuit.

"And before you ask, no, they do not know that I'm here."

"Ah, I see," said Trudy, who didn't, really.

"I can't have them thinking I'm getting myself embroiled in things and nor do I want them pestering me to come for visits and such."

Trudy felt a flush rising to her face. That had been the question she couldn't bring herself to ask.

Feargus saw her distress and said, softly, "It's best we don't draw too much attention to your being here, you see. This was all very much down to Cernach's machinations and it's always wise to hold these things very lightly, if you get my meaning."

Trudy stared down at her hands, which were cradling her mug. She hadn't had time to scrub her nails. Self-conscious, she let go of the mug and tucked her hands in her lap.

"But I couldn't have got here without your help," she said,

her voice quiet but steady. "You gave Mr. Jamison that box, with the books and with the faery cloth..."

Feargus shifted uncomfortably in his chair, drumming his fingers on the tablecloth.

"Yes, yes, I suppose I played a minor role..."

"Not minor at all!" said Trudy, her eyes wide, "If it wasn't for that box I never would have been able to come here and you know it."

Feargus waved a hand, avoiding her eyes. He made a fuss of pouring himself another cup of tea.

"Oh," he said, gesturing to a wooden crate that had materialized next to the door of the cottage. "I brought your plants. I was checking on your flat and a few of them were looking a bit bedraggled. I thought you'd rather we didn't try and keep them alive in your absence. None of us are terribly blessed with a green thumb."

"Thank you," she said, "but don't change the subject. Why can't you acknowledge what you did?"

Feargus groaned.

"Because, dearest girl, long ago – and no, I won't tell you how long ago – I made a promise of my own and by assisting in these matters, I'm rather breaking that promise. I would prefer to not keep doing that."

"Is that why you're, well, Feargus, then? Instead of being like Cernach? I mean, you're both gods..."

Trudy faltered, feeling a twinge of cognitive dissonance. It was hard to reconcile the portly figure, dressed in a yellow tartan waistcoat and tweed trousers, pink and white spotted handkerchief protruding from his breast pocket, as a powerful deity of the sea.

Feargus grinned, seeing the confusion on her face.

"It's hard to imagine, isn't it? Yes and no, my lamb. I chose this persona for a multitude of reasons and am quite happy to remain so. Times have changed, you see. I don't believe there's a place for the likes of us in this brave new world of yours and so I've hedged my bets." He held up an admonishing finger. "And that's the last we shall speak of this, yes? Consider me only as Feargus O'Rourke, humble shopkeeper and former thespian."

Trudy sighed, allowing the rest of her questions to dissipate. She nodded her head. "So, you won't be telling me about the faery cloth, then? What it is, how it worked?"

Feargus shook his head.

"That, my dear, is a story for another day. Let us, instead, chat about common-place things, shall we? Tell me, is Moss as thoroughly tryrannical as Frances says?"

* * *

The sun was descending below the horizon as the two friends stood at the border between the worlds. The sky was a soft, pink and periwinkle haze. Somewhere in the distance, a fox barked.

"You'll give them my love?"

"Of course, I shall. And they shall know it to be true and deep."

Feargus wrapped his arm around Trudy's shoulder and pulled her close, sensing her thoughts.

"A year and a day will pass in no time at all. Before you know it, you'll be back in Glencarragh listening to Cliona's tirades and fending off Angus' muddy paws."

Trudy smiled a small smile.

"And if I don't want to go back?"

Feargus stiffened for only the briefest of moments, before squeezing her shoulder and letting her go.

He turned her to face him, bending slightly as his blue eyes searched hers. She held his gaze until he gave an almost imperceptible nod.

"Then we shall deal with that when the time comes, won't we?" He cleared his throat and smiled brightly. "Now, get yourself back to that lovely wee cottage before I hear Moss bellowing you to your dinner."

"Will you…"

Feargus shook his head.

"No more words, darling girl. I can't bear goodbyes, so it's best we just part company without saying anything else. Let me just have this vision of you walking back down that hill, to a warm fire and a good meal."

Trudy swallowed hard before reaching up to place a kiss on his smooth cheek.

"Thank you," she whispered. "For everything."

The old god watched as she made her slow, careful way over the tufts of grass, down to the rose-covered cottage by the edge of the sea.

About the Author

Melanie Leavey was born and raised in the north-east of England before emigrating to Canada with her family at the age of nine. An aspiring hermit and passionate gardener, she likes nothing better than drinking tea and thumbing through the latest David Austin rose catalogue. A country mouse turned town mouse, she lives with her husband, two children, a badly-behaved Jack Russell and a cat named George on the Territory of the Haudenosaunee Confederacy, Fort Erie, Ontario.

You can connect with me on:
🌐 http://www.threeravens.ca

Subscribe to my newsletter:
✉ https://landing.mailerlite.com/webforms/landing/a6v1h6

Also by Melanie Leavey

A world without magic is a world without hope…

Skelly
The first book in the Sea Glass Trilogy

Wind Singer
Book Two of the Sea Glass Trilogy